Flirting with Death's Grace

by

B.B. Swann

Flirting with Death's Grace

Cover Art by *The Wild Rose Press, Inc.*

The Wild Rose Press, Inc.
PO Box 708
Adams Basin, NY 14410-0708
Visit us at www.thewildrosepress.com

Publishing History
First Edition, 2022
Trade Paperback ISBN 978-1-5092-4416-4
Digital ISBN 978-1-5092-4417-1

Published in the United States of America

I hung, waiting for the rock I clutched to pull away from the soft soil and send me plummeting to the bottom. Instead of screaming in fear, I laughed. Kali had told me we should have met at the bottom of the quarry, and I'd even reminded myself of the possibility before I came here. Maybe it was inevitable. I pictured Kali's beautiful face. Seeing her Hollywood smile when she greeted me might be worth the pain of death.

Then new visions filled my mind. Grace laughing on the playground at recess as I spun her on the merry-go-round. Grace chasing me through the woods behind our house, letting her catch me so she could tickle me and I could feel her touch. And Grace hugging me after I told her about my parents' divorce, her arms tight around my waist, head on my chest as she cried with me. The thought of dying left me as cold as the stone I clung to. But the visions filled me with a burning heat, heat I wanted to feel and taste before I died.

Movement from above sent a shower of pebbles bouncing off my head and face. I closed my eyes until they stopped and looked up again—into Kali's dark eyes.

"Hey, Asher."

Relief flooded me. "Thank God. Please help me out of here."

"Sorry." She shook her head. "That's not why I'm here."

Praise for B.B. Swann and...

FLIRTING WITH DEATH'S GRACE

"An emotionally gripping story of redemption and love. It's never too late, and this is an expertly woven tale of hope."

~Shami Stovall, author

~*~

"This story of first love and second chances will keep you turning the pages until the emotional end."

~Chris Cannon, author

~*~

"Get comfortable because you're going to want to read this in one sitting! Intense, romantic, and a great escape. I couldn't put it down."

~Lynn Stevens, author

Dedication

For my dad, who taught me to love reading, and for Mick, who made me feel loved as an author. They may not be here to see this moment, but I wouldn't be here without their influences.

Chapter One

I had a date with a death angel once.

I took her out for pizza and a movie. Who knew reapers liked comedies? I wasn't surprised she wanted to meet me. Up to that point, my life had been pretty freaking hilarious, in *A Midsummer Night's Dream* sort of way, where the Fates jerked people around just to laugh at them. And I gave them plenty of material to work with.

My parents divorced me years before they divorced each other. Long nights at work, office parties, and too many happy-hour "business meetings" let me know where I stood in their lives—in the way. The reaper's pity must have been what drew her to me. Or maybe she just needed a good laugh, too.

Though some minds thought outside the box, most portrayed reapers as cloaked masculine figures with big scythes and quiet dispositions. When I met my death angel, she sat on the hood of my car outside my best friend Connor's house, wearing jeans and a pink tank top, snapping her gum behind a Hollywood smile.

"Hey, Asher Jacobs. How's it goin'?"

"Hey." My voice only cracked because I tried not to intimidate her.

I'd never had trouble talking to girls—well, except for one, but only because she hated me. Still, I wasn't ashamed to admit I was okay looking, had more compliments than complaints. Maybe I wouldn't get the lead role in a feature film, but I'd sure kill it in the B-rated movies.

Dark hair, blue eyes, and a strong six-foot frame got me lots of easy action—not from the one I wanted to be with. I'd ruined that a long time ago. But seeing this girl, red hair glinting with gold flecks in the sun, white teeth shining, and mile-long legs untangling as she hopped down to greet me, I had to admit I'd have to put forth more effort—and I didn't know if I had what it would take.

She sidled over to me, stopping close enough I could smell her gum. She exhaled, and I almost tasted the mint.

"I'm new in town. Wanna show me around?"

I checked to make sure Connor wasn't playing a joke on me. Nothing out of the ordinary—quiet street, soft breeze rustling the new spring leaves, cookie-cutter matchbox houses lined up like tired ants along the sidewalk.

I swayed a little on my feet. After the case of beer I had shared with Connor instead of going to school, my reflexes weren't the greatest. I took a step back to hide my wobble. She followed.

"Well, sure." I blinked a few times. "How do you know my name? And who are you?"

"A little bird told me." She slid her hands onto my hips and pulled herself closer. "And, like I said, I'm new. Let's take this car of yours for a ride, see what she can do."

When a hot chick grabbed a guy by the hips and said, "Take me for a ride," okay was the only reasonable response. And when that hot chick was a fiery redhead with the best body he'd ever had the privilege of almost touching, anything but okay made him an idiot.

I gestured to my midnight-blue Mustang. "After you." I even opened the door for her. I was a gentleman like that. Actually, I just hoped to get some at that point. And to look at her legs again.

She slid into the passenger seat, and I closed the door. I got in and revved the engine to show off. Peeling away from the curb, I swerved onto the street.

Too late, I realized I shouldn't be driving. Connor and I had woken up prepared to spend the day at school in higher learning. Instead, when I came to pick him up, we'd spent the day high. With his parents at work and a refrigerator full of beer, who needed reading, writing, or arithmetic? Skipping school also saved me from seeing...her.

I gained control of the car, then slowed my speed, gripping the wheel with both hands. Wouldn't it be great to have the hottest girl in town dead in my car because I crashed like a drunken dipshit before I got to touch her?

I glanced at her out of the corner of my eye. "Where are you from?"

"Oh, here and there. I've been lots of places."

Mysterious *and* hot. Maybe I'd passed out on Connor's couch, and this was all an alcohol-induced dream. "Okay. Tell me *something* about you. Like maybe your name? You just show up, know my name, and hop in my car. I'd like to get to know you."

I smiled my most charming smile, which always worked to get me what I wanted. Especially when I used it on my mom. She could never tell me no.

She smirked. "That smile won't work on me, Asher. I'm not your mother."

Whoa. "How do you know that?"

"I know a lot about you. I've met your type before—a time or two." She flashed her bright white teeth. "I'm Kali."

I chuckled. "For a second, I thought you knew my mom."

Kali laughed. Tinkling bells, shimmering notes, silvery peals, every cliché came to mind. None of them fit. Her laugh lit a fire inside me, only the fire was made of ice. It splintered through my body, like frost forming in a time-lapse video. I couldn't wait to hear it again.

She laid a hand on my leg. My heart sped, melting the ice with one hard beat.

"I do know her. But that's not why I'm here." She pulled her long hair onto one shoulder. "I handle the younger crowd."

Her velvety voice filled my head. My tires crunched on the gravel shoulder, and I forced my gaze back to the road. "Why are you here?" Her hand still rested on my thigh, and I tried not to react below the belt.

Didn't work.

She tilted her head. "Somebody put in a good word for you, so I came to meet you." She slid her hand toward my knee, then leaned back in her seat, folding her hands on her lap. "I didn't want our first meeting to be the last. I'm glad I did. You remind me of someone I used to know."

I exhaled my pent-up breath. Focusing on her words was impossible while my body reacted to her touch. My vision blurred, and I blinked to clear my eyes. *Damn Connor.* I told him we should have stopped after the first twelve-pack—and the second bowl.

I gripped the wheel harder and shook my head, trying to clear it. "Want to go to The Cliffs?"

Our small suburb of Chicago was flat. We called our hangout The Cliffs because of the drop-off into the quarry. Staring down from the edge made it look like a mini Grand Canyon.

Kali nodded. "That sounds interesting."

No, it was lame, but so was most of my town. I had planned to go there and finish my bag of weed before she showed up hot and sexy on my car. Maybe if I shared it with her, she'd share something else with me.

I took the turn onto the dirt road leading to The Cliffs. My car skidded, and I eased off the gas pedal. "Stupid tires." I glanced from the corner of my eye.

She laughed, and the ice re-formed. Again, it melted with her hand on my leg. Her touch also turned the heat up down under, and my body strained against my jeans.

"It's not the tires, Asher." She let go, and I exhaled again.

The quarry's abandoned feel added to the weirdness with Kali. Mine was the only car in sight. A small building covered in flaky white paint sat behind us, like an island in a dusty parking lot surrounded by patchy brown grass not even checkered with the green of spring yet. Combined with the wind whistling through the nearby woods, carrying the scent of last year's rotting leaves, it was the perfect setting for a murder mystery— or maybe a ghost story.

Lucky for me, I was drunk, high, and too focused on the girl next to me to worry much about it.

I parked the car away from the edge of the cliff, not close like I normally would. I was really buzzed, and I didn't want to miscalculate where the front tires stopped. This was the third car my mom and her husband had bought for me. Two previous wrecks because of "deer" had been forgiven. But at some point, they would tell me no more. Maybe. Besides, even though I'd thought about it before, I didn't want to die today. Life had just gotten interesting with Kali in the picture.

We got out, and I followed her toward the edge.

She looked down into the old quarry, narrowing her eyes. "That's a long way down." She raised those eyes to mine. Black as midnight, with only a slight hint of blue encircling the pupil.

I rubbed the raised hairs on the back of my neck. "They don't use this quarry anymore. I think it's about three hundred feet deep." I joined her at the edge, standing behind her. She confused the hell out of me, and not because I was drunk. Anyway, I didn't want to talk— I wanted something physical to happen. My muddled brain struggled to come up with a good line.

"So you want to hang out for a while?" *Brilliant*. I sounded like a ten-year-old. "Or we could—" She turned to face me, and my breath caught in my throat. *God, she's hot.* "—could go out. On a real date."

She smiled, and the hairs on my neck rose again.

"Oh, don't worry. I already have our date penciled in." She rubbed her hands from my chest to my shoulders. "But it's not tonight."

Damn. "You sure? I've got some stuff in the car, and I'm good at sharing."

She released me and laughed, harder than before. The ice raced like an avalanche through my body. I couldn't move. Without her touch, the avalanche buried me. Had I known what was coming, I would have grabbed her hand or waist or some other part of her. My new predicament proved she gave a whole new meaning to the phrase "hot body."

"Asher, you are one lucky boy. Living up to your name, right?"

She laughed again, and the ice spread until my eyes were all I could control.

"Now, I want you to listen to me. Got it?"

When a hot chick rendered a guy immobile by freezing him with her laughter and told him to listen— well, I knew the drill. I listened.

Intently.

The perfect arch of her eyebrows collapsed between her pitch-black stare. She turned, moving to the edge of the quarry. I followed her with my eyes, drawing shallow breaths around the ice in my lungs. Her toe bumped a loose stone and sent it over the edge. Instead of fading away, the echoes increased in volume on the way to the bottom, ending with loud peals of thunder. Or that might have been my heart in my ears.

"It's like this. I'm not supposed to be here. Yet." She kicked another rock into the quarry, and it thundered to the bottom. "The rules are set in stone, and I always follow them, except this time. Like I said, I've heard about you." Kali whipped around, her long red hair flaring out like fire.

No, wait, it was fire. Flames crackled on the ends of her hair like tiny orange snakes. I gagged on the rotten stench of sulfur, and if I hadn't been frozen, I would have bolted. Who the hell was she? *What* the hell was she?

She raised her hand and crooked her finger, calling me to her. She knew I was frozen, right? If I hadn't been, I was *pret*-ty sure there was no chance in hell I would go near her.

Then I moved. Rather, she moved me, like a piece on a game board, sliding me to the edge of the cliff. My

7

right foot touched the ground, but my left hovered in the empty air. With a twist of her hand, I leaned over the edge, dangling for a minute, staring at the bottom of the quarry three hundred feet below. My heart beat in time to the name I couldn't form earlier... *Grace. Grace. Grace.*

Maybe I should have gone to school instead.

"If I'd followed the rules, that's where you and I would have met." Kali jabbed a finger toward the bottom of the quarry. "And I don't mean driving down the service road in your sweet car to party at the bottom. I mean one small step and a fast trip with a quick hard stop. Because you think you have all the answers. Because you think that will solve all your problems. Because you keep feeling sorry for yourself and blaming everyone else for *your* bad decisions. Decisions you better change if you want to stay off the bottom of the quarry."

Staring into the nothingness, I gasped and struggled to get enough air to scream. Another twist and I righted, both feet on the ground. Good thing my bladder was frozen, too. She reached for me and stuck her hand on my chest. The ice didn't melt. It ceased, like it had never existed.

I wobbled toward the edge of the cliff, flailing my arms, trying not to fall over. Kali pushed me back, and I landed on my ass in the dirt. My heart raced now that it wasn't encased in a block of ice. My lungs worked now, too, so I sucked in deep breaths of the warm late-spring air. I searched the area, frantically wheeling my gaze from side to side at the deserted grounds surrounding us.

She smiled but thankfully didn't let loose with her freeze-ray laugh.

What the hell did she mean? That I would kill

myself? I squinted and shook my head. She didn't know me if she thought I could do that. *Ridiculous*. Wanting to die and killing myself were two different things.

"Who are you?" The tremor in my voice made me sound less assertive than I had hoped for.

She pursed her lips and rubbed a slim finger under her chin. "Guardian angel? Yeah, let's go with that."

If I weren't scared shitless, I would have laughed. Of course, my guardian angel would be a smart-ass. I scooted back farther from the edge with a flailing backward crab walk, then wobbled to my unsteady feet. *God, please let this be a dream.*

"It's not a dream, Asher." She walked closer and caressed my shoulder, the warmth of her skin bleeding through my shirt. "I told you I didn't want our first meeting to be our last. You intrigue me."

She stared at me, black eyes narrowed, shining like the eyes of a crow. Fire filled my veins, spreading faster than the ice had before. I cried out, falling to my knees in front of her. She placed her other hand on my shoulder, and the fire increased. Tiny stars appeared in my vision. I squeezed my eyes shut and focused on not passing out.

What the hell? Why was she trying to kill me after she'd just said she came to save me from pitching myself over the side of the quarry?

She released me, and I fell forward, palms in the dirt. The pain faded, and my head cleared, the buzz from my earlier binge gone. For the first time in a couple of weeks, I was totally sober. The unfamiliar feeling made me almost as disoriented as the twelve-pack. I raised my face to Kali. "What did you do to me?"

"We barely made it here. I couldn't let you drive

home drunk." She stepped away from me.

I rose to my feet, steady this time, yet it didn't stop my hands and knees from shaking. "Is this really happening?" The buzz was gone, but I still thought this could be a dream. I reached out to touch her, to make sure she was real.

But she moved farther away, her dark eyes twinkling like wet ink on paper. "It's real. But now I have to go." She turned to walk away.

"Wait!" Even though she had frozen my drunk ass and dangled me over the cliff, I didn't want her to leave. She had some explaining to do. "Will I see you again?"

She turned back, wearing her Hollywood smile. "Of course. I told you I have our date penciled in. But it's up to you what we do on that date. I can only give you one option."

I glanced at the edge of the quarry. Something told me her idea of a date wasn't something I'd want to do.

Hips swaying above her long legs, she walked toward the edge, turned to face me, and raised her arm. Something whizzed past my head. The weed. She caught it in her hand, winked, and flipped backward into the quarry.

I ran to the brink, afraid to see her smashed against the rocks. But when I got there and leaned over the side, rocks were all I saw.

Once my heart slowed from its running-from-an-ax-murderer rate, I left The Cliffs and drove toward home. What was she? My guardian angel? *Yeah, right.* Guardian angel my ass. She sure looked like an angel, but what kind of angel dangled a drunken teen over the edge of a cliff? *Nope.* She was definitely something darker. And what did she mean by someone had told her about me? As far as I knew, nobody in my life was a mad scientist or worked with secret government agencies. Though I did know plenty of drugged-out teens who had the potential for doing stupid shit like jumping off The Cliffs for fun. She seemed to know a lot about me. But the longer I thought about her words, the more pissed off I got.

"I do not feel sorry for myself," I scoffed. Why would I? If I played my divorced parents against each other when I needed something, I could have anything I wanted. Their guilt made them eager to one-up each other and be the "good" parent.

No reason for me to feel sorry for myself, though.

The mansion I pulled up to left little room for self-pity. Not that it was home, I only lived here. Mom had scored big when she married Terry. He did well for himself, was nice to her, and was sometimes polite to me...if Mom was around. Whatever. I didn't need another dad. The one I had was bad enough.

I pushed aside thoughts of Kali and parked my car in my allotted garage space next to Terry's SUV. I entered through the door and into the gourmet kitchen that rarely got used. Holding my breath, I tried to rush past the arched dining room doorway before Mom could see me.

"Asher, come here for a minute."

I stifled my groan and turned back. The controlled tapping of her manicured fingernails on the shiny top of our large, cherrywood table seemed out of sync with the muscle twitching in her clenched jaw. Her short blonde hair was impeccable, her designer clothes wrinkle free, but her blue eyes had plenty of lines around the edges. Her plastic surgeon must have been out of town.

"What's up, Mom?" I smiled *the smile* and stood in the doorway, ready to make a quick escape.

"How was school today?" Her left eye twitched.

She knew. If I lied and said it was fine, she'd blow, and I didn't have the patience to listen to my mom bitch at me for an hour. I chose a different path.

"I didn't go." I looked at the floor and shook my head.

Mom stood barely over five feet tall and might weigh one hundred twenty pounds, but she crossed her arms and tried to look intimidating. It might have worked if she'd ever punished me before.

She tapped her foot under the table on the hardwood floor. "And why not?"

I cleared my throat. Connor and I had this rehearsed, so I knew the script. "I had to help Connor. This morning, I went to pick him up, and he was…" *Wait for it.*

She raised her eyebrows. "He was what?"

I sighed and joined her at the table. "Drinking again. Something happened with his dad, and I stayed with him to talk through it." Technically, it was true. His asshole dad always caused problems for Connor. Mom didn't need to know our *talk* involved us both downing beers while we bitched about the jerk.

She rubbed her forehead, and the foot tapping stopped. "Poor Connor. He has it rough, doesn't he?" She patted my hand. "You're a good friend for him, Asher. But I hate for you to miss school."

I bit back a laugh. She'd swallowed the lie, as usual, wanting to believe I was a good boy because then it meant she'd done her job. If she looked deeper, she'd realize the truth. I shouldn't laugh.

"What was I supposed to do, leave him alone and let him get drunk?" *Without me?* "He might have done something stupid." *Like drive a hot, freaky redhead to The Cliffs, thinking he would get laid, and instead have her scare the piss out of him.*

"No, but maybe he needs professional help."

"No. If his dad finds out, it'll just get worse." I hurried to the door. "We'll go to school tomorrow. Sorry." I ran up the stairs, her groan following me.

I blew out a breath as I entered my bedroom and closed the door. My room—my suite, actually—was professionally decorated and decked out with blue walls and dark furniture, roughly the size of a studio apartment, with my own bathroom and even a refrigerator in the corner. I could live up here and never have a reason to go downstairs or talk to anyone. Until I needed clean underwear or food. Even then, Mom washed, dried, and delivered.

I threw my backpack on the chair in the corner and fell onto my bed. I stretched out, easy to do on a king. Rubbing my head, I pictured Kali.

The image of her body didn't make me forget the other weird things about her. Had she really frozen me with her laughter? In the safety of my room, the whole thing seemed like a bad dream.

Yeah, at first sight, I wanted her, but screw that. My *guardian angel* was batshit. I'd be better off with anyone else at school. Even Grace would—

Nope. Jumping from my bed, I cut that thought off before I could finish it. What I had with Grace was over. She'd made that perfectly clear.

I headed for the shower. The sun blasted through my bathroom window, sparkling off the gray granite tiles. I

13

flipped on the shower and waited for the water to heat. Stripping off my clothes, I pictured the scene at The Cliffs and laughed. *Yeah, it must have been bad weed. A bad trip. Sure, that's what happened.* Maybe, if I kept repeating the lie, I'd believe myself. Steam poured out of the stall as I opened the glass door, but I stepped into the shower and turned up the heat. Even that couldn't erase the chills on the back of my neck.

****

The next morning, I left for school like I'd promised, stopping by Connor's house to get him, too. If I had to go, so did he.

Connor pushed his way out the front door and strode toward my car—torn jeans, black wrinkled sweatshirt, his short brown hair a dark messy wreck. And a fresh purple bruise surrounding a lump on his forehead, not quite hidden by the hair he pulled over it.

My stomach ached, and I shook my head. *I wish his dad would drop dead.*

Connor wasn't small. At six feet and about one hundred eighty pounds, he should have been able to defend himself from his asshole dad. But for some reason, he never fought back. I never asked why, and he never volunteered the reason, but I think he didn't want his dad to retaliate by beating his mother instead of him. Not that his dad needed a reason for that either. Connor's mom sported her own bruises whenever I saw her.

He slammed the car door and launched into his complaints. "Man, what the hell. I don't want to go to school. This is bullshit, Asher."

I pulled away from the curb and didn't comment on the bruise. He would just blow it off. "I know, but it's almost over. Two more months and we graduate."

"Yeah, then what? At least you have a plan. I got nothing." He lit a cigarette.

I jabbed a finger on the button and opened his window. "Dammit. You know I don't want you to smoke in here."

He laughed and sucked in another drag. "Fuck off." He blew his smoke in my face, and I coughed. He laughed even harder.

"I won't pick you up, and you'll be the only senior on the bus." I hit a button, and my window opened with a quiet hum. Cold air billowed around us.

"Shit, fine. If you're gonna freeze me out, I'll throw the damn thing out the window." He took one last drag, then tossed the butt to the shoulder of the road.

I shivered as the windows hummed closed, visions of Kali and ice coming to my mind. "Speaking of freezing, did you notice the hot redhead sitting on my car when I left your house yesterday?" As much as I tried to convince myself Kali was nothing but a bad trip, I couldn't shake what happened completely. Maybe if Connor confirmed her existence, it would make her seem less...spooky.

He raised an eyebrow in confusion. "How does freezing make you think of a hot chick?" The words barely left his mouth, and he laughed. "Oh, I get it. The hot redhead froze you out and didn't give you any."

"Whatever, asshole. Did you see her, though?"

"Dude, you left the shed and got into your car. I didn't see a hot redhead."

Dammit. I swiped a hand over my face.

"Her name is Kali. Said she's new in town." I shivered again, remembering her amazing body, her minty scent, and the magical way she'd disappeared into the quarry with my bag of weed.

"Whatever, you probably dreamed her up. Was this before or after you smoked the rest of your stash?"

I gripped the steering wheel harder. "I didn't smoke it."

His eyes lit up. "Oh, then let's go, man. We can take a toke before school. That should make it more fun."

Talking to him about Kali was a mistake. He'd call me crazy if I told him the weird shit that had happened. Besides, I didn't want to tell him she had bungeed without a cord into the quarry with my weed. He'd never believe me.

"I don't have it with me."

He sagged in the seat. "Great, there goes my day."

"Can't you make it one day without getting high?" I pulled into the school lot and parked near the front. Senior privileges.

He lifted an eyebrow. "Why would I want to do that?"

I chuckled, but my concern flared. I liked to get high, but for Connor it was an obsession. Then again, he had a good reason to escape with drugs and alcohol. But I didn't know what to do about his dad using him for a punching bag. Not like I could stop his old man from being an asshole.

So I did what I could. I drank and got high with him to help him forget his shitty life. At least I bought the pot. That's what Dad's child support was for, right?

When I went away to college in the fall, Connor would be on his own. He might not handle things alone. Ignoring the squirming in my stomach, I brushed it off. Again, nothing I could do.

I scanned the parking lot, looking for Kali. The only

redhead was a stupid freshman cheerleader who'd come on to me last Saturday at Dan's party. All the same old people. The same old girls. Nothing ever changed around here.

From the corner of my eye, I caught a glimpse of strawberry-blonde hair that punched me in the gut.

Grace King sat behind the wheel of her car. She covered her face with her hands but pulled them away just as I drew parallel to her. Our gazes met through the glass—hers was filled with tears.

I slowed my pace and frowned. Why was she sitting in her car crying? Maybe I should—

Uh, no. I'd be the last person she would want to talk to. And I didn't want to talk to her either.

But as I continued to walk toward the school, I couldn't stop from looking back over my shoulder.

Grace had recovered and gotten out of her car. She half ran, half skipped through the cars, grinning as she tapped her friend Britt on the shoulder from behind. Britt turned back and greeted her, wrapping an arm around Grace for a quick hug. They fell into step with each other and headed for the school, chatting, smiling, friends to the end—just like she'd promised me once upon a time.

"What's eating you?" Connor asked, glancing toward Grace.

"Nothing." At least, nothing I could do anything about.

The warm weather of the last couple of days had spoiled me. A brisk breeze cut across my face, and I shoved my hands in the pockets of my jacket. I picked up my pace as we walked to the school and climbed the steps toward the student entrance. Grace disappeared inside the building through the door to my left.

"Hey, Asher."

I paused on the top step and turned back around. "Hey, Vikki." I glanced into the school to see if Grace could see me, but she wasn't there. Not that I had anything to hide. Or that her opinion of me mattered.

"Great," Connor mumbled.

Jogging up the final two steps, Vikki grabbed me around the waist and pressed her lips on mine—and ground her hips against me.

"See ya later." Connor rolled his eyes and followed the crowd into the building.

"You want to skip today?" She wiggled her hips again, biting her lip at my body's reaction.

I breathed deep, pulling her sweet perfume into my lungs. "Can't. I skipped yesterday. My mom will kill me if I do it again."

She pushed out her full lower lip, and my mind flashed back to what she'd done with those lips last weekend. Her thick brown hair tickled my hands as I held her waist and pulled her closer.

"Come on, Ash." She leaned in and kissed my ear. "I won't tell."

"Wanna meet after school? We can…study together."

She licked her lips with the tip of her tongue. "Is that all you want to do?"

"Well, I'm sure I can think of something else."

"So can I." She held my cheeks and pulled my mouth to hers, her tongue slipping between my eager lips. She wasn't my girlfriend, and she knew this was just for fun, but Vikki always kept her promises—unlike Grace.

I pulled back before my body passed the point of no

return and I skipped school with her.

She stepped away. "I'll meet you at your car after school. We can go to The Cliffs for a while, to *study*." She winked on the last word and walked into the building with a swish of her hips.

The Cliffs. The scent of mint surrounded me, and the excitement from Vikki's kisses faded. The hair rose on my neck, and my heart pounded in my chest.

Kali.

We were meant to meet at the bottom of the quarry. I had a strange feeling if I went there today, that's exactly where I'd end up.

Chapter Two

Despite telling me she'd see me again, Kali hadn't showed up at school. Not that I expected her to keep her word. Whatever. Her criticism of my life was just a bunch of bullshit. My life was great. I enjoyed everything in it.

Did that sound like I felt sorry for myself and blamed others for the shit I did? I did it because I wanted to—and changing was stupid. I had nothing to change.

Walking through the hall between classes was an art form. I stayed in the flow of traffic traveling forward on the right side until I reached my final class for the day—senior seminar.

Every senior had to take the ridiculous course their final semester. The administration claimed it was their way of "preparing" us for college and life beyond high school. Students knew it was the school's way of boring us one last time and making us think we weren't ready to be grown-ups yet. Like balancing a checkbook or paying bills wasn't something we could figure out on our own.

I moved to my seat at the back of the room. Sliding onto the molded blue plastic, I glanced around at the other victims. Connor sat two rows over with his head on his desk, fighting a hangover. I would be too if Kali hadn't burned the alcohol out of my body for me. Guess I should be grateful for that.

Vikki concealed her phone from the teacher's view,

holding it between her knees under her desk. She tapped out a text, then stuck her phone into her waistband. Raising her brown eyes to mine, she blew me a kiss.

My gaze traveled past Vikki to the only girl in this school who might be hotter than Kali. No, the only one who *was* hotter than Kali—Grace.

I was the king of the potheads at our school, the ladies' choice for the easy girls, but in the hierarchy of high school royalty, Grace was the queen bee.

She was beautiful and smart and hot and friendly and sexy and sweet. She had it all. Looks, intelligence, and an awesome personality. The fact she didn't flaunt it made most of the guys—and even some girls—drool when she walked by. Me included.

Too bad she hated me.

Just like almost every other time I saw her in class, I couldn't stop from remembering what it was like when she and I grew up together. We used to play games, ride bikes, climb trees. Inseparable. Same ideas, same dreams, we even had the same freaking weird blood type. Maybe it happened when we were kids before I really knew what it meant, but I fell in love with her between eighth grade and freshman year.

After youth group, we'd all gone out for tacos, and Jimmy Petrowski flirted with Grace. He teased her, joking about her being the preacher's daughter and asking if she'd ever be allowed to date, and if so, he volunteered for the job. I wanted to punch him in the face to make him shut up. But Grace just held my hand. Jimmy had given up after her kiss on my cheek.

I swallowed the sudden lump in my throat. That had been before my parents divorced, before I met Connor and the numerous Vikkis in school…and other vices.

21

After hanging my backpack on the seat behind me, I slammed my folder onto the desk as a memory blasted its way into my head—Grace's face the day she'd caught me drinking my dad's bourbon in our old fort by the trees between our backyards.

At first, she tried to get me to stop. Told me I didn't need drugs and alcohol to help with the pain, that she would be there for me. Right. It didn't take her long to give up on me like my parents had. The more I drank, the less she helped. She'd stopped coming over, stopped answering my drunken phone calls in the middle of the night, stopped caring.

I clicked the end of my pen over and over, glaring at the folder. *Fuck her.* I didn't need her approval. But as I sat there in class comparing Grace and Vikki—strawberry blonde to brunette, sweet and clean to fast and dirty—my stomach tightened. I couldn't lie to myself. I knew which one I'd rather be with after school today.

Someone bumped me, and I jerked forward in my seat. "What the hell?" I glared up at Dirk Davis—Dork—our senior class president.

"Sorry. Didn't see you there." He smirked, then slid into the seat next to Grace. "Hey, Grace. Got a minute?"

She turned her head and met my stare for a second.

I scowled, and she looked away.

"What is it, Dirk?"

He leaned forward across the aisle. She leaned back in her chair.

"You busy after school today?" He reached over and tucked a strand of her hair behind her ear.

I clicked faster.

She untucked her hair and shrugged. "Well, sort of. I have a lot of homework I've been neglecting."

Right. Even I knew that was a lie. She never neglected homework. Grace rejected Dork five times a day, and he was too thick to get the hint.

"Well," he pressed, smiling his goofy smile, "we can study together if you want. Then maybe get a bite to eat?"

Pink faced, she looked at her hands.

I caught the scent of mint, and a chill raced down my back.

Kali.

Was she here? A quick glance around the room told me she wasn't, yet I was sure I felt her heated touch, heard her icy laugh. My heart raced.

I wiped my face with my hands and swore underneath my breath. "I must be fucking crazy."

"I have the cure for that," Dan said from behind me. His gaze scanned the room from side to side. "I've got an eighth right now I can give you for thirty bucks."

I cocked my eyebrow. He always overcharged me. "Why you gotta be such a jerk? Just because my mom's husband has money doesn't mean he shares it with me."

He rubbed a thick hand through his curly blond hair. "Fine, twenty, but that's the lowest I'll go." He reached into his pocket and pulled out a small plastic bag, keeping it tucked into his palm. I handed him the money, and he nodded, passing me the bag in a handshake.

I stuffed it into my backpack, and Vikki's gaze caught mine. She wiggled her eyebrows.

Zipping my bag closed, I lifted my gaze right to Grace's. She gave the pocket where I'd stowed my contraband a pointed look, and her face flushed red. I looked away, but it was too late. Sludge filled my chest, and my cheeks grew warm.

"C'mon, Grace," Dork said. "We could go to The Other Place and get some pizza."

His desperation eased my embarrassment at getting busted by her. I smirked. Seeing him get rejected made me feel like less of a jerk. *Good luck, asshole.*

She turned her attention to Dork. "Actually, Dirk, that sounds great. I'd love to have a study partner. I'll meet you in the student lot after school."

What! I glared at her.

Dork lightly ran a finger along her cheek, and I almost launched myself at him, linebacker style. She glanced in my direction and narrowed her eyes, first at my backpack, then at me.

I crossed my arms and glared back. She lifted her chin and turned away with a flip of her ponytail.

My stomach churned. But why should I care what she did when she didn't care about me? Whatever we'd had ended a long time ago, and she wasn't there for me anymore. Just like my parents. I didn't need Grace. And I didn't need Kali either. She was just another name on the list.

****

"Wow. That's good." Vikki leaned her head back on my passenger seat, closing her eyes while she held in her smoke. She blew it out after a few seconds.

I brought the bowl to my lips and paused. Grace's angry green eyes flashed before me. They brought a vision of Dork running his fingers through her long strawberry-blonde hair. They were probably making out right now, his hands touching her soft skin. I scowled and drew in a deep puff, mentally telling the eyes and hair to piss off.

So easy now, inhaling, holding, waiting. The

tingling started in my chest, moving to my brain. Vikki was right. Dan always delivered the best.

I exhaled, my worries leaking out with the smoke. Vikki leaned on my chest and kissed me. Her acceptance eased the loneliness from Grace's dismissal. I kissed her back, my tongue on hers. She took the pipe from my hands and inhaled another toke. She held it for a moment, then her lips went back to mine, and she exhaled her smoke into my mouth.

She wants to get messed up.

She passed the pipe. I took a drag and exhaled into her mouth. She sucked it in, then grabbed my shirt and moaned. She kissed my neck and slipped her hand to the waistband of my jeans, popping the button before I could blink.

"Slow down." I grabbed her hand, Grace's angry scowl rolling through my mind.

"Why?" Her lips went back to mine for a second. "I want you, right now."

"Let's…finish the bowl first."

"Is that really what you want?" She pulled her hand from mine and ran her fingers along the inside of my thigh.

My stomach clenched, and I opened, then closed my mouth. What I wanted I could never have—I didn't deserve it.

She pushed out her lower lip. "Fine, you smoke. I have a better way to use my lips."

Her chocolate-brown eyes held mine for a few heartbeats. I longed for a different pair of eyes to gaze at me like that, a different set of lips to smile and set my heart on fire. Closing my eyes, I took another drag from the pipe.

Vikki leaned toward me, unzipping my jeans. She stroked me, then her lips traced a path along my neck, down my chest, then lower still. I gave a low moan and leaned my head back on the seat. I probably should stop her. Should drive her home. Vikki didn't deserve to be used just because I was so desperately lonely. But that was my biggest problem—I was so desperately lonely. With my eyes still closed, I let strawberry blonde capture my imagination.

After, Vikki grabbed the bowl, inhaling deeply. She exhaled, and smoke encircled her flushed face. "You're welcome. And there's more where that came from, whenever you want it." She passed me the pipe.

I inhaled, glancing at her. "What's that mean?"

"It means I treat my boyfriend very well."

I coughed. "Boyfriend?" *What the hell? When did that happen?*

She giggled, waving at my crotch. "Come on, Asher. You don't think I'd do that for just anybody, do you?"

We'd had this conversation the first time we hooked up. "I'm not your boyfriend." I lowered the window and dumped out the remaining ashes from my bowl.

Her forehead wrinkled. "What?"

"This was just for fun. You knew that." I wasn't boyfriend material—not anymore.

"No, it's not *for fun*. At least not anymore. I know you said that, but we've hung out a few times now, and I thought—" Her eyes glittered with tears. "Don't you want me?"

Her warm lips covered mine, her other hand stroking me again. My body responded. Wanting her wasn't the problem. Physically, it was easy. The emotional baggage she'd share would take more effort, effort I didn't want to give. Only one person worth that effort, and it wasn't Vikki. Hell, Grace had already proven I wasn't worth the effort either.

I needed to make myself clear on this issue. Zipping my pants, I told her, "I'm *not* your boyfriend."

"Sure you are."

"No, having sex doesn't mean I want to go out with you. You'd be dating half the senior class, including Dan and Connor, if that were true."

She gasped.

I felt bad for saying it but not bad enough to give her what she wanted.

"Go to hell, Asher." She jumped out of the car and slammed the door.

I should have looked away. I should have closed my eyes. Instead, I watched her walk toward the edge of the cliff.

I jumped from the car. "Vikki, what are you doing?"

She stumbled and stutter-stepped to the edge. Wobbling for a moment, she finally caught her balance and turned to glare, tears oozing from her bloodshot eyes. "What do you care? Let me relieve the pressure. You'll never have to worry about fucking me again."

As she turned back to the cliff, I broke into a run. Before she could take the step that would send her falling to the bottom, I reached her and grabbed her by the back of her shirt. But she leaned, and her momentum pulled us both forward.

I yanked her back toward safety, and she fell to her knees in the dirt. My grip on her slowed my forward progress but not enough. I spun my arms, grasping at the air. My feet went over the edge first, and I slid down the side of the cliff, scraping my chest and face on the rocks.

My hands caught a rocky ledge, and she screamed.

I clutched the rock, my sweaty hands shaking. My feet dangled below me, and I kicked the air, trying to find a place for them to catch. The sheer face of the quarry offered no relief. I raised my face and looked toward the top.

Vikki peered over the edge, her face white. "Oh my God. Hang on, Asher. Please don't fall. I'll find something to help." She pulled back and disappeared from my view.

Great. I'm hanging from the edge of a fucking cliff with nobody to help me but the pissed-off stoned girl I just insulted.

The Fates rolled on the floor right about now. I hoped they choked.

I hung, waiting for the rock I clutched to pull away from the soft soil and send me plummeting to the bottom. Instead of screaming in fear, I laughed. Kali had told me we should have met at the bottom of the quarry, and I'd even reminded myself of the possibility before I came here. Maybe it was inevitable. I pictured Kali's beautiful face. Seeing her Hollywood smile when she greeted me might be worth the pain of death.

Then new visions filled my mind. Grace laughing on the playground at recess as I spun her on the merry-go-round. Grace chasing me through the woods behind our house, letting her catch me so she could tickle me and I could feel her touch. And Grace hugging me after I told her about my parents' divorce, her arms tight around my waist, head on my chest as she cried with me. The thought of dying left me as cold as the stone I clung to. But the visions filled me with a burning heat, heat I wanted to feel and taste before I died.

Movement from above sent a shower of pebbles bouncing off my head and face. I closed my eyes until they stopped and looked up again—into Kali's dark eyes.

"Hey, Asher."

Relief flooded me. "Thank God. Please help me out of here."

"Sorry." She shook her head. "That's not why I'm here."

My fingers cramped, and I shifted my grip on the rock. It wiggled, more pebbles falling on my face. Sweat from my forehead burned my eyes. "What do you mean? Why can't you help me?"

"Because this is our date, Asher." She pursed her lips, then whispered, "The one when we were *supposed* to meet."

"You mean…" My heart dropped to my stomach. I glanced over my shoulder into the empty air behind me and wheeled my gaze to her face. "No, please," I croaked with my dry throat.

"I told you, you had to make better choices to change this date." Her tears dripped onto the back of my hand. "My option isn't any fun."

Closing my eyes, I pictured Grace again. Her smile. Her laugh. The way she used to hold my hand while we ran around the playground at school. How I'd sat next to her in the grass at church and listened to her favorite songs, teasing her about the twangy country voices.

Then the memory I'd repressed most haunted me— our first and only kiss. Neither of us had known what to do. It had been sloppy and wet, and I'd done everything wrong. I'd wanted it so bad I went in way too hot and almost chipped a tooth. But I'd give anything, *anything*, to do it over again, because I had ended it—ended everything—with my stupidity.

The next day my parents had announced their divorce, and the pity party I'd celebrated with began. It was all my fault. Now it was too late to fix everything?

No. I wouldn't leave Grace to remember me like this, drunk and high, falling off a cliff.

"Kali, please." My arms trembled from the strain of holding on for my life. "Please let me have another chance."

"I can't. I already broke the rules by trying to clue you in to what would happen." She bit her bottom lip. "I'm not allowed to save you."

"I don't want to die." I meant to shout, but my voice only came out as a shaky whisper. "Please, I have to fix things with Grace. I have to fix myself." The rock I held wiggled again, and I yelped. More dry dirt coated my face, clinging to the cold sweat on my forehead.

She frowned. Then, still chewing her lip, she nodded. Hope flooded my chest.

"I can't help you get out." She stuck out her chin. "Since you've made the choice to change, you need to do this on your own."

"What's that mean?"

"It means you have to save yourself."

She stood, and I had to tilt my head farther back to see her.

"If you can climb out of there, you'll get your second chance. Then I can help you. If not…"

I didn't need her to finish. Breathing deep, I thought of Grace. I could do this. For her. For us.

If I could grab the larger rock just above my right hand, I could reach the one above it and eventually haul myself up the side, like the rock wall at the gym. At least

I had taken care of that aspect of my life. It might just save my sorry ass.

I concentrated for a moment, then swung my hand toward the stone. My hand slipped, and I yelped again, but then I hit my mark, and I grasped it with a death grip. Snail slow, arms shaking and chest heaving, I moved my hands from rock to rock and climbed for my life. For Grace.

Kali bit her lip and watched me work my way back up the three feet I had fallen. Before I got to the top, she stepped backward, and I lost sight of her.

I grabbed the side of the cliff and used my feet to push myself out. I flopped onto the grass along the edge and rolled onto my back, sucking in the sweet minty air. Vikki stood a few feet away, holding a large stick in her hands, frozen like a statue.

"Glad you made it. Now please stop driving under the influence." Kali placed a hand on my sweaty forehead. I closed my eyes and gritted my teeth against the flames seeping through my veins. I opened my eyes to a clear head, but Kali had disappeared.

With a jerk, Vikki unfroze and ran to where I lay.

"You're okay." Crying, she dropped the stick and knelt in the grass beside me. "I'm so sorry. I didn't mean for you to fall. You didn't need to... I wasn't going to jump."

I stared at her, trying to catch my breath. "What?"

"I thought you would run to the edge and grab me." She sniffled. "I just wanted you to go out with me."

My heart already raced from the fear of falling and exertion of climbing the wall. Anger pushed it harder. "I could have fucking died!"

She sniffled. "I love you, Asher. I'm sorry."

31

I wiped my hand across my face. The Cliffs had lost all their allure. They felt ominous, out to get me. I needed to get away before a freak gust of wind blew me back over the edge.

"You don't even know me." I pushed off the ground and stood, wiping my dirty hands on my jeans. "Get in my car. I'll take you home."

She curled her top lip. "Forget it. I'll walk." She turned toward the exit.

I grabbed her arm. "No, it's too far. Come on, Vikki."

She crossed her arms and frowned. "Fine, take me home."

We walked through the dirt back to my car, and the swirling dust erased the mint from the air. Vikki cried, and I squeezed my hands into fists. I was an idiot for coming here with her. My never-ending bad decisions. Not a great beginning for my second chance.

Chapter Three

At her house, Vikki didn't even say goodbye. She jumped out of my car and then ran up the front sidewalk without glancing back.

As I pulled away, Grace replaced Vikki in my mind. The trees blurred past my window, and I frowned at myself in the rearview mirror. "What the hell, idiot?"

I'd almost died today. Why had I gone to The Cliffs if Kali had told me I should have already died there? The Fates wanted a piece of me, and going where they wanted me to go made it too easy for them. I would never go back.

My stomach rumbled, and I made a plan. Shower. Food. Bed. Instead, a surprise waited at home. My dad's car sat by the curb.

"Shit."

I parked and got out. Dad had waited in his car but joined me on the driveway. No wonder my mom sometimes looked at me like I was the devil. She'd told me enough times my father was evil, and I looked just like him.

"Hello, Asher."

I nodded. "What's wrong? You never visit me here."

He ignored my question. "You want to go get something to eat?"

"Really? You're volunteering to spend time with me? If something is wrong, just spill it."

A shadow crossed his face, but he hid it with a smile. "I just wanted to take you to dinner. Do you want to go or not?"

"Can I go change first?" I'm surprised he couldn't smell the pot on my clothes. Or maybe he could and just didn't care enough to complain.

"Yes, I'll wait out here." He smirked. "I'm sure your mom doesn't want me to come inside."

I shook my head. "I'll hurry." I ran toward the door, telling myself I was only excited because I wanted to know what was going on, not because I was glad to see my dad.

I took the steps two at a time, then ran to my room and straight into the bathroom. I cranked the shower and stripped out of my torn, dirty clothes. Scrapes covered my chest, and a long thin scratch cut across my left cheek.

"Dammit." I traced the cut on my cheek with my finger. At least I wasn't smashed like a dead cockroach on the bottom of the quarry.

I jumped in the shower, wincing as the hot water scalded my injuries. I lathered and hurried through the routine. Dad's appearance after two weeks of silence had my stomach rolled tighter than a joint.

I dressed in jeans and a long-sleeved shirt, yanked on my shoes, and ran back down the stairs. Mom banged pans in the kitchen, getting dinner ready. She'd be pissed about Dad being here.

"Mom," I yelled from the front door. "I'm going to eat with Dad. Be back later." I ran out before she could complain.

Dad fiddled with the rearview mirror of his '65 hotrod. Cherry red and in mint condition. Not that he'd had anything to do with the car's restoration, only his checkbook did. He smiled as I pulled the seat belt across my chest.

"Where should we go? You pick."

My stomach dropped. The news must be really bad if he was willing to leave the choice up to me.

"Pizza sounds good." A true test of my dad's intentions. He hated pizza.

He started the car. "Pizza it is, then."

Maybe he's dying.

We drove to The Other Place, the best pizza restaurant in town. Stupid name, but when the deep-dish pie's cheese dripped from my chin, the name didn't matter. My mouth would have watered if I wasn't so worried about Dad's news.

The hostess showed us to a booth in the corner of the store. The dim lighting helped conceal the worn leather seats and graffiti on the walls. Dad slid into one side, and I sat across from him.

His gaze traveled around the old room. "You've always liked this place. We had your seventh birthday party here, remember?" He smiled, tiny creases bursting from the corners of his eyes.

Reminiscing? Holy shit, he is dying.

"Okay, Dad. You got me here. Now spit it out."

The waitress interrupted us to take our order.

After, Dad sighed. "I do have some news, Ash. I thought it would be best to give it to you in person."

I tilted my head. "So tell me."

"You're just like me. Get down to business, never mind the small talk." His grin faded. "Sometimes, Ash, the small talk is important, too."

Dad letting me choose the food? Dad giving me life

35

advice? Dad smiling like he actually wanted to see me?

Maybe I'm dying.

He leaned back in the booth and folded his hands on the scarred tabletop. "I've been offered a promotion at work, and I've accepted. I'm moving to the office in Seattle. I leave next week."

My brain whirred for a minute before the news registered. Before its effect on my life seeped in. Okay, moving was better than dying, I guessed. But if he moved to Seattle, I'd never see him. He lived ten minutes away now, and we only saw each other once a month, if I was lucky.

So this was it. Dad's final event in the father-of-the-year contest—complete abandonment. I clenched my jaw and curled the corner of my lip. "Why did you feel the need to let me know in person? Sounds like I should get used to not seeing you anymore."

The briefest hint of a crease formed between his eyes, and I knew I'd hurt him. *Good.* He'd earned it.

"Ash, you know I don't want that. I try to see you when I can. My job's busy, though, and—"

"And it's more important. I get it. You don't need to explain." I grabbed my pop.

"No, it's not more important." He rubbed his forehead. "I know we haven't spent much time together since the divorce. But I'm trying to make an effort here. Can't you do the same?"

I stared at him. I'd *made* the effort when I was seven and ten and fifteen. Now he was leaving, and he thought we could make up for lost time with the week we had left? All the wasted years filled my chest like wet cement. I didn't have time for his bullshit, guilt-ridden attempt at making amends.

"Dad, whatever. Let's just eat and forget about it." I took another drink of my pop, wishing it were a beer. I bet I could guilt him into buying me one.

His forehead wrinkled, and he nodded. "I'm buying you a plane ticket to use whenever you want to come visit. Just let me get settled, and you're welcome anytime."

"Great. Sounds fun."

He pressed his lips together. Watching my dad deflate shouldn't be so satisfying. My indifference was like a pin popping a bubble—sharp and destructive. He deserved it.

The waitress arrived with our food. Dad tried to restart the conversation a few times but finally gave up. At least the pizza was good.

I should have been used to him letting me down. But like the idiot I was, I let my hopes rise only to have them crushed. Every. Fucking. Time. This time would be the last. This wasn't just a new position at work—it was the final goodbye.

I welcomed it. I was tired of his shit. Tired of him ignoring me. I hoped I never saw him again.

He drove me home, the hum of the engine the only sound. He stopped in the driveway, and I shoved the door open.

"Ash, wait. I don't want to leave this way."

I met his crinkled gaze with narrowed eyes. "Don't worry, Dad. It's no worse than any other time you've left. It's better. At least I won't have to wonder if you'll come back. This time, I know you won't."

Pain flashed across his face, but I climbed out of the car and slammed the door. He didn't deserve my pity.

Anger bubbled in my chest, and the subtle scent of

mint filled the air. I ran to my room and called Connor. My dad might be unreliable, but his wasn't. His dad always had a refrigerator full of beer.

****

"Both our dads are total dicks." Connor tossed me another beer. He popped the top on his, and my mouth watered at the fizz.

I relaxed back into the worn-out recliner, my usual seat in Connor's hangout. The rusty aluminum shed sat at the back of the small yard, resting far enough away from his house that his parents didn't bother coming to see what we were doing. Having to cross the patchy, dirt-filled lawn took too much effort.

I opened my beer, looking around at the ratty chairs and the saggy, stained couch where Connor chilled. He held an ice pack to his black eye—his dad's latest gift.

Swallowing a large gulp, he squinted, then pointed his beer at me. "But at least yours doesn't slap you around."

The stories I told my mom to cover for our beer fests were true. Connor's dad drank a lot and would get pissed at him for anything—not cleaning his room, not filling the car with gas, breathing. I hated seeing him bruised up by his old man, but I didn't know how to help.

"My dad would have to be there to beat me." Thinking of my dad and his latest news, I chugged. My second beer went down faster than the first.

Connor took another gulp, then frowned at me. "Slow down, man. We have a limited supply tonight. The old man hasn't refilled the fridge yet."

"Sorry, my dad's bullshit pisses me off, but at least he never hit me." I crushed the can between my fingers and waved it in the direction of his bruised face. "Did your dad notice the other beer we drank?"

He rubbed his cheek and winced. "No, he thinks he drank it. He cussed my mom out and accused her until she yelled that he probably drank it last weekend when he got wasted Saturday night with his friends." He took a long drink, then reached into his pocket and tossed a small plastic bottle at me. "Here. This should help you relax."

I caught it, even though my head already spun. I turned the bottle and peered in at several round white pills. "What's this?"

"That is your new friend. It's oxycodone, prescription meds like my grandma's. Take a couple. You'll love it."

"You're crazy. I'm not taking these." I threw the bottle back at him, but it bounced off his fingers and hit him in the face. I snorted out a laugh.

"Dammit!" He glared at me. "What's wrong with taking a few pills? They're safer than weed."

"You've killed too many brain cells, Connor."

He shrugged his shoulders. "They come from the doctor. Why would the doctor give my grandmother something dangerous?" He opened the bottle and shook a couple pills out onto his palm.

"Hey, idiot. Don't you pay attention in health class? Those drugs are addictive." I grabbed a third can from the cooler.

"Don't be such a pussy. You won't get addicted from two pills." He popped the pills in his mouth and took a drink of beer. He tossed the bottle back at me and raised his eyebrows. "Come on. It's no big deal. My weed is gone, so unless you have some, these can fill the void."

I rolled the bottle in my hand. The pills clicked against the brown plastic like teeth on a skeleton.

I thought about my dad, Kali, and of course, Grace. I'd begged for a second chance with her without even considering if she'd want it. I watered my doubt with a gulp of beer. Grace already thought I was a waste, Kali knew I was, and my dad didn't care enough to stick around and find out.

I tossed back two pills. *Fuck them.* I might as well feel good while I could.

"I'm proud of you, Asher." Connor pretended to wipe his eye, then he laughed. "I thought you were going to wuss out." He chugged the rest of his beer and picked up his phone. He tapped his fingers across the screen.

"Who are you texting?" I took the first gulp of my fourth beer. *Damn, maybe I should slow down.* Somehow, I doubted the doctor had told old grandma it was okay to toss a few back while she was taking the pills.

"Vikki."

I groaned. "Do *not* ask her to come over."

"Why not? She and Trina texted me before you got here." He opened another beer. "Come on. I'm horny."

"Vikki literally almost killed me today." I thought about how I'd treated her and winced. "If she comes here now, she might finish the job."

His eyes widened. "What happened?"

I told him about Vikki and falling into the quarry.

"I warned you not to mess with her. She's obsessed with you." His phone lit up, and he glanced down. "Sorry, they're here. They were probably stalking the house, waiting for me to text them back."

I rubbed my eyes. "Does Vikki know I'm here?"

"Yes, I told her. Maybe she'll kiss your boo-boos and make them all better." He laughed at my glare.

"Shut up. I should go." I stood to leave but fell back into my chair. "Holy shit."

Grace and I had once spun each other on the merry-go-round until we both puked. The pills and beer had the same effect.

He nodded. "I told you they were great. Relax and enjoy it. Don't want to waste them by freaking out for no reason."

Two knocks on the door echoed in the small shed, and the vibrations rippled along the aluminum walls. Connor ran a hand through his hair, messing it even more. He swayed his way over to answer it.

Vikki's face came into view, and my heart raced. She wavered like a mirage in the desert, and I blinked to hold her still. Connor wasn't lying. The pills made me stoned worse than weed ever had. Must have been from the beer, too.

"Hey." Trina wrapped her arms around Connor's neck. She laughed, hanging on him. Vikki stumbled toward the couch and fell into it. Great, they were both messed up already.

I stood again to leave, but the cotton in my head had thickened. If I drove home now, Kali and I would have a late dinner together in Hell, or wherever she'd come from. I sat back in my chair.

"Ladies, it was nice of you to join us tonight. Beer?" Connor pulled Trina to the couch, then sat between her and Vikki. He reached into the cooler.

"Thanks, babe. Got anything to go with it?" Trina ran her hand along his leg.

"Sorry, fresh out of weed. By the looks of it, you've

already had some appetizers." He smiled at me.

Vikki stared at the floor, sipping on her beer. She raised her gaze to mine and licked her lips. "Asher and I had ours earlier."

I raised my eyebrows. Didn't she have any self-respect?

Connor and Trina weren't listening to us anymore. His hands twisted in her long blonde hair. She hugged his neck, practically climbing on top of him as she kissed him.

Jeez, get a room. I threw my empty can at the wall behind Connor's head. It crashed into the metal, and they jumped apart.

"Don't mind us."

Connor laughed and grabbed Trina's hand. "Come here for a minute. I want to show you something." He pulled her toward the back section of the shed.

He'd added what amounted to a bedroom by shoving another smaller shed against the back of this larger one. The "door" consisted of a hole cut into the wall with a blanket tacked along the top to form a curtain.

Great. I hoped he had at least fixed the bed from squeaking. I didn't want to listen to what they were going back there to do.

Trina giggled and followed him. "What is it? Will I like it?"

"Oh yeah, you'll love it." Connor tugged her hand.

They disappeared, and I grimaced at Vikki. "Sorry, guess we should turn on some music to drown them out."

I reached for my phone and pulled up a playlist. I scrolled through two phones with twenty fingers. The music finally started, but the twangy voice was unfamiliar. *How did I get a country song on my phone?*

Vikki watched me, then set her beer on the rickety TV tray that served as an end table and straddled my lap.

"What are you doing?" I would have pushed her off if I hadn't treated her like dirt earlier. And if I could see well enough to make sure she didn't get hurt. I could barely blink without feeling like I was on a roller coaster.

She kissed my neck, running her tongue along my skin. "I'm sorry about before. Let me make it up to you." Her lips met mine again, cherry lip gloss teasing my tongue.

Forgetting where I was, I kissed her back. Then Grace's green eyes floated through my mind. This wasn't Grace. I pushed Vikki away with my hands on her slim shoulders. "You're wasted."

She rubbed her hand along my chest to the bottom of my shirt. Then she slipped her fingers underneath, and her warm skin met mine. She kissed me again, her mouth moving urgently as she slid her hand between my legs. "But I want you."

I grabbed her hand. "Stop. *I* don't want you."

"Sure you do. We didn't get to finish earlier today." She laughed softly and leaned closer. "Come on, Asher, we belong together."

Hell no.

Her reminder of my near death was like a bucket of cold water over the head. She wasn't the one I'd climbed out to be with. I pushed her off my lap and stood. "I don't want to be your boyfriend, and I sure as hell don't belong with you."

She swayed. Or maybe it was me.

"You're just upset," she said, hugging my waist. "We can talk about this tomorrow."

"No." I stepped away from her. "Forget it, Vikki.

Just leave me alone."

Tears welled up in her eyes. "I thought you were different, Asher. But you're just like the rest of them."

I couldn't argue with her.

She ran through the door of the shed, and I fell onto the couch.

"Dammit." I ran a hand through my hair. Grimacing at the squeaks coming from the other room, I stood and chased after Vikki. As wasted as she was, she'd probably wrap her car around a tree—or another car. Outside, I caught up to her in front of Connor's house. She fumbled her keys, dropping them in the gutter.

"Vikki, wait."

She turned to glare at me, then bent to retrieve her keys, nearly falling over in the process. I grabbed her around the waist and held her steady.

"Let me go. I'm fine." She pushed me away with a hand on my chest and fell back into the driver's side door.

I snatched her keys. She reached for them, but I pulled them away, and her hand swiped through the air.

"You can't drive. You're going to kill yourself."

"So?" She crossed her arms, blinking her glassy eyes. "What do you care?"

Good question. Why did I care? She wasn't Grace. But part of me—the drunk and stupid part—felt bad for her. Maybe because I was just like her.

"I'll walk you home." I clicked her key fob until her car beeped. "You can get your car tomorrow." She and Connor lived in the "rough" side of town, but it was quiet tonight. Still, I couldn't send her off alone. With my luck, she'd get mugged and blame me.

"I'm not walking." She reached again for her keys.

"It's only a few blocks. Don't be stupid. Besides, I can't drive either."

Sniffling, she lifted her chin, lips trembling. "Fine."

She turned on her heel and stomped away. It would have been impressive if she hadn't stumbled. I shook my head and followed her, tripping on a huge divot in the cement.

We walked in silence along the cracked sidewalk. Was she thinking about what had happened today at the quarry? The tears on her cheeks told me she probably was. Each time she sniffled, it sent ripples of guilt through my gut, like pebbles thrown in a mud puddle.

She reached a hand into her jeans pocket and pulled out a joint and a pink plastic lighter. I rolled my eyes. She didn't need any more pot. She could barely walk as it was. Then she lit up, and the smoke blew across my face, igniting my own cravings.

She held it out to me.

I twitched my hand in my pocket. "Nah," I said with a shake of my head.

She took another puff. "Can I ask you something?" Her voice shook, but her gaze narrowed.

No. "I guess."

"Why don't you want to be with me?"

"Don't, Vikki. We've both been drinking and—"

"And you don't think I'm worth answering." She turned her face away, glaring at the weed-filled sidewalk under our feet. "Whatever. Forget I said anything."

"That's not it."

"Right." She sniffled again, then took another drag. "It's not you, it's me. I need space. Let's just be friends. But I can't even get that, can I?"

Her voice cracked, and she smoked some more. The

45

smell of the pot coming off her brought back memories of us in my car. She was right. I didn't want to be her friend, not when I needed to change. *And I'm doing such a fine job of that.*

"I know you still like Grace."

I jerked my gaze to her stony face. "What?"

She rolled her eyes. "I've seen you look at her. Like she's a fucking goddess."

"We weren't talking about Grace."

"You're right." She shook out her hair and drew a deep breath. "We're talking about us."

"There is no us." Maybe I should have sent her home alone. The neighborhood looked deserted, houses all dark. Nobody would mess with her. Probably.

I glanced at the joint in her hand.

"Face it, we're more alike, have more in common."

I'd already had that thought, but everything inside me wanted to tell her she was wrong. She didn't know me. Didn't know Grace. I opened my mouth to argue, but the taste of beer on my tongue glued it shut again.

"She's not the reason I don't want to date you." Even I didn't believe that lie.

Vikki stopped, turning toward me. She held out the joint and raised her eyebrows. I took it and put it to my lips to pull in a drag.

She grabbed my hips. "Think about it. We both have families who don't care about us, both want to be needed, both know how to have fun." She slid her hands to my shoulders and pressed her hips closer. "Why can't you see I'm better for you?"

Swallowing hard, I stared back into her dark, hopeful eyes. With my head spinning from the drugs and beer, I tried to come up with an argument. But she had a point. Everything she said was true, and my foggy brain drew a blank.

"I know I'm not perfect either, Asher. But there's a reason we keep ending up together like this. It's because you and I are so much alike. We belong together." She took my hand and continued walking toward her house.

I didn't pull my hand away.

We walked in silence again, and my mind went back to earlier. The Cliffs. Falling. My *date* with Kali. Vikki wasn't the one I'd begged for, and she wasn't the one I wanted to be with. But just because Kali gave me a second chance didn't mean Grace would. Still, if there was even the slightest hope…

"We both like to get high. That doesn't mean we should go out, Vikki." We stopped in front of her house, and I pulled my hand from hers, raising the joint back to my mouth.

She frowned and stepped closer. "That's not what I'm saying. What I mean is I accept you for who you really are. But she won't."

Again, I met her gaze, blinking to focus my spinning head. Who I really am? Which me was the real one? Which one did I want to be? And did I really have a choice?

"C'mon. You know I'm right. We'd be so easy together." She dropped her gaze to my lips and raised up on her toes to kiss me. But as she drew closer, mint blew across my face, bringing with it a green-eyed vision.

Even with the reminder, though, icy spikes of doubt pierced my heart. Today was a perfect example of how weak I was, running off to get wasted with Connor because of my dad. What made me think I could change?

Vikki closed the gap, her lips soft against mine. She

was right. It would be easy, and I wouldn't have to change at all. Wouldn't have to stop partying. Wouldn't have to give up anything—except my integrity. But I never had that to begin with.

She slipped her tongue between my lips and held my shoulders. I kissed her back, ignoring the guilt and focusing on the warmth of her acceptance. I sucked as a person, but she knew it and didn't care. Maybe that was the best I could hope for. The best I deserved.

Then the mint grew stronger, almost gagging me. *Great, now I pissed Kali off. Disappointing everyone, as usual.*

I held Vikki away with my hands on the tops of her arms. "I gotta go."

She nodded and rubbed her fingers on my cheek. "Just think about what I said. And make sure Trina gets home."

"Yeah. Sure."

She took the joint and walked into her house.

The only one I wanted to think about was Grace, but what did she think about me? And did it really matter? Kicking pebbles, I turned to walk back to Connor's. The breeze blowing in my face cleared away the mint, chilling my face and my heart.

I picked up my pace, hunching against the cold, hoping Connor and Trina were finished. If not, more beer would drown out their squeaks—and hopefully, I could drink enough to silence the doubt screaming in my head.

Chapter Four

"If you ever give me those pills again, I'll beat your ass," I told Connor. Last night I'd been stupid, and I paid for it today—in more ways than one.

I'd finally made it to senior seminar, last period. All day some little dude on a jackhammer had worked overtime inside my skull. I sat in the chair beside Connor before class so I could bitch at him.

"Whatever. It's not my fault you can't handle the big stuff." He smirked.

I bit back the curse I wanted to say. He didn't deserve my anger. After I returned from walking Vikki home and kissing her and listening to her bullshit—and pounded a few more beers and pills—I'd passed out. Luckily, Connor had texted my mom with my phone, or I'd be in even more trouble.

—*Mom, Connor needs me to stay. He's feeling rejected and abused.*—

He was the furthest from rejected as I'd seen him in a while. He was in a great mood today, thanks to Trina.

He shrugged. "Dan's having a party Friday. We going?"

"I guess. But if Vikki's there, I'm leaving." I'd avoided her today, not wanting to talk about the "us" she wanted. In the hungover light of day, her argument still made sense and made me hate myself even more.

"Whatever. Dan's brother bought a keg. That's all I

care about."

My hangover disagreed. I went to my seat in the back before he could say any more. Laughter floated across the room, and I looked in its direction. I shouldn't have.

Grace sat with a group of friends and Dork, laughing like the world was filled with rainbows and puppies and shit. She looked perfectly happy. Maybe the other day she'd been crying about a bad grade or a hangnail or a sappy commercial on the radio. She didn't have any problems now that I wasn't a part of her life.

Her strawberry-blonde hair was pulled to the side in a ponytail that hung over her shoulder. It stood out against the deep-blue, skin-tight shirt hugging her chest. Her skin glowed, like she had a light inside. It radiated from her smile and set her green eyes on fire. She exuded health and happiness.

Vomit burned the back of my throat, and I swallowed it down. Before I could look away, her gaze met mine. My fight-or-flight instincts kicked in, and I wanted to run from the room. Almost like I couldn't bear to have her look at me. No, not almost.

What made me think I deserved a second chance with her?

She rubbed just above her knee for a moment and frowned at me.

I looked away.

Our teacher, Mrs. Kumar, walked to the front of the room, her long skirt and wild curly hair swaying with her quick steps. She clapped her hands together. "Let's go, ladies and gentlemen. Take your seats. I have a surprise for you today."

My groan wasn't the only one in the class. Once

everyone sat, Mrs. Kumar pulled a large flowery hat from behind her desk.

Dan chuckled behind me and tapped me on the shoulder. Leaning his fleshy elbows on his desk, he whispered, "If she makes us take turns wearing that thing, I'm telling her I have head lice."

"Today is a very important day for all of you, class." Mrs. Kumar grinned. "It's your wedding day, everyone. Congratulations!"

Oh shit. I knew what this was. This was the final project. I looked around. Some, mostly girls, were smiling. The guys all had the same look I probably did—unadulterated dread.

Mrs. Kumar continued. "Inside my flower hat are girls' names." She reached behind the desk and pulled out a black top hat. "Here are the boys. Unless anyone wants a same-sex marriage, I will choose a name from each hat, and that couple will be partners for the final project of senior seminar."

Grace raised her hand. "What is that project?"

Really? She didn't know? I thought she knew everything about this stupid school.

"Good question. For this project, you and your partner will simulate a married couple. You will all get jobs, buy a house, pay bills, and most importantly, raise a child."

Half the class groaned. The estrogen half cheered.

Mrs. Kumar picked up a stack of papers and handed some to the first person seated in each row. "Settle down. I have an instruction sheet with the information you need. Take one and pass the rest back. There are due dates listed for various components. Look it over while I draw names." She reached into the hats, and I wiped my sweaty hands on my jeans.

"Li and Heidi."

I took the stack of papers and laid mine on my desk without looking at it.

"I hope I get Grace for my wife," Dan said, taking the papers from me. "She'll probably do all the work so she doesn't get a bad grade. And she's hot."

He was right. She would never let her partner slack off. Dealing with her judgmental rejection wouldn't be worth it to me, though. Then again, I didn't want Vikki for my fake wife either. We'd end up in fake divorce court and fail the class. Or maybe fake prison when she killed me.

"Dan and Gina."

Dan groaned and crossed his arms over his chest. Gina rolled her eyes.

The throbbing in my head increased with every heartbeat.

Each time a pair was made, the chosen couple laughed. A few got rowdy and made catcalls until Mrs. Kumar quieted them down again.

"Ashley and Dirk."

I squashed down the relief that Dork didn't get Grace for his partner. As Mrs. Kumar created marriages, I laid my head on my desk. *This sucks balls.*

"Grace and…" Mrs. Kumar paused.

I lifted my head.

She fumbled her fingers through the black top hat. In slow motion, she held the slip of paper, peering at it through the reading glasses balancing on the bridge of her thin nose. Right before she read the name, mint enveloped me, and I knew whose name she'd picked.

"Asher."

Why did the Fates hate me so much? What had I ever done to them?

I looked at the side of Grace's face. She stared blankly ahead, her lips pressed together. Her friends hid their smiles, darting glances at me. Mrs. Kumar flounced ahead, oblivious to the gigantic can of worms she'd opened in the classroom.

Connor whispered, "Sorry about your luck."

Mrs. Kumar pulled out two more names. "Connor and Vikki."

I snorted, and he flipped me off. The way they partied, they'd be lucky if their house had a roof and their baby had all four limbs.

After all the names had been called, Mrs. Kumar clapped her hands to quiet everyone down again.

"Today, you and your spouse will get together to figure out how and when you will meet to complete your projects." Mrs. Kumar cleared her throat. "*Together* is the key word in that sentence. You are to share the duties of the project, just like a real married couple should share those same duties."

Connor raised his hand. "Does that mean the girls should perform their wifely duties every night? A healthy sexual relationship is important in a marriage."

Most of the guys laughed and a few of the girls, but Mrs. Kumar glared at him. "No, Mr. Martin. This is all hypothetical. That's a big word that means fake, in case you didn't know."

Then all of the girls laughed.

"Get with your partner and discuss your project. If your partner isn't here"—Mrs. Kumar looked at Connor—"come see me, and we can discuss other things."

I smirked at his back. Karma was a bitch.

Laughter erupted, and voices raised as everyone changed seats to meet with their new spouse. Grace didn't move, so I left my seat. I stood next to her, and she glanced up.

"Hi." My voice cracked, and I cleared my throat.

"Hi, Asher."

I checked her lips for icicles. "I'll bet you never thought we'd end up married."

She curled her top lip. "No, not after the way you turned out."

What the hell? I knew she hated me, but she was never mean. "Yeah, time changes everyone. You used to be a lot nicer."

She blushed and scratched the bridge of her nose. "You're right. Sorry."

I didn't expect her to apologize. She was right. I had changed a lot. I sat in the seat next to her, tapping my fingers on the desk, unsure what to say.

Grace met my gaze with her clear eyes and pointed to the cut on my cheek. "What happened? That looks like it hurt."

"Nothing. Just fell." I pointed to the syllabus. "So what should we do about this?"

She flipped through her papers. "It looks like we'll need to meet quite a bit. Let's figure that out first. The only days I have free are Saturdays."

There went my next few weekends. "Couldn't we meet during the week? I usually have plans on Saturdays." Like partying. I didn't want to spend them doing homework.

"Mondays I have student council, Tuesdays I do volunteer work, Wednesdays and Sundays I have church,

Thursdays I have French club, and Fridays my family has family night. Saturday is the only day I can meet with you." She crossed her arms and leaned back. "What do you have that's so pressing on Saturday you want me to rearrange my schedule?"

I narrowed my eyes. Damn, what happened to being polite? Then guilt gnawed my insides. She was truly busy. I was just lazy. "Nothing I can't do another night, I guess."

Grace's blush deepened. "Sorry, again. I shouldn't assume your plans aren't important, too. I've been under a lot of stress. My temper's a little short these days."

She massaged her knee again.

Her apology made me feel even guiltier. And pissed me off. I didn't need her pity.

"Whatever. Saturday is fine. Where do you want to meet?" I glared at her.

She frowned, staring back into my eyes. I looked away, afraid of what she'd see if she looked too closely.

"How about the library?"

"Sure, it's fine." The jackhammer picked up its tempo in my brain. Maybe I was having a stroke. Would that get me out of this ignorant assignment? I rubbed my forehead.

"I'll meet you there Saturday at ten o'clock?"

"Why so early?" We had Dan's party Friday night. I'd barely get to bed before five a.m.

"Early? That's late." She looked at the desk, and her voice dropped to a whisper. "We used to get up before the sun to play when we were kids."

Her gaze returned to mine and sucked me back in time to tire swings and bike rides, pirate games and adventures in the creek behind our houses and staying up

55

late to look at the stars and laughing and friendship and love and *dammit*—I wanted it back.

Then I smelled mint and knew that world was gone. Because of me. Despite Kali and her second chance, I'd never recover it.

I narrowed my eyes against the pain. "Ten o'clock is fine."

She nodded. "Good."

We didn't talk the rest of class. She wrote in her notebook, taking notes on our upcoming marriage. I watched the other, happy couples talk and laugh around us with a hollow pit growing in my gut. Grace deserved better, something better than me.

****

I entered my house through the garage and into the kitchen. Throwing my keys on the cold, granite countertop of the island, I slammed my book bag into the metal back of the barstool.

"Dammit." I hopped onto the other stool, leaned my elbows on the counter, and squeezed my head between my hands.

Mom's heels clicked against the slate tiles as she strode into the room. "Rough day?"

I raised my head. "Nope. Everything's great."

She chuckled at the sarcasm in my voice. "Want to talk about it?" She grabbed her purse and slung it over her shoulder, tapping her shiny nails on the counter.

Yeah, she really looks like she's interested. "I'm not in the mood to talk."

Glancing at her watch, she nodded. "Okay. Well, I need to run and meet with a caterer for the English wedding next month." She rolled her eyes. "Georgia insists on having sushi at her reception, even though her future mother-in-law is allergic to shellfish. Grab whatever you want for dinner. I'll be late. I'm meeting Terry for dinner and a movie after he leaves work. Money's on the counter."

She waved, then rushed out the door I'd just entered. I snorted a laugh. *Yep.* Mother of the year. Bet Georgia had the same relationship with her future in-law. That would explain the poisonous reception menu.

Food wasn't what I wanted. I had something else in mind. Ignoring the money, I went through the arched doorway and into the dining room, walking right up to the cherrywood hutch sitting on the wall opposite from the kitchen.

LED lights from the top of the case reflected off the crystal decanters lining the glass shelves inside. I stared at the multicolored hues of brown and gold filling the bottles. On the far right, a green bottle sparkled brighter than the others, drawing my gaze—and tightening my chest.

Emerald green. Shiny. Judging me. Just like Grace's eyes.

I reached for the door and froze. Usually, Connor stole the beer or alcohol for us from his parents, or I paid Dan's older brother to buy it. I'd never drunk here because I didn't want to get busted. Mom would kill me if she found out. Dad would get pissed and tell me what a fuckup I was. Mom's husband Terry would probably call the cops and press charges for stealing.

"What the hell am I doing?" I turned away and stepped toward the stairs to my room. Expecting mint to slap me in the face, I took another step. The only scent I found came from Mom's plug-in air freshener next to the cabinet. Flowers, not mint.

Flowers, like the kind I smelled when Grace passed by me in the hall at school laughing with her friends and not looking my way. Ever.

Pressure filled my chest, and I blew out a breath to release it. Swallowing the extra saliva pooling in my mouth, I turned back to the cabinet and grabbed the green bottle, not even bothering with a glass. I squeezed my eyes shut, but her face wouldn't leave. I took a swig to drown her, but I came up coughing.

Peppermint schnapps. Great. Probably a joke by the fucking Fates. Or Kali. I replaced the bottle and grabbed another. Clear, filled with brown liquid. Whiskey this time to erase the minty taste in my mouth. I'd had enough mint to last a lifetime.

Carrying the bottle, I took another drink as I climbed the steps. In my room, I went to my dresser and yanked open the bottom drawer. Reaching in the back, I pawed around under my neatly folded shirts. My hand came to rest on the plastic bag I'd stuffed inside.

Pulling out my weed, I grimaced, then crossed the room to my bed and opened the side-table drawer to grab my pipe. My head already spinning, I took another shot of the whiskey and prepared my smoke. I flicked the lighter, staring at the bright yellow flame dancing by my thumb.

I raised the pipe to my lips and—stopped.

Wait.

What was I doing? Drinking. Getting high. Everything I said I wouldn't do anymore because I was supposed to be changing. For Grace. My second chance.

Vikki was right. I was just like her.

A fuckup.

No wonder Grace hated me.

I lit the bowl and took a deep toke. Why bother changing when Grace wouldn't want me anyway? I took another toke, breathing it in deep and holding it for as long as I could.

After three more tokes and a few more shots, my pity party went into full swing. Like lampshade-on-the-dancing-drunk-Uncle-Joe's-head mode. Only the drunk wasn't the crazy uncle. It was me. And my dance took on a darker tone.

I grabbed the lamp from the side of my bed, gripping the base like a bat. I pictured Grace's face today as we'd talked in class, her cautious gaze, her disdain when she asked what plans I couldn't deign to break for her royal highness. Her fake concern when she pretended to actually consider my feelings.

With the precision of a four-year-old playing T-ball, I bashed the lamp against the nightstand, cracking it and the wood below. Shards of white ceramic sliced my fingers, blood coating my skin, but I didn't feel any pain. Gulping air, I looked for something else to destroy, like Grace had destroyed my hope today.

"Fuck!" I yelled. I grabbed the alarm clock from my cracked nightstand and threw it across the room. It shattered with a satisfying explosion of plastic and wires, leaving a divot in the wall.

I laughed, and even to my ears I sounded deranged. Energy from my anger fed the need for more destruction. But the best thing to destroy would be myself, because nobody would care. I sat on my bed and grabbed the bottle again, chugging a few gulps. The burning in my esophagus was more satisfying that the clock exploding.

"Having fun, are we?"

Jumping, I dropped the pipe on my bed, scattering a

few ashes on my blanket.

"Shit!" I patted the embers, burning the palm of my hand, then whipped my head around to meet her glare.

Kali stood at the end of my bed, arms crossed and eyes narrowed. "How's the bud? Is it everything you wanted?"

Ignoring the heat in my face, I glared back at her. "Yep."

She shook her head, curling her lip. "Really? 'Cause I *thought* you wanted another chance with Grace." She bit out the last word with a snarl.

My gaze made a blurry circuit from the bottle to the pipe and back to her angry eyes. I curled my own lip. "Shut the hell up. What do you know? You have no idea how I feel or what it's like to want what you can never have."

I grabbed the bottle and lifted it to my lips, letting the alcohol burn away the guilt she dredged up in my chest.

She uncrossed her arms and clenched her fists. "Hmm. You think so?" The flames crawling along her arms belied the calm in her voice.

I rose from my bed and backed away from her. "Why did you even come here? Just leave me alone."

"Right. Let me guess," she sneered. "You can handle things on your own. You don't need my help. You're in control." She glanced at the pipe and bottle in my hands. "That's obvious."

I glared at her and lifted the bottle. "Yeah. This is me being in control." I tipped the bottle back and took a long drink. Wiping my mouth with the back of my hand, I smirked. "See, didn't spill a drop."

I was being an asshole, but I couldn't stop. Like I

was on autopilot, channeling my inner Connor's dad.

Kali made a noise in the back of her throat. "You're ridiculous."

"Oh, sorry, where are my manners?" I tried to give her a mocking bow. Stumbling forward and catching myself on the bed ruined it. I tossed her my pipe. "Want some?"

She caught it and narrowed her eyes. "Now you're just a jackoff."

"Yeah, just like that guy I remind you of, I suppose." I gave her a harsh laugh. "Was he a jackoff, too?"

"No, it was a girl. And you're making all the same stupid mistakes she did." She set my pipe on the cracked nightstand. Her eyes sparkled like black lava rocks in the sun. "And believe me, she pays for those mistakes every day."

"Probably because you tried to help her, too." I took a drink to put out the burn of my self-disgust.

She took a step forward, and the flames grew brighter. "I offered you a second chance. I broke the rules for you."

"So?"

"So there are consequences when you don't keep your end of the bargain." She waved to the bottle.

"Consequences. Aren't there always? Then un-break the rules! Take what you came here for!" I said with a laugh. "It's not like anyone would care if you did. Not even me and especially not Grace."

My head buzzed like a chainsaw. *Screw the guardian thing. Did I just tell a death angel to kill me? Yep. Total fuckup.*

The flames dissipated with a sizzle, and Kali took a step back, frowning. "Enjoy your hangover tomorrow.

I'm sure it will be worth it."

She raised her arms above her head, and blue fire engulfed her body, scorching my retinas. I covered my face with my forearm and turned my head away, gagging on the sulfur stench. When I opened my eyes, she was gone. I sank back onto my bed, still holding the bottle, and took another toke from the pipe.

Glancing at my nightstand, I caught my breath. I set the bottle on the stand and picked up the paper laying there, unable to look away from the face smiling at me from the picture that used to be hidden in the drawer of my nightstand. Grace's face. Happy. Clean. Beautiful.

Unforgiving. Just like Kali. Had she dug this out to encourage me or to punish me? Punishment seemed more likely.

"Fuck you, Kali." Crumpling the picture with a shaky fist, I raised the bottle and drained it, then stuffed it under my bed. Maybe oblivion could hide the real me from Grace's eyes and hers from mine. But as I lay there a few moments later and tumbled over the edge, my vision filled with green—and the air filled with mint.

Chapter Five

The next day, the man with a jackhammer returned to my head—with forty of his closest friends.

Connor slammed the door as he got in my car, and I cringed.

"Shh." I rubbed my forehead. "Please just be quiet."

He grinned. "What the hell happened to you? You look like shit."

"Nothing. I just don't feel good today. Guess I got a bug or something." I pulled away from the curb.

"Right. A bug." He laughed. "Is it the JD bug?"

"JD?" With the throbbing in my head, I didn't have room for riddles.

"Yeah. The Jack Daniels bug." He slapped my shoulder. "You should have called. I would have helped you drink it, then you wouldn't be so hungover."

"I'll remember that next time." Should have known better. I couldn't hide this from the master drinker.

"What were you celebrating?" He gave me a sideways glance.

"Nothing." I tightened my grip on the steering wheel and glared at the car in front of me.

He nodded. "I got one guess. Getting Grace for a partner?"

Hmm. He paid closer attention than I thought. Still, I tried to cover my feelings with a shrug. "Nah, just wanted to get wasted on a Thursday night. Had the house

B.B. Swann

to myself and all Terry's expensive liquor."

He snorted. "Thought he didn't drink."

"He doesn't. But Mom does, and he likes to keep her happy. Now please. Shut up. My head is killing me." He laughed, and I groaned. Finally, I pulled into the student parking lot and parked. We got out, and I squinted in the bright sunlight.

We walked toward the building, and Connor elbowed me in the side. "There's your muse."

I followed his head nod to Grace standing on the steps, talking to Dork. Little Jack in my head turned up the speed on his hammer party. I glared at Grace, then sucked in a breath as her gaze found mine. She lifted her chin and looked back at Dork.

"Asher, wait for me!"

Bile burned the back of my throat as I turned toward Vikki's voice. I glanced back in time to see Grace glaring at her.

The Fates must be working overtime today in the let's-screw-with-Asher game.

"I'm outta here." Connor chuckled. "I don't have time for this shit show."

"Thanks." I smirked as he walked toward the building.

Vikki replaced him, wrapping her arms around my waist. She raised her eyebrows. "What's the matter? You don't look so good."

"Yeah." I glanced at Grace. She leaned against the building facing me but seemed to still be focused on Dork. I narrowed my eyes at his back, then tried to focus my attention on Vikki. "What do you want?" I asked, pulling away from her arms.

She frowned, then stepped closer again. "Did you

64

think about what I said?"

Movement caught my eye. Grace lifted a hand and touched Dork's arm, her laugh carrying to me across the grass. I swallowed.

"Well?" Vikki asked. She moved even closer, grabbing the strap of my backpack and raising up on her toes. The scent of her perfume surrounded me, and my stomach rolled. I clenched my teeth to hold back the nausea.

"Sorry, been busy."

"With what?" She leaned in, wiggling her hips against me and biting her full bottom lip. "Anything I can help with?"

"Not really." God, why had I drunk all the whiskey? I tried to step away from her, but her hand tightened on my shoulder strap.

"I'll bet I can think of something you need." She kissed me, pressing her body into mine.

I held my breath to fight the rising vomit. Then again, maybe I should let it fly. Barfing on her face would get my message across. She pulled away, and my gaze instantly found Grace.

She watched us from the step, arms crossed, then turned, stumbled a bit, and disappeared inside with Dork hot on her tail.

I waved Vikki away. "I have to go. The bell's about to ring." And I seriously needed to get to the bathroom.

Vikki's lips pressed together, and a wrinkle marred her forehead. Then she nodded. "See you in senior seminar."

I dashed toward the building and headed for the nearest bathroom. Kali was wrong. Nothing was worth feeling this hungover. But then again, I deserved it.

****

End of the day. Last hour. Then I'd go home and crash. At least I'd stopped throwing up between classes.

I slid into my seat and heaved a sigh, rubbing my temples with my fingertips.

"Have a rough day?"

I raised my gaze to Grace's cocked brow. She sat in front of me, not her usual seat, and I frowned. Her smile faded as her gaze moved over my face. I rubbed the stubble on my chin and self-consciously cleared my throat. She seemed to see right through to my thoughts and, from the disgusted grimace on her face, didn't like what she saw.

"Yeah, you could say that." I swallowed, glancing to my left as Vikki sat at her seat in the next row, shooting daggers with her eyes at Grace.

"Hmm." Grace drew a deep breath. "Sorry to hear that. Can I help?"

"Not really. Besides," I said, as guilt started its landslide from my throat to my stomach, "I don't think you really want to help me."

Fight hurt with hurt. The biggest lesson I'd learned from watching my parents play the blame game.

She flinched, sitting straighter in her chair. Then she narrowed her eyes and jerked her head toward Vikki. "You're right. You have Vikki anyway. She's more your speed."

"Don't you mean my *type?*"

"No, I said what I meant. She's more your speed. You know—fast and easy."

Game. Set. Match.

I frowned. Grace stood, turned with a flip of her strawberry-blonde ponytail, and walked away.

Second chance. Third chance. Hundredth chance. No matter how many Kali gave me, it wouldn't matter. I was out of chances with Grace, and nothing would convince me otherwise—not even the mint around my head strong enough to burn the tears from my bloodshot eyes.

****

After school, I drove to the quarry. I was an idiot that way. I had tempted the Fates here twice, and they hadn't gotten me. Maybe the third time was the charm. Maybe I'd help them out.

I parked my car next to the edge and stepped out into the sunshine, squinting my eyes against the brightness. A pair of sunglasses lay on my passenger seat, so I grabbed them and slapped them on my face. The clear liquid in the bottle I'd bought off Dan after school sparkled in the sunshine. A little hair of the dog. Just what I needed.

I gazed around the empty quarry. Most kids only came here on the weekends to mess around. The quiet suited me fine. I didn't want to talk to anyone. I had something to consider, and I didn't want anyone else to bug me while I did it.

I took off my jacket and threw it on the seat. The weather had warmed since the cool early morning, and my T-shirt was all I needed. I closed my eyes and tilted my head back. The warm sun prickled my skin, almost making me feel alive again. I was dead long before I climbed from the side of the quarry for a second chance.

I approached the cliff, picturing Vikki near the edge, my hands gripping the rock as I hung there, begging. I picked up a handful of rocks and threw them, one by one, into the quarry. After taking a sip from the bottle, I winced as the vodka burned its way to my gut.

I sat with my legs dangling over the side against the background of the massive hole. My feet seemed insignificantly small, like me and how I fit in the world. My unsteady gaze fell to the bottom of the quarry. It was too deep for me to see it well, but I'd been there before. Sometimes we'd drive the steep, curved road used for carrying out the quarried rocks and party at the bottom. Years of scraping and digging had left the walls smooth, flat, nothing to get in the way if someone fell—or jumped.

Would anyone know if I was gone? Would anyone care?

My mom might care a little, shed a few tears. My dad would have his secretary send flowers. Connor would have a party to celebrate my memory and have a reason to get fucked up. Vikki would get high.

What about Grace? Would she care? Would she speak at my funeral, remember games we had played, stories we had made up, tell everyone what I had been like before I became an alcohol-guzzling pothead? Picturing her face hurt the most because it meant the most to my battered heart.

I didn't want to face any of them again. Jumping would solve that for me. Vikki, Mom, Dad. And Grace. I'd disappointed her the most. But I hesitated. Waiting for something, just not sure what it was.

The minty scent reached me, and her footsteps followed, crunching in the gravel behind me.

"This was stupid, Kali." I couldn't look at her. My stomach churned with the sludge of shame and what was left of my hangover.

She joined me on the edge. She placed a hand on my

leg, and the heat from her touch warmed my icy blood. At least it didn't hurt.

"Talk to me," she said.

I raised my gaze to hers, the blackness tempered by the blue—and concern even a blind man could see.

"Why didn't you help me, stop me from doing the stupid shit? You said you would, but you haven't helped at all." I lashed out at her for the neglect I'd been given from everyone important in my life. I let the alcohol burn away my hurt.

I swallowed, then wiped my mouth with the back of my hand. "You said I could have a second chance, that you'd help me, but you lied. You haven't done anything to help me change." I raised the bottle to drink again, but instead, I threw it into the quarry. The sound of breaking glass never reached my ears. I even fucked that up. *Can't even throw an angry tantrum right.*

She slipped her hand into mine. "Asher, I can't make decisions for you. You're a big boy, and you have to think for yourself."

I thought of all she had seen me do, all the terrible things I'd said to her, and heat filled my face.

A hawk flew across the gaping maw of the quarry, swooping down, aiming straight for the side of the cliff. Just before he crashed into the side, he extended his feet and snatched something from the rocks. His powerful wings pumped him higher until he disappeared in the sky. I would like to imagine myself as the hawk, strong, in control, but that would be a lie. I wasn't cut out to be the predator. I'd always been the prey, cowering in fear and self-pity.

I met Kali's gaze and wondered what she saw in mine. "Why did you bother? I can't change. I *hate* myself too much."

A silent tear slipped between her lashes and rolled down her cheek. Who knew a reaper would cry for a broken piece-of-crap teenaged boy?

"I don't want you to hate yourself. But you've hit what experts call rock bottom. There's no place to go but up."

My sarcastic laugh echoed off the cliff. "Right." I ripped off my sunglasses and rubbed my eyes. "Up is impossible, Kali. Up is the sky. I'll never make it."

She squeezed my hand, and a wave of heat rippled through my body.

"You're stronger than you know. I have faith in you."

"You shouldn't. I sure as hell don't." The weight of all I had done crashed down on me on the side of the quarry. It crushed me, smashed my lungs, cracked my back, until I was too weak to stand, too broken to move.

I hadn't cried in years, not since before my parents divorced, back when I still had hope for a happy life. Sadness was just existing, meaningless without the foil of happiness to show what was missing.

Talking to Grace, watching her laugh with other people, remembering what happiness used to feel like, and finding out how far away I was from it, I'd realized how horribly sad I was. And I didn't want to be sad anymore, but how could I change? With my death angel holding me in her arms, I cried. I cried for lost time, for lost opportunity, for lost life. But most of all, I cried for lost love, because I'd never known I had it until I drank it away.

The tears eventually stopped, and Kali smiled. She held my face in her hands. The warmth filled me up again and replaced the cold hollow emptiness I had lived with for so long.

"What are you going to do, Asher?"

The choice had always been there. It wasn't Kali's to give or hers to make. I had messed up my life. My parents hadn't done this to me. Their indifference, or maybe their misunderstanding of me, wasn't to blame.

Bad things happened to everyone, and nobody's life was perfect. What we chose to learn from those bad things, what we chose to do *despite* those bad things, defined who we were. I was tired of throwing my life away, tired of destroying myself slowly with drugs and alcohol. And I was tired of feeling sorry for myself.

I wanted to be someone Grace could love, because I'd never stopped loving her. On the edge of the quarry where I was supposed to die, I chose to redefine my life. But I needed a new dictionary. Mine was ripped to shreds.

Kali's dark gaze demanded an answer. I gave her the only one I had.

"I don't want to die, but I'm not sure how to live."

She tightened her grip on my cheeks before letting go. "Deciding is half the battle. You took the first step. I'll help you with the rest."

She pushed herself up from the ground and held out her hands. I stared at her, then placed my shaky hand in hers. My legs were steady, but inside I shook like a flag in a tornado.

"What do I do?" I tried to act positive, but my question sounded hopeless to my own ears. Her much keener senses would see right through me.

"You have to promise if I try to help, you'll listen. I have rules, too, you know, and there are consequences when I intervene."

I nodded. *I hope I don't let her down, too.*

She pulled me toward my car. "The first thing is easy, though."

"What's that?" Baby steps sounded good.

She smirked. "You need to cancel plans with Connor. That boy is nothing but trouble."

Chapter Six

"Get your ass over here, Asher. Dan's party starts soon. I need a ride." Connor wasn't one for small talk. It was Friday night, and that meant one thing—*let's get wasted*. It couldn't be my motto anymore, but he always made beer sound good.

I melted farther into my mattress and knew I'd fall asleep soon. I'd made my choice to follow a new path, and I'd stick by it, but I couldn't tell Connor. Warm fuzzy moments weren't his style. "I'm staying home tonight. I feel like shit." That part was true.

"Come on, don't be such a wuss. Take some aspirin and get over here." His laugh pierced my eardrum. "Don't bail on me now—I need to get out of here."

I frowned. "What's up?"

"My fucking dad." He groaned. "He's already wasted, bitching about his shitty life. I don't want to give him the chance to take his anger out on me."

Now what? I couldn't leave him to deal with his dad alone. "Why don't you come hang out here tonight? We can order a pizza."

He giggled like a girl. "Omigod! Can we have a pillow fight and paint our nails, too?"

"Very funny, asshole. I just don't feel like going out tonight."

He laughed. "C'mon, man—don't let me down. I really need to drown myself in cheap beer. We can't do that at your house."

He was scared. He would never tell me about his dad if he wasn't. But I couldn't go to a party and not get drunk or high.

"I told you I'm not going. Besides, I have to meet with Grace tomorrow at ten for that project." My stomach flipped. Pretending Grace was my wife hit every level of weird I could imagine, but my heart raced every time I thought about it.

"Ugh. Screw Grace. Let's *go*," he said.

I gritted my teeth, and my concern for him faded with his insult to Grace. "No. I'm hanging up now. Call someone else for a ride." I tossed my phone on the nightstand and closed my eyes. My mood must have been how people felt after they had a good cry, like I could sleep for a week.

I cringed, thinking about how it would have looked if someone saw Kali holding me when I boo-hooed on her shoulder. Not that anyone else could see her. She'd told me only the people about to die—and that she was supposed to collect—could see her. I could only see her because I'd been on my way to plummet into the quarry and end up an Asher pancake on the bottom.

My phone vibrated on my nightstand. *Damn it.* Connor would need to make friends with a new driver if I wasn't taking him to parties anymore. I pressed my fingers into my eyes and answered.

"Connor, I'm not going to the damn party."

"Wise decision, but this isn't Connor."

I bolted up in bed, heart racing, and smoothed my hair with my hand. "Hey, Grace. Sorry, thought you were Connor calling me back again."

She chuckled, and I fell backward in time to us

watching cartoons on Saturday morning, eating sugary cereal, and planning our next adventure in the creek.

"Believe it or not, I figured that out on my own. Can we meet later tomorrow? Something came up, and I won't be able to make it at ten."

"I guess." Something. Probably a date with Dork. "What time can you meet?"

"How about noon? We can meet for lunch."

I laughed. "Do I have to treat?"

Cringing at the silence, I took a gulp of air and waited for her to respond.

"I'll pay my own."

"Sure, sure." I struggled to find a topic to fill the awkward silence. "Uhm, so what do you have going on?" *Nosy much?* "I just mean…is noon late enough for you to make…whatever it is?"

"It's just…something I gotta do."

So secretive. Whatever, not like I had anything else to do. "Where should we eat?"

She cleared her throat. "Let's meet at The Other Place. Their pizza is awesome."

"I'll be there at noon." I grimaced. Maybe I should have suggested McDonald's. Thanks to Dad, the pizza place had bad memories.

"See you then."

"Grace?" My breath caught, and I struggled again to find words. I didn't want this call to end, but I didn't have the right to talk to her like a friend.

She sighed. "What, Asher?"

"I'm…I'm sorry about what I said earlier." *Sorry about everything I've ever said.*

My mind filled her silence with the years of pain I'd given her.

"Sure." She cleared her throat again.

"Never mind. I'll see you tomorrow."

Her soft breath blew through the phone speaker in my ear, music playing in the background. Country. It had always been her favorite.

"Have a good night."

"You, too." I remembered game night. "Have fun hanging with your family."

"Uh, thanks. Good night."

I chuckled at the surprise in her voice as my phone went silent. I added her to my contacts and searched through my phone for a picture of her. The ones I had were two years old, from when we were still together. I scrolled through them and stopped on one where she stuck out her tongue. I laughed, then tapped it and added it to her profile. Maybe someday I'd be ready to call her.

I tossed my phone back on the nightstand and clicked off my lamp. Mom must have replaced it, and I figured I'd still be on the receiving end of her lecture about taking care of things. At least I'd been able to put back the empty whiskey bottle.

I threw back the covers and slid under my cool sheets. The last time I went to bed this early on a Friday night, Grace and I had still been friends.

I guessed some of her goodness had rubbed off on me. But despite her good influence, my dysfunctional ways were sure to cause tension. I'd find some way to fuck it up. Still, as I eased into the deepest sleep I'd had in a long time, I smiled. And in my dream, Grace smiled back.

****

The screeching buzz of my phone's alarm jerked me awake. Eyes closed, I slapped at it to turn it off. It fell to the floor and bounced under my bed, still making the god-awful shrieking noise. I opened my unwilling eyes and groaned at the sunlight blasting my face. Rolling, I fell out of bed, landed on my stomach, and pawed at the soft gray carpet, trying to grab the stupid phone. I fumbled with the screen. The noise cut off, and I laid my head on the floor.

"Happy fucking Saturday. Well"—I rubbed my eyes—"at least I'm up." I pushed off the floor, then stretched my arms over my head and glanced at the phone. Eleven o'clock, an hour until I started my new marriage to Grace. Heart racing, I grabbed my clothes and rushed into the bathroom.

Lathering my hair with shampoo, I thought about Kali. Was she able to influence my life, the stuff that went on every day? She said I had to make my own decisions, but I suspected she had helped with a few key events, like making Grace my fake wife.

I toweled off and got dressed. The warm weather continued, so I threw on a black concert T-shirt with jeans and pounded down the stairs, hopping over the last three steps. Mom and Terry stood from the couch in the formal living room.

"Asher, come in here for a moment, please." Terry's voice was polite, but it grated on my nerves. He was only polite if Mom was around, and even then, it didn't last long. I sighed and altered my steps, heading for them instead of the door.

Terry's appearance always shocked me. His short frame, salt-and-pepper hair, and general nerdiness contrasted with my dad's movie-star look. Why Mom had chosen him for her affair stumped me. It couldn't have been his personality. Maybe it was his overly large bank account.

Ignoring him, I focused on Mom. "What's up?"

She lifted her chin and held her hands behind her back, hiding something. "We need to talk. Sit down please."

The *something* wouldn't be good for me. With my luck lately, she had a forty-minute lecture planned. Not that I didn't deserve one. I checked my phone. "Mom, I have to meet Grace in fifteen minutes. Can't this wait?"

Her eyes widened. "Grace King?"

I pressed my lips together and rolled my eyes. "Jeez, surprised much?"

Her face reddened.

"We're doing a project for senior seminar. She's my wife, and we have to make plans for our marriage."

She lifted an eyebrow at Terry.

He snorted. "That's a stretch."

I glared at him. "What the hell does that mean?"

Mom patted his arm and gave him a warning glance before turning to me. "Nothing. Go meet Grace. We can talk later."

He pressed his lips together.

I cocked my eyebrow and smirked. Asher one, Terry zero.

"See you later, Mom." I ran out the door into the bright sunshine. I climbed into my car, then cranked the music up and rolled the windows down. I reached the restaurant and parked, then walked up to the building and pulled the door open right at noon.

My eyes adjusted to the dingy darkness after a few moments, and I scanned the room. I found Grace and caught my breath. She sat at the same booth where Dad and I had sat.

With my heart pounding in my ears, I checked her out as I approached the table. Her long hair gleamed, pulled back in a ponytail again. Her pink T-shirt hugged her body, and black leggings clung to her perfect legs. I swallowed to wet my suddenly dry throat.

She absently massaged her thigh, then looked up from her menu as I drew closer, a small smile playing on her lips. "Hi. Thanks for meeting with me."

Maybe it was a trick of the light, but her eyes looked puffy, like she'd been crying again. *Does she hate having me for a partner that bad?* I shrugged. "It's not like we had a choice."

Her face flushed. She glanced back at the menu. "True."

What the hell was wrong with me? I finally get a shot with her, and I said stupid shit.

"I didn't mean that the way it sounded."

"Then what did you mean?" She tilted her head.

"I meant you don't have to thank me for doing what I'm supposed to be doing." God, that wasn't any better.

She narrowed her eyes. "You're right. Let's get this over with."

I dipped my head and bit the inside of my lip.

She reached into her bag on the seat beside her and slid out a crisp plastic folder. After wiping the table free of crumbs, she set the folder on the scarred surface and lined her purple pen and green highlighter up next to the edge of the plastic. She flipped open the folder and pinched the syllabus between her index finger and thumb, then slapped the folder closed. She placed the paper on top, tapping everything straight.

"I've outlined what we need to do each week and when it's due. We'll start today by choosing our jobs and where we want to live. We need to research probable pay and create a mortgage budget based on our salaries. Next time we'll decide on a house and how many children we plan to have. It looks like Mrs. Kumar will throw problems at us, which we have to solve by working together."

I listened to her with a growing smile on my face. She hadn't changed at all. When we were kids, she'd known where to go first on the playground based on how many kids liked the swings versus the slide and how best to avoid the most-crowded areas.

I'd always done what she told me. I never should have stopped listening.

She looked up from her notes and frowned. "What's so funny?"

"Nothing. You reminded me of when we were little, that's all."

A red blush spread from her neck to her hairline, and I smiled even bigger.

"Is that a nice way of saying I'm being bossy?"

"No, just organized." I got lost in her emerald eyes, then blinked to break their hold.

She drew a deep breath. "Well, one of us has to be."

I wanted to argue with her. My grades were better than she gave me credit for, even if they weren't at her level. But she was right. She was far superior in every way. My stomach fell, taking my spirits with it.

"You're right." I dropped my gaze back to the table. I should just keep my mouth shut and let her do all the talking.

Her sigh floated across the table. "I think we need to talk."

"Isn't that what we're doing?" I met her gaze and

raised an eyebrow.

Her white teeth bit into her bottom lip, and I couldn't help imagining the taste.

"I mean, we need to talk about…us."

"Grace…" There was no "us," and the blame was all on me. I didn't need to rehash it.

She raised her hand. "We're here for the assignment. Just because you and I are partners doesn't mean things are okay between us."

Hope rode on a landslide from my heart to the sticky floor at my feet. Stupidity must have been my superpower. I was stupid to think this assignment might lead to that second chance with her. Stupid to think she had any feeling left for me other than hate. Stupid to think I mattered to her like she still mattered to me.

"I know this is just for class. Did you really think that I thought this meant we could be friends again?"

She slouched her rigid posture and leaned toward me. "I didn't mean that the way it sounded."

"Sure." I grabbed the syllabus from her notebook and flipped through it, acting like my world wasn't crashing apart.

She reached out and laid her hand on mine. "Let me explain."

My heart reacted to her touch, pounding against my ribs. I yanked my hand back and bit out a bitter laugh. "Go ahead."

Maybe I should have gone to the party last night and skipped this shit. At least Connor and his friends liked me. I didn't want to sit here and have her tell me what a loser I was. I already knew. I clenched my hands under my arms to stop the tremors, eyeing the pitcher of beer at the next table.

"I...I meant this assignment teaches us about life and responsibility. I don't think we can move ahead without repairing our foundation. Maybe we can fix our past first, and it will teach us to be better in the future."

I glared at her. "You mean you hope you can teach me how to behave."

"No, that's not it." A tear cut a path down her cheek. She wiped it away with the back of her shaking hand.

We'd starred in this scene before. She still thought she could fix me. Our old argument picked up where we left off. Back when my parents first divorced, and Grace and I fell apart. Back when I pushed her away.

Even though I wanted the same thing she did, anger flared in my chest. "I'm not a broken toy. You can't fix me to make yourself feel better."

"I'm not trying to fix you. I want to fix our friendship or at least learn to forgive each other." Another tear joined the first.

Friendship? Did she still have feelings left for me other than disgust and hate? Her tears were like acid on my heart. I slipped out of the booth. "You should ask Mrs. Kumar for another partner."

"Asher, no. I didn't mean to push you away. Please don't go."

Grace grabbed my hand just as the mint arrived. I grimaced. Great, I could almost feel Kali pushing me back in my seat.

No, she *did* push me. Her invisible hand pressed on my shoulder, and I slid back onto the worn leather.

Her whisper crackled like electricity in my head, bringing with it white-hot pain. I held my breath. *Give her a chance. This is something you both need.*

The pain faded, and I exhaled, responding to both of

their requests with a sharp, "Fine."

Grace's shoulders hunched forward a little as she sniffled. "Thank you. And I'm sorry." She rubbed a hand on her forehead. "I guess I thought we could try to make amends."

I raked my gaze over her pink face. "What does that mean, though? You want to hang out? Want me to go with you to your student council activities? Catch a movie on the weekend, go to church with you on Wednesdays and Sundays?"

"I would love to have you at all those places. But only the old Asher, not this jerky one." She glared at me. "Why don't we start by trying to be civil and stop freaking out if we hear things that touch a nerve?"

Kali's fingers dug into my shoulder, and I winced.

Returning Grace's glare, I replied, "Okay. Fine. But promise you won't point out all my faults because I already know what they are."

Her mouth pulled up at one corner. "I promise. I'll try not to nag."

I studied her face for a moment, torn between the desire to run and my need to be with her. A middle-aged woman with a messy bun and a grease-stained apron stopped at the end of the table. She glanced between us. "Are you ready to order?"

"A veggie calzone with an iced tea, please." Grace smiled and looked at me.

My mouth went dry, and I couldn't swallow. I probably wouldn't be able to eat with all the knots in my stomach. And she was a vegetarian, so I didn't want to order meat in front of her. My other choices offended her enough. My face grew hot, and I blurted out the first lame thing that came to mind. "I'll have the same."

The waitress raised her eyebrows and walked away.

Grace exhaled a deep breath. "Should we talk about our jobs?"

"You mean our fake ones, right?"

Her giggle hadn't changed since we were kids. It was still cute and contagious. It eased the tension in my head.

"Yes, unless you want to tell me what you want to be when you grow up."

Glad she had changed the topic, I grinned. "I guess for this assignment I'll be a doctor."

Her pencil scratched across the paper. "What kind of doctor?"

"Hmm. A surgeon. They make good money. I'll be able to support our family, be a good provider."

She raised her eyebrows. "Money isn't everything. You should love what you do for a living, or you'll hate going to work."

The waitress returned with our drinks, frowning, then walked away again.

Grace nodded at her. "See? She hates this job. But she probably has no other options, so she's stuck here."

I looked around the restaurant, smirking at the help wanted sign in the window. This place was dark and crowded with years of pizza and stale beer scenting the stuffy air. I'd hate to work here, too. Not many applicants for that, I'd bet.

"What's wrong with wanting to have money? Everyone needs to pay the bills." I pointed at the syllabus on the table. "And our bills are due in a couple weeks."

"Well, I want to be a counselor. I'd like to help people with their problems."

"I knew it." I smirked. "You're using me for on-the-job training."

She laughed and patted my hand, making my pulse race even faster. "I'm not allowed to talk about that. Remember?"

She turned her gaze to the notebook and made a few more notes.

Her hair fell over her shoulder, glittering in the soft light. Her long lashes feathered over her cheeks. *Dammit.* She looked incredible. I wished we *were* here on a date instead of for homework.

But the things I did on dates weren't things she would like. My stomach burned with shame, and I grabbed my drink, glancing again at the beer on the next table.

She raised her head. "Congratulations, you're a doctor. The fastest guy ever to graduate med school."

I tried to smile, but I was pretty sure it didn't happen.

She bit her bottom lip and looked back at the syllabus. "We can pick anywhere to live, but I think it might be easier to just say we live here. At least we know how much things cost. We won't have to make up or research the finance end of the assignment." She glanced at me. "Is that all right with you?"

"Sure." I waved a hand.

A crease formed between her eyebrows. "We can move somewhere else if you want."

"I don't care where we fake live." I rolled my head between my shoulders.

"Then why are you upset?"

Because I'm not good enough to be sitting here with you.

"I'm not."

She shook her head and laid her hand on mine. "You

still tap your fingers when you lie."

I craved her touch, but I sure as hell hadn't earned it. It wasn't fair she remembered me when I had forgotten myself. I pulled my hands away and placed them in my lap. "I'm fine. Let's keep going."

Our food arrived, saving me from Grace's steady stare. She'd make a great counselor someday. Those electric eyes would drag out anyone's deep dark secrets.

She turned her smile on the waitress. "Thank you, it looks great."

The waitress walked away with more pep in her step. Grace had that effect on people.

Her eyes caught me mid-stare, and red flooded her face. "What?"

"Nothing." I glanced at her notes. "Is there anything else on the schedule for today's meeting?"

"No, we did enough. Let's eat. I'm starving." She cut off a bite, then pointed her fork at my plate. "Since when do you like veggies?"

"I'm trying to eat healthier," I lied.

She paused mid-chew and raised an eyebrow. "Eating healthy is important, but there are other ways to take care of yourself, too."

Right. Like not doing drugs and drinking alcohol. I chewed my calzone. Telling her about my decision to change might make her smile, and I would love to see that. But what if I failed and disappointed her again?

Better to stay safe.

"What ways are you thinking of?" I asked instead.

She took a drink. "Well, exercise."

"I exercise."

She smirked. "Really?"

"Do I look soft?" I flexed my bicep, tapping it with

a finger. "Do I need to add more weight to my routine?"

My heart sped as her gaze roamed over my chest and arms.

"No, you don't look soft. You look…" She blushed again, and her gaze dove to her calzone. "I didn't think you would be the type to hit the gym. I mean…"

"You mean potheads aren't supposed to care about their bodies?" My face burned.

"Let's drop it. I shouldn't have said anything."

She took another bite from her calzone. Her face stayed red, and my stomach twisted into a pretzel. Awkward didn't even begin to describe this meal. The waitress walked by, carrying a pitcher of beer to the table next to us. My mouth watered.

Kali's mental voice seized my mind. *Focus on Grace.* My head throbbed in response, and I rubbed my temple. Was this the consequence for her help that she had mentioned? Great, her help meant more pain.

Tell her, Kali commanded. She left my head, and the throbbing eased. I looked at Grace. A lost lifetime of memories shone in her smile, trailed through her hair, danced on her gentle hands. I wanted her to be there, to support me, to help me fight my demons. But the words wouldn't come. I didn't want to talk about the person I'd become when she was still the person I'd fallen for—the one I'd let down.

Kali was right, though. Grace was the reason I wanted to change. And Kali would throw me into the quarry herself if I didn't listen to her advice. I cleared my throat. "Grace?"

She looked up from her food and stared with those magnetic eyes.

"I need to tell you something." My pulse pounded in

my throat, and I took a sip of tea to stall.

"What is it?" She cut into her calzone, oblivious to the terror racing through me.

"I know I hurt you. And I'm sorry."

A muscle on her jaw twitched, and her knife scraped across her plate. She pressed her lips together and glanced at me. "Okay."

"I made all the wrong choices. Even with you there to tell me I was stupid." I took a deep breath and blurted it out. "Would you believe me if I told you I want to change?"

Sagging a little in my seat, I took a deep breath through my nose. Too late to turn back now.

She held her fork midway to her mouth. Her jaw hung open, and her eyes widened. "W-what did you say?"

I dropped my gaze to the table. "I know I've made a mess of things. My life. Your life. And I'm tired." Tired of being a piece of crap. But I couldn't look at her, couldn't bear to witness the hope I'd see in her eyes, hope swirled with disbelief.

"Asher," she whispered. "Do you mean that?"

Yep, she had hope, and I would only let her down again. "I mean it. I just don't know if I can do it." I stared at the scarred tabletop and traced a gouge in the wood with my trembling fingertip.

She shoved aside her plate and reached for my hands across the table. "Yes, you can."

I glanced up and drowned in her tears. I'd done nothing but disappoint her for the last two years, and I didn't deserve her faith. I dropped my gaze again, ashamed of what I'd done, what I still wanted to do.

Her soft voice broke the silence. "I'll be here if you

need me."

"Why?" I raised my gaze to hers. "You don't owe me anything."

"Because I've never stopped being your friend." She squeezed my hands. "I couldn't make decisions for you, but I've waited for you to make them on your own."

She sounded like Kali.

I shook my head. "Would you still want to help if I told you I've been sitting with you and thinking about needing a beer because you stress me out?"

She laughed. "I'd be more surprised if you told me you didn't feel that way."

The tightness in my chest eased a little with her laugh. "Been working on that counselor training?"

"No. I help my dad at church on Tuesdays." She frowned, glancing at the table. "That's the night he meets with the AA group."

Heat filled *my* face this time. I pulled my hands from her grasp. "I'm not an alcoholic."

Her sharp green eyes twinkled under the light hanging above our table, and I couldn't meet them all the way.

"I mean, I like to drink, but it doesn't control me. I can stop if I want to." I gulped and poked my calzone with my fork. "But I'm afraid I don't want to."

She nodded. "Would you like to come with me Tuesday?"

I looked away from her knowing eyes, avoiding the disappointment I knew I'd see there. "No."

"Okay. Maybe next time." She brushed a stray hair behind the curve of her ear. "Let me know when you're ready."

"Sure." *That'll never happen.* I pushed my plate

away. Veggies and guilt didn't mix well.

She checked her phone. "I need to go soon."

Dammit, I didn't want her to go, not when I had let her down. I tried to lighten the mood with a joke. "Got a big date?"

She frowned. "No, it's not a date."

"Anything I can help with?"

She shook her head. "It's family stuff. We have…another appointment."

Yeah. Her family wouldn't want to see me. Especially her dad.

The waitress appeared with the check and two boxes. I grabbed the bill.

"How much is my half?" Grace pulled out her wallet.

"I got it."

Her head snapped up. "No, I'll pay for my own." She tried to grab the check, but I pulled it away. "You're not buying my food."

"Why not? I want to."

She glared at me. "This wasn't a date. Even if it was, I would still pay."

"If you'd been on a date with me, we wouldn't be spending money at a restaurant." I laughed. "Trust me, this is a better way for me to use my resources."

Her cheeks flared. If she kept hanging out with me, they'd stay that way.

I tucked the money in the folder with the bill. "It makes me feel good to do something normal. Besides, we're married now, so my money is your money."

She nodded. "Thank you."

"You're welcome."

We boxed our leftovers, then I slapped on my

sunglasses before walking with Grace out into the blinding sunshine.

Turning, she placed her hand on my arm. "Call me when you need to talk. I'll answer, no matter what time it is."

"Thanks." My stomach twisted, and my heart raced at her words and soft touch. I shifted on my feet, fearing what I'd do left alone.

She pulled me into a hug, her arms holding me together. "You can do this. One step at a time, Asher."

Her whispered words gave me a spark of hope. I hesitated, then squeezed her waist. "I'll try."

She stepped back, and my arms ached to hold her again. She patted my cheek and walked to her yellow Bug—perky and happy, like her.

She pulled away, waving. I sat in my car, unsure where to go, where I'd be safe from myself.

I turned the key. Only one place would let me hide from everything. Ready to face Mom, I turned my car toward my house, knowing what her talk would be about and what would come from it. I'd seen what she'd held behind her back, what she'd found in my room.

I pressed on the gas, ready to face this problem and take that first step toward freedom. Toward Grace. I laughed to myself, looking forward to being grounded. That was one sure way to keep me in line.

Chapter Seven

Dad's car sat in the driveway. Seriously? Mom thought she needed backup, and *he's* the one she'd called?

I parked in the garage and cut the engine, staring at the shelf-lined wall in front of me. Stalling. Inside, more people waited for me to disappoint them. I entered the house through the empty kitchen and walked to the living room.

My parents sat on opposite sides of the room. Mom on the cream-colored suede couch and Dad in the brown leather side chair, like if they got too close, they would spontaneously combust. Considering their volatile relationship, they might. The glass coffee table between them wouldn't survive the showdown.

"Hey, Asher." Dad smiled, but it didn't reach his eyes.

I crossed the room, feet slapping on the polished wood floors. I flopped into the matching chair next to him. "Let's get this over with."

"This?" Mom raised her perfectly arched eyebrows. "So you know what I'm about to say?"

"Yes." I glared at her. "You're about to tell me I'm a loser, like Dad."

He chuckled, and she whipped her face to his. "This isn't funny, Michael."

"No, it isn't, Beth. But he has a point."

She ignored his comment and snapped her gaze back to me. "I found this in your room."

My bowl bounced on the glass table, and I winced at the loud crack of the metal on glass.

She crossed her arms. "What do you have to say?"

"What do you want me to say?" I narrowed my eyes, glancing between them. "You both had your own when you were younger."

She gasped. He cleared his throat.

"How do you know that?" Red blotches spread across her face and neck.

"You and Dad used to talk about it with your friends. Guess you should have been more careful if you didn't want me to know." This conversation had taken on the feel of a cheesy made-for-TV movie about drug addiction.

"This is about you, not us." He sighed. "We don't want you making the same mistakes we did."

"Your father's right. What else are you doing?"

Hearing Mom say Dad was right about anything was almost worth getting caught. "What does it matter?"

"Answer her question." His voice rose a few notches. His dark eyebrows mashed together over his glaring blue eyes, eyes like mine.

I curled my lip. "I'm not on crack if that's what you want to know. I smoke weed and drink. Just like the two of you."

Mom shook her head. "We're adults. What we do is not the concern right now. You're still a child, and you shouldn't be doing any of this. I want to know where you get these things."

"You don't need to know." I refused to get Dan busted.

"It's not important where you got it," Dad said.

Mom jabbed a hand toward him and opened her mouth.

He shook his head. "What's important is that you stop getting it. We don't want you to ruin your life. Drugs and alcohol are the quickest way to do that."

"You're such a hypocrite," I yelled, releasing years of pent-up anger.

"Like your mother said, what we do is not the issue here," he bellowed. "You have a problem, and you need to deal with it."

I jumped out of my seat. "You don't care what happens. I see you once a month, maybe, and then you tell me you're moving to another state. Now you're trying to be a dad? Spare me the lecture."

I crossed the room to the window and walked into a cloud of mint. *Jeez.* I braced for the headache.

They were right about what the drugs and alcohol would do. I was only still here because Kali had given my ass a second chance. I had already chosen to quit, so why didn't I tell them?

Maybe because I was still pissed at them for getting divorced and making my life hell. For them not caring enough to notice I'd been drinking for two fucking years. For them always putting their needs ahead of mine and getting mad at me for not praising them when they finally remembered to think of me.

"You're moving? You said you would help with this problem." Mom looked at Dad with raised eyebrows, then scoffed. "I should have known better. Your job always comes first."

"This isn't about you either, Beth. Leave your issues with me out of it."

She smirked. "Sorry if the truth hurts, but it obviously affected Asher."

Whoa. Mom blaming Dad, what a shocker. My parents played the blame game like a tennis match. Back and forth, and I was nothing more to them than the damn ball.

A muscle in his jaw twitched. "I will help."

"How? By calling once a month? Having your secretary send a memo telling Asher you're rooting for him?" She shook her head. "It's just like you to run away when things get too difficult."

"Like I said, this isn't about *you,* Beth." He stood and joined me at the window. "I'm not moving."

Fighting against the hope threatening to build in my chest, I snorted. "Yeah, right. Did they rescind the promotion? Or maybe the apocalypse has come? The end of the world has better odds of happening than you choosing me over your damn job."

"No, I *passed* on the promotion." He ran his hand through his hair. "I told them today I need to stay here for family reasons."

I stared back, the forbidden hope threading its way through me like the ice from Kali's laugh. My last words must have hurt him more than I thought.

Mom glared at him. "So you're not moving?"

"No. I'm staying here to be close to Asher." He laid a hand on my shoulder. "You're the most important thing to me. And yes, I want to be a dad. Your dad."

The bad memories splintered into my head. Riding to little league games with whichever team parent could pick me up, going to church with Grace and her family because Mom and Dad had too many things to do, struggling through my algebra homework with YouTube videos because nobody was home to help. The weight of those memories and a hundred others strangled the moment.

Mom left the couch and stood by Dad's side. She caressed my arm and wiped her eyes with her other hand. "Please, let us help you."

My heart pounded as the mint swirled through the air. *How can they not smell it?* I swallowed, staring into their eyes. Could this time be different? The past tugged on its chokehold a little more.

"Help me what? Quit drinking? Quit smoking weed?"

She flinched, but I kept going.

"How can you help? What are you going to do, ground me?"

Please ground me. If I leave now, I know where I'll go.

She sniffed. "Oh, you're grounded. If keeping you home is the only way to keep you away from drugs, then yes, you'll stay home." She rubbed the bridge of her nose. "But you need to be the one to make this work."

Right, that won't happen. I'm not strong enough to do this alone.

"Are we finished? Can I go to my room?"

She exhaled. "Will you stop?"

I wanted to change. For Grace, not them. But even now, standing here with my parents fighting for me for the first time, Kali hovering invisible by my side, Grace probably praying for me wherever she was, I still wanted to pick up that bowl and light up. My hands shook from the stress, and if someone handed me a beer, I'd guzzle it down.

"I'll stop." The promise burned my throat.

Mom hugged me, crying on my shoulder. Dad smiled. I glanced away before he could see my lie.

****

"Fuck." I fell onto my bed and groaned. I snatched the remote from my bed and punched the power button. The TV on the opposite wall flared to life, and I flipped through the channels, stopping on a movie I'd already seen. The movie ended, and I found another, trying not to think about my pipe, which Mom had confiscated and no doubt thrown away.

What I wouldn't give for just one more chance to feel nothing, to have the anxiety filling my chest wiped away in a cloud of smoke. I wanted to make Grace happy. Kali, too. And I didn't want to die, but my craving fast overtook my desire to be who we all wanted me to be.

"Dammit." I looked at my dresser. I knew what was in there and what it would do for me. Unless Mom had found that, too. Since I was the idiot who'd left the bowl lying on my nightstand on accident, I doubted she had searched any farther.

My phone buzzed, and I jumped. Connor's name flashed on the screen. *Speak of the devil.*

"Hey. What's up?"

"How's the sickie? Feeling better?" He laughed.

"No." I'd never felt worse about myself, knowing my next action would break all my promises.

"Well, you missed a kick-ass party last night. Everyone was there, including Vikki. I guess it's good you weren't there if she's on your shit list."

"Yeah, I don't want to see her."

"She asked about you. I told her you were sick, but I don't think she believed me. You'll be glad to know she hooked up with Dan, so she must be over you."

I laughed. "Thank God."

"How was your homework date with Grace? I'll bet she bossed you around. Did she tell you she'd do all the work so you didn't fuck things up?"

"No. I mean, she has it all under control, but she's making me pull my weight." An image of Grace's sparkling green eyes entered my head, and I grinned. "I completed med school, and she became a counselor. Next time we'll buy our house and have a few kids."

He grunted. "You're lucky you got Grace. With Vikki as my wife, I'll end up divorced. She's useless with school."

"True. Grace will keep us on task." If only he'd keep talking about Grace. Hearing her name eased my anxiety, made me think I could stay away from the pot in my dresser.

His voice changed, excitement replacing the dullness of talking about school. "What're you doing tonight? Up for a little smoke at the shed?"

I should have known better than to count on Connor to help me behave.

I eyed the dresser. "No, I can't go anywhere. My parents grounded me today."

He barked out a laugh. "What are you, like, ten or something? Just leave. You have a car, you know."

"Well, they were serious." I paused, bracing myself for his laughter. "My mom found my bowl. Now she and my dad think I'm a drug addict. I'm on house arrest."

"Man, that sucks. Want me to sneak you supplies?"

Temptation—the more it happened, the harder it was to ignore. He could get me beer and a new pipe, and I already had the weed.

"Uh, nah." My gaze settled on the drawer, and I cleared my throat.

"Sounds like you're thinking about it." He laughed. "I can be over in ten if you want."

"No, thanks." I stood from my bed and paced the room. Each step took me closer to the drawer. "You know, maybe I should lay off for a while."

"Dude, that's stupid. You're not addicted. Why would you want to stop?"

Because the hot redhead told me I had a date with the bottom of the quarry. Because I don't want to disappoint Grace again.

"I don't know. It's just a thought." I stopped pacing at the foot of my bed. "Listen, I need to go."

"Whatever. Let me know when you get out of jail. Later."

"Bye." I stabbed the screen with my fingers.

Connor was my friend, but it seemed like all we ever talked about was getting high. His voice was like some weird mind-conditioning thing. He spoke, and I wanted weed. He was right, though. I wasn't addicted. I didn't need it. I wanted it.

And I wanted it now.

I walked to the dresser and pulled the drawer open. I pawed around until my fingers connected with the bag under my neatly folded shirts. My hand wrapped around the plastic, and a vice wrapped around my stomach.

What the hell was I doing? I'd promised Kali, I'd promised my parents, and most of all, I'd promised Grace. Shame burned in my throat, the fire traveling down to the pit of my stomach.

I don't want this.

I don't want this.

I don't want this.
Fuck, I want this bad.

I sat on my bed holding the weed, waiting for Kali to stop me. The air remained clear of mint. My dad had left hours ago, and Mom had left not long after him. I was alone. Nobody to stop me from getting high but myself. And I wasn't strong enough to do that.

With my bowl gone, I grabbed my papers and rolled a joint. I searched through my nightstand for a lighter and caught the glow from my phone. A missed call. Grace stuck her tongue out at me.

Maybe it was divine intervention or Kali's way of helping. Hell, it could have been a butt dial. But I looked between Grace's beautiful face and the shit in my hand, and my chest caved in like one of our mud castles in the creek.

I crushed the joint in my fist and threw it on the bed. I picked up my phone and, using my thumb, scrolled for her number and tapped a call. Grace answered on the third ring.

"Hello, Asher. What's up?" Her voice sounded clear and clean, the opposite of me—muddled and dirty.

Embarrassment made my voice gruff. "You said I could call."

"Yes, *anytime*." Her breath whistled through the line. "What do you need me to do?"

My life was a huge shitastrophy. I didn't deserve to ask her for help. And she didn't deserve to be dragged into my mess. But I needed her. Shame filled my whisper. "Talk me out of it."

"You can do this." A door slammed in the background on her end of the line. "I'm coming over. Stay on the phone with me. Tell me what happened."

"How do you know something happened?"

"Something made you want to get high. There are other ways to ease your stress. You have to learn new habits."

I looked at the joint laying on my bed, wishing it were that simple. "You don't have to come over. I'm grounded anyway. My mom found my…stuff."

Her engine revved in the background. "Too late. I'm on my way. And it's a good thing your parents know. That'll help you, too."

I rubbed my eyes. Her voice watered the seed of strength she'd planted inside me. "Hmm. New habits, huh? What are we going to do when you get here?"

She laughed, and my heart sped faster.

"Not what you're thinking. We'll get your mind where it needs to be. No husband of mine will get himself into trouble with drugs. What would your patients think?"

Now I laughed. "Thanks, wife."

She snorted into the phone. "Asher, you're stronger than the drugs. You don't need them."

You're stronger than the drugs—I repeated her quiet mantra in my head, but the words didn't sound as good coming from me.

She should hate me for abandoning her, for choosing drugs and alcohol over her. I whispered the question burning in my mind. "Why are you helping me?"

She was quiet for a moment. "You know why."

Shit. I should hang up, end this before I hurt her again. But I was too selfish, too weak to think about what she needed. "You don't have to do this."

"I do. It's something I've prayed for every day since you left."

I swallowed my fear, struggling to find hope I wouldn't ruin everything. Again.

"I'm pulling into your driveway now."

"I'll meet you at the door." I hung up and ran downstairs, taking the steps two at a time, and yanked the door open before she even knocked.

Grace lowered her raised fist. "You weren't joking about the on-the-job training."

Embarrassment and shame washed over me like a tidal wave. The corners of my lips twitched, but I couldn't return her smile. "Dealing with me may inspire you to change professions."

She stepped in and closed the door. She wrapped her arms around me, and damn, she felt good, like playing catch on a Saturday and climbing trees in the backyard. I clung to her, the warmth of her body easing the coldness in my own. I inhaled the rain and roses from her hair.

"Asher, you're my friend. I want to help you. We need to let go of what happened in the past, or it will keep getting in the way." She left my arms but held my hands. "I forgave you a long time ago."

"I was an ass and—"

She covered my lips with her fingers. "No, you were hurting, and I didn't know how to help you then. But now I do, and I will."

I nodded, and she pulled me into the living room.

"Now, tell me what happened."

I sat beside her on the couch, my elbows resting on my knees and my head in my hands. "My parents were getting on me, arguing. Blaming each other for my problems, for their problems. You know, the usual. Then Connor called to tell me about the party last night. He kept asking me to meet him or let him bring me stuff. And dammit, I didn't want to say no. I grabbed my weed and didn't even try to fight."

I clenched my hands together, and she laid hers on top. I marveled at the difference between them—hers soft and gentle, mine weak and filled with excuses.

"But you did. You called me. There's no shame in asking for help." She squeezed my hands, and I closed my eyes.

I hadn't been the one who fought. Kali had done it, forced Grace's contact to light up my phone. She knew seeing Grace's face would be the only thing to make me stop. I couldn't tell Grace, though. She'd think I was insane.

"Your picture opened on my phone." I raised my gaze to hers. "You made me stop."

She lifted her chin, her green eyes filled with determination. "Where is it?"

"Upstairs." I looked away and stared at the hairs on the backs of my hands.

"Let's go."

I raised an eyebrow. "To my room?"

Red crept into her cheeks, and she nodded. "We have to get rid of it."

Having her in my bedroom was like a dream come true, but I didn't want her to see me with weed.

"I can do it. You don't need to see it."

"I'm not afraid of seeing it." She walked toward the stairs, and I followed.

"Maybe I don't want you to see my messy room." At the bottom step, I grabbed her shoulder. My blood pounded in my ears.

"I have a brother. I've seen messy boys' rooms

before, too."

Was I worried about her seeing me with drugs, or was I worried about her getting rid of them? They both scared me. And I didn't know how I would react to seeing her on my bed. That image stirred my blood in a different way.

"Let me help you." She twisted her fingers with mine, and my resistance melted under the touch of her warm skin.

"Okay." I led her to my room where the pot still lay on my bed. Instead of the disappointment I expected to see on her face, she wore a huge smile.

"It's clean." She studied the room. "I was expecting at least a few pairs of underwear lying around."

She walked to the bed and picked up my weed. I cringed seeing it in her hand.

"Do you trust me?"

"Yes," I answered, without hesitation. At that moment, I only trusted two people, and the other one was dead.

She walked backward toward the bathroom. Her gaze never left mine. "Come on."

I gulped and followed her. She handed me the bag of weed and the joint, then pointed to the toilet bowl.

I widened my stare. "You want *me* to do this?"

"This is your battle. It's better if you destroy it yourself."

I nodded, but as I dumped the contents of the bag into the bowl and threw the joint on top, my stomach lurched. The handle jiggled under my shaky hands, and the swirling water swept away my demon.

"I'm proud of you, Asher."

My shame flared. "Why? I could just go buy more."

An image of Dan's house seeped into my head.

"Then let's do something about that." She pulled me through the door and back into my bedroom.

"Where are we going?" Not that it mattered. I'd follow her anywhere to see her smile at me like that.

"I have something in mind. But first you have to change." She paused just inside the door to the hall.

"Isn't that what I'm trying to do?"

Her laugh had the opposite effect of Kali's. A delicious heat flooded my chest. I was already planning my next stupid joke just to hear it again.

"I mean change your clothes. You need a distraction. Let me show you how I get high."

"Uh, what should I wear?" Thoughts of Grace nearby while I was naked did nothing to cool the heat in my chest—or anywhere else on my body.

"Whatever you wear to work out." She rested her hands on her hips. "We're going for a run."

"Like, outside? On our feet?" Too busy admiring her face, I hadn't looked closely at her body. She wore tennis shoes, leggings, and a blue athletic shirt. All of which clung to her toned body, at which I now couldn't stop staring. My body reacted in its usual way, and my jeans grew a little too tight for comfort. I was so going to Hell for lusting after the preacher's daughter.

"I was about to go running when you called. We can go together." She leaned against the doorframe and crossed her arms. The corners of her pink lips pulled up. "Unless you're afraid you can't keep up."

My heart raced, and I swallowed, returning her grin with the most confident smirk I could force on my face. "I think I can manage."

I opened my dresser and grabbed a pair of shorts and

a workout shirt, then pulled off my T-shirt.

Her gaze widened, darting around my bare chest. She cleared her throat. "I'll just… I'll…wait out in the hall." Her cheeks flared red, and she ducked out, closing the door behind her.

I didn't even try to hold back my laughter.

Chapter Eight

My heart raced, but I wasn't sure if it was because of the tinkling sound of Grace's laughter at having outrun me or the side effect of my body attempting to keep pace with her.

I bent over in the driveway, trying to breathe. Fire filled my chest, and my legs wobbled like a rubber eraser. Almost dying on a run was worth it to have her smiles instead of glares and looks of hopeless disappointment.

"You're not nice. I'm dying, and you're laughing at me."

She laughed harder. "It's not my fault if you're out of shape. Next time it'll be easier."

I panted with my hands behind my head. "Next time, I'm tying your feet together and making you watch TV instead."

"Only if you can catch me. Which you obviously can't."

I reached for her but missed. She giggled.

Running had been torture. But I'd do it over again. She hadn't smiled at me this much in years, and I'd do anything to help it continue. Running also distracted me from my problem. Plus, focusing on getting enough oxygen left little room for smoking weed.

"Let's get some water." Holding her hand was so natural I didn't realize I'd done it until we walked into the kitchen and came face-to-face with my mom.

Her eyes widened, and she smiled at Grace, staring at our hands like she'd just won the lottery.

"Hello, Grace. It's good to see you again." Mom's gaze flashed to mine, and I let go of Grace.

"Hello, Mrs. Andrews. It's good to see you, too."

I raised an eyebrow at Mom. "Sorry I left. We went for a run."

She laughed, waving a hand. "It's no problem. I'm glad you had fun."

Bet she wouldn't be so okay with it if I'd gone with Connor.

"I didn't say it was fun. She almost killed me." I winked at Grace. "She's fast, and I'm in bad shape."

Grace's eyes twinkled. "You need to run more often."

"Maybe you should work on that," Mom said. "You could whip him into shape in no time, I'll bet."

Subtle much? "Now my mom's trying to kill me, too. I'm getting water before you two succeed." I took two glasses from the cabinet and filled them with ice and water from the fridge. I handed one to Grace.

"Thanks." She took a long sip and wiped her mouth with the back of her hand. "I haven't been able to run much lately either. Today felt great."

I tsked at her and shook my finger. "You can't lecture me about staying healthy and neglect your workout routine. What's the problem? Too many volunteer nights in the week?"

"My parents think it could—" She opened and closed her mouth for a second, then she wrinkled her nose and shook her head. "Never mind. It's no big deal. But what about you? Was running with me that bad?"

If Mom wasn't standing there watching us like a soap opera, I would have told Grace I could walk through hellfire with her by my side.

Instead, I shook my head. "It was fun."

"Then I'll meet you tomorrow after church for our next session. Unless you want to get up early and go before?" She bent to tie her shoe.

"That's okay. The afternoon is early enough for me." I took a drink and widened my eyes at Mom in a silent plea.

"Would you like to stay and eat with us, Grace? I ordered a pizza. It should be here soon."

Grace stood and checked her phone. "No, thank you. I need to get home. My parents have a meeting at church, and I have to watch my little brother."

I clenched my glass, my pulse increasing with my breath.

Please don't leave.

"Maybe next time," Mom said. "I'm glad to see you again."

"Thanks." Grace switched her gaze to me, and her smile faltered.

"Well, I'll be upstairs for a few." Mom walked toward the stairs. "The money for the pizza is on the counter, Ash."

I wondered how long it would take her to call my dad and give him the good news that their drug-addict son was back with the ex-girlfriend he'd shit on.

Not that we were back together. One trip on the Asher Hot-Mess-Express was enough for anybody. Right? I didn't want to put her through that again. Part of me believed the lie. But the part that wanted Grace back told it to shut the hell up and gave it a throat punch.

Grace's gaze rested on my face. "What are you thinking?"

That you're beautiful. That I wish we could forget the last two years. That I want to be the person you loved before. That I'll love you forever even when I know you shouldn't love me.

"Nothing."

She stepped closer and covered my tapping fingers with her soft hand. "You'll be fine. One step at a time. I'm right here if you need me."

The funny thing was I hadn't even thought about weed or beer. I just didn't want her to leave.

"Thank you for helping me." My lips tingled, and I craved a taste of hers. But I didn't want to ruin this second chance. The odds of that happening were great enough without me adding to them by letting my hormones get in the way.

"Anytime." A crease ruined the smoothness of her forehead. "I have to go."

She placed her glass in the sink and walked toward the door. I followed her outside to the porch, trying to keep my cool and not fall to her feet begging her to stay and keep me in line.

"Rest up tonight." She tucked a loose strand of strawberry-blonde hair behind her ear. "I'll be back tomorrow, and we'll hit the pavement again. I know a few hills we can spice up our run with."

"Should I be scared?"

"Terrified."

She patted my cheek, then bounced down the steps, skipping to her yellow Bug. The sun had set, but the night was still warm. Fireflies danced along the edges of the driveway, scattering when she passed by. She rolled down her window and pulled away waving, the twang of a country song fading with her taillights.

I sat on the creaky porch swing. Rocking back and forth, I frowned, wishing I was strong enough to do this without her. Maybe then I'd earn the right to be with her again. Instead, I depended on her to help me. I was such a wuss. The bitter taste of self-hate filled my mouth.

Kali replaced it with mint.

"I can't do this to her, Kali."

She squeezed my leg. "She's good for you."

"But I'm bad for her." I rubbed my forehead. "I'll only hurt her again if I let her down."

"You chose to live, and this is life. Sometimes there are risks. Some things are worth it, too." Her dark gaze found mine. "You need her, and believe it or not, Grace needs you."

"She doesn't need me."

"Yes, she does." She turned her gaze toward the sky and closed her eyes, tears trickling into her hair. "She needs you more."

"What are you saying?" Her words left a hollow pit in my stomach. "What is it you know?"

She shook her head and wiped her eyes with the back of her hand. "You're not ready, and neither is she."

She stood and peered down at me with her liquid eyes, no hint of blue now that the light had left the sky. The darkness sent a shiver of dread down my spine.

"What the hell kind of remark is that? Tell me what's going on."

She laughed, but the sadness lurking in the inky darkness of her eyes remained. Even with her hand on my arm, the icy tendrils tickled my nerves. "Sorry, you'll have to wait."

She took a step toward the stairs, and my heart lurched.

"Are you leaving, too?" With every step she took, my heart sped faster, and my body shook like when I hung from the cliff.

"Yes, I have a job to do, you know." She winked. "I have a few people I need to go see."

Right. Reaper. I grimaced. "You mean people you have to kill."

"I don't kill people. I told you, I only collect them after they die, and the ones I collect do it to themselves." She frowned. "I'm only their guide."

Kali's smooth skin shone in the late afternoon sun, long red hair billowing on her shoulders. Her mysterious eyes hid the secrets of death. Seeing her face after dying wouldn't be so bad. Better than seeing the traditional grim reaper, I guessed. I thought of the people about to die right now.

"You said you've never given anyone a second chance. Why me? What makes my life worth more than any of theirs?"

She walked back to hold my face. Fire bloomed in my heart, fire that burned away the loneliness and pain.

"All souls have the same value, and I can't answer this question yet, either. But when it's time, you'll know."

"Kali, please."

She shook her head and her hands fell to her sides. "No, not yet. Focus on changing your life. That's enough for now."

I ran a shaky hand through my hair. "I don't want to be alone. What if I do something?"

"This is your battle. I'll help when I can, and so will

Grace. But in the end, it's up to you."

"I was afraid you would say that. Maybe I should learn how to play solitaire."

Her eyebrows pulled together, and she pursed her lips. "We all have to face our demons alone in the end."

I smirked. "Why me?"

She gazed at me for a moment, unblinking, then she smiled. "Like I said before, you remind me of someone I used to know. And my boss is a nice guy. He believes in giving second chances. At least to the living." She walked toward the stairs again. "Why don't you go take a shower and relax with some TV? That should keep you out of trouble."

"Are you saying I stink?"

"You said it, I didn't. See you later, Asher."

My chest constricted, but I gave her a nod.

She raised her hands, and that Hollywood smile lit up her face. Then fire spread from the ends of her fingers, the ends of her brilliant hair, engulfing her in bright orange and yellow flames. The heat blasted my face, and I gasped. She met my gaze and winked.

Then with a soft hiss, she disappeared, leaving the night once again filled with darkness and silence.

"Show-off." I laughed and walked toward the door. Kali's fiery image still burning in my mind and on my retinas.

****

I woke up on Sunday before my alarm with Grace on my mind. Her smile, her laugh—her legs. Then I stretched *my* legs, and pain bled into the pleasure of thinking about her. No way running did this to me. Someone had beaten me with a bat while I slept. Holy shit, maybe I was dying.

I pulled myself out of bed and grabbed a pair of shorts and a T-shirt. Grounded for the rest of my life, I wouldn't need to get dressed to go anywhere, and I wanted to be ready for my run with Grace later.

In the kitchen, Mom looked up from her tablet, sipping on her coffee. Terry ignored me as usual.

"Good morning, Ash. You're up early," Mom said. "What do you have planned for the day?"

Terry snorted behind his paper. "I thought you grounded him."

I glared at the comics hiding his face. Asshole, he couldn't even look at me when he made his rude comments.

"Grace is coming over later to run again." I flexed my legs under the table and grimaced. "I don't know if I can take the pain. She about killed me yesterday."

Mom lifted an eyebrow, and I smirked. She knew I was lying. I would run naked through school in high heels if Grace wanted me to.

"Maybe another run will loosen your legs up. It's nice to see you doing things with her again." She blew on her coffee, then took a sip.

"Yeah." I turned away so she couldn't see my shit-eating grin. "She's cool."

I limped to the pantry to get cereal. Returning with a bowl, the box, and milk, I got a spoon and ate while Mom and Terry read.

My phone buzzed, and I grabbed it. Instead of Grace, Connor's brown-eyed face stared up at me, flipping me the bird—his idea of a good contact picture.

Mom frowned at the screen, and I stood.

"I'll be right back." A call from him this early meant he hadn't been to bed yet and would be drunk. Mom didn't need to hear either end of this conversation.

I walked to the couch in the other room and tapped the screen. "What's up?"

"Duuuuude! You missed an awesome party!"

I could almost smell the beer on his breath through the phone. "Yeah, sounds like it."

"Hey, I'm coming over to bust you out. A couple people are heading to my house, and you might want to be there for some, uhm…relief." He laughed.

"I'm not going anywhere. I'm grounded." A vision of Grace intruded, and I smiled.

"So what? Tell your mom you're staying in your room and sneak out the back. We'll park down the street, and you can meet us there."

"Can't. Grace is coming over later to…work on our project."

"Ha, right. To *work*. I'm sure you could get the preacher's daughter to put out or at least give you a blow job, then she could still say she's a virgin."

Anger filled my chest. "Is that all you ever think about?"

"No, I think about beer and weed, too. Both of which I'm sure you're dying for."

Only because you won't shut up about them.

I rubbed my eyes. "No thanks, it's too early for that."

"Early? I haven't been to bed. It's still Saturday night to me." He laughed. "Well, if you're not coming over, I guess that means I'm coming twice. Thanks."

I didn't even want to know who he had with him. Whoever it was, she wasn't Grace, and Grace was the only one I wanted to be with.

"Have fun. I'll talk to you later."

"Later."

I returned to the table, and Mom frowned. "What did Connor want?"

Stuffing in a bite of cereal, I shrugged. "Nothing much. Just wanted to talk."

She looked at me over the rim of her coffee cup. "I don't think you should hang out with him."

"Why not?" I jammed another bite into my mouth.

"He's the one you drink with, isn't he? All those times you said you were helping him, you were joining him."

Heat filled my face now, too. "Yes. Don't worry, I told him I couldn't hang out."

Terry folded his paper and smirked from the end of the table. "That reminds me. I know I'm not your dad, but I think I have the right to ask where you get the money for your habits."

What the hell?

"You're right, you're not my dad, so butt out. The money didn't come from you. That's all you need to know."

He narrowed his eyes. "It won't come from your mother either."

I looked at her.

Her face grew red. "I'll handle this, Terry."

He shrugged, hiding behind his paper again.

She set her cup on the table and folded her hands. "I think it's time for you to get a job."

I wanted to yell at her and say she was being unfair. But she wasn't.

"Fine. Whatever." I weighed the benefits of impressing Grace with a job and the con of losing time with her to go to it. "Since I'm not allowed to go places with my friends, I might as well go to work."

Terry snorted.

I sent him a go-to-hell stare.

Mom's shoulders relaxed. "You can go places with Grace. She's one person I know who'll be a good influence on you."

"I agree." My heart beat faster. "I'm not sure it's a good idea for her to be with me, though."

"She's tough. You won't change her. And despite your bad choices, you're a good person. She knows that."

Most times Mom either complained about the things I did or pushed me away with a nod and some money. Hearing her praise was surreal. I didn't know what to say, so I just frowned at her.

She patted my hand, then stood and placed her cup in the sink. "I've got to go check on flowers for a wedding I'm planning next month. I'll see you both later. Have fun with Grace, Ash."

After she left, I cleaned my mess and ran up to my room. I'd rather sit with Hitler than Terry. I looked around my cell, I meant my room, and my gaze fell on my backpack lying on the chair. I picked it up and took out my math homework. Might as well use my time wisely.

I tried to concentrate on statistics, but Grace kept getting in the way. She *was* tough. But I still worried about the effect I would have on her. Thinking about the way she reacted to my bare chest yesterday, I grimaced.

I might not get her to drink and smoke weed, but the way she excited me, I wasn't sure I wouldn't try to ruin her in other ways.

Chapter Nine

At one o'clock, I lay on my bed and checked my phone. Grace hadn't called or texted. Was her dad preaching extra long today? Maybe she'd gone to lunch with the family. When we were kids, I'd sometimes get invited to go with them. I'd loved hanging out with her family since they weren't messed up like mine. They liked each other. Her dad liked me, too. He always had a smile and a joke.

That had ended when I hurt Grace. I knew he wanted to hate me. Too bad he wasn't allowed. Pastors should love everyone, right? For all I knew he hated me anyway.

I pulled up her contact and stared at her picture. I could call her, right? She'd said anytime. She'd meant when I needed help to say no to drugs, but this time the withdrawals were for her.

I sat against the headboard and hesitated. What if she hadn't called because she'd changed her mind? What if she didn't want to talk? Maybe she regretted getting involved, regretted helping me.

I argued with myself until my phone buzzed in my hand. Grace's number flashed on the screen, and I clicked it. "Hello. Is this my running coach?"

She giggled. "No, this is your conscience."

My heart sped with her laugh. "Oh, great. We haven't spoken in a while. I thought you might have quit." How many stupid jokes could I think of to make her laugh again?

"How are you?" She breathed like she'd already run five miles.

"Fine, now. How was church? Your dad must have had a hell of a sermon today."

"You know Dad. He got caught up in the moment."

"Well, I'm ready to run if you are."

And ready to see you. And ready to touch you. And ready to make you laugh.

"I, uh, can't run today."

"Oh." My stomach fell. "What's wrong?"

"My leg is killing me." She gave a soft laugh. "I think I pulled a muscle yesterday. That's what I get for teasing you."

"That's good. Uh...I mean...not good that you're hurt, but good that..." I took a deep breath and blew it out. "I thought maybe you changed your mind. You know. About...helping me."

"Never." She groaned. "I wanted to run with you again, but I can hardly walk. Nothing helps. I've taken eight ibuprofen already."

"Want me to get you something else?" I grinned to myself. "I know something that will make you feel better."

"That's not funny," she whispered in a rough voice.

"Fine, if you don't want ice cream..." I teased.

After a heartbeat of silence, she laughed. "Ice cream sounds good, but you don't have to bring me any."

"It won't bring itself. I can be there in a few minutes. Do you still like strawberry?"

"I do, but really, Asher, don't..."

I waited for her to finish, and doubt crept back in like a sucker punch to my gut. "Your dad doesn't want

"He's just worried."

Yeah, worried that I'll rip apart your heart again.

"I know."

Silence filled the line. Then Grace cleared her throat. "How about if we go get that ice cream?"

"You don't have to."

"I *want* to go."

"Your dad will get mad, and I know you don't like to disappoint him."

She whispered, "I want to see you."

I closed my eyes, hope rising a few inches. "You do?"

"I said so, didn't I? Let's meet at Southside."

"You shouldn't drive with a sore leg. I can pick you up."

"Well…" Her voice rang with uncertainty again.

"Unless you don't want your dad to know you're with me."

"Hmph. My dad will just have to get used to it. He preaches about acceptance and forgiveness. It's time he listened to himself."

"If someone dumped my daughter for beer and weed, I'd hate them, too. He has every right."

"No, he doesn't. If I can forgive you, then he should, too." She blew out a breath. "I'm ready when you are."

"I'll change and be right over. See you in a few."

I hurried into a pair of jeans and a long-sleeved flannel. The day wasn't warm like yesterday. Besides, clean-cut clothes would hide my dirty past, right? I checked my hair in the mirror, brushing my fingers through to calm the mess. Good thing it was short, and the mess looked intentional.

I ran down the stairs. Well, tried to. My thighs screamed, and I slowed to a trudge, glad ice cream waited instead of more miles.

Mom had returned from her flower meeting, and I met her in the living room. She sat on the couch sifting through files.

"Mom, Grace and I are getting ice cream." I blinked a few times and added, "Is that okay?"

"I thought you two were running again?" She smiled. "Did you convince her not to go?"

Laughing, I shook my head. "Her leg is sore today. I thought ice-cream therapy would be better for us than running."

"Can we talk for a minute first?" She patted the seat. "I promise, just a few minutes. I don't have a lecture planned."

Sitting next to her, I checked the time on my phone. "What is it?"

"I noticed that you two picked up where you left off." She twisted her hands in her lap. "Do you think it's a good idea to have a relationship right now? This is a hard time for you. You have things you need to work on in your life."

"I am working on them, and she helps me."

She studied my face for a moment, then patted my knee. "Then I hope it works out this time. She's a great girl."

"I know. Can I go now? I've kind of been waiting for this all day."

"Go." She laughed. "Just don't go anywhere you shouldn't."

"I won't. See you later." I ran to the door, headed for the first place Pastor King would consider somewhere I shouldn't be—to Grace's side.

****

Pulling into their driveway, I had a flashback to freshman year. Instead of driving then, I'd ridden my bike to her house, but it felt the same. My heart pounded, and I grinned like an idiot.

I cut the engine and swallowed the nervousness from my throat. I hadn't been face-to-face with her dad in two years. Not since I'd let her, and them, down. I'd never told Grace, but her dad's opinion meant a lot. He'd treated me with more care and respect than my dad. Maybe that's why my betrayal had hurt Pastor King, too, and why I feared facing him again.

I walked up the sidewalk to the little brick ranch-styled home, so different from the ginormous houses I'd lived in. A line of bushes sat under the front picture window in the neat and tidy yard. White flowers lined the walk leading to the red wooden front door.

Nothing extravagant, nothing special—except for the love on the inside, love that used to include me. I rang the bell, feeling like the prodigal son returning home at last. But I wouldn't bet money on her dad setting a feast for my return. I'd have to settle for buying my own ice cream.

After a moment, Grace answered the door. My nervousness evaporated from the heat of her red face.

"Hi." The little word almost exploded from the depth of my emotions packed inside of it.

"Hey, Asher. Come in." She stepped back, holding the door open.

Her parents sat on the couch. Her dad stood, and the anger simmering behind his stare made me feel like a kid again, about to get in trouble for running in church.

I walked nervously toward them and nodded. "Hello, Mrs. King, Pastor. It's good to see you again."

Her dad raised his eyebrows. "Hello, Asher."

Her mom smiled and gave me a hug. "It's good to see you, too."

"Thanks." I hugged her back. My heart rose to my throat with her warm welcome—a welcome I didn't deserve.

She let go and darted a quick glance at her husband, then back to me. "How have you been?"

High. Drunk. Stupid.

"I'm good. How about you?"

"Oh, you know, the church keeps us busy." She gestured to Grace's dad. "Paul is always coming and going. Sometimes he sees himself at the door."

He gently kissed her cheek. "That's the truth. There's always something to do. But that means we never get bored or lonely, right, Ann?"

He looked back to me with a frown. At least I knew he still had it in him to be happy, just not with me.

Grace brushed my arm with her hand, and his left eye twitched.

"Asher and I are going out for ice cream."

Her dad raised an eyebrow and studied my face for an uncomfortable moment. "I don't recall you asking permission."

My heart hammered against my ribs. *Awkward.*

A muscle flexed in Grace's jaw, and she raised her chin. "Since when do I need permission to get ice cream?"

Since you want to go with me.

Her dad pursed his lips, and I could imagine the words he had for me in his head.

Her mom gave a soft cough, covering her mouth with her hand. "It's fine, Grace." She looped her arm around the pastor's and nodded. "Just come home in time for youth group."

Grace still glared at her dad but then turned to smile at her mom. "Sure. I'll be back in time."

Her dad narrowed his eyes at me, and I swallowed. He didn't argue with her mom, but I'd lay odds on him calling a family meeting later to discuss her acceptance of the pothead hanging out with their daughter.

Grace crossed her arms and cleared her throat. "Would you like to join us?"

What? Hell no. Why did she ask them that? Guilt for defying her dad must have rattled her brain.

Her dad cocked an eyebrow in my direction, like he thought tagging along to ruin the trip was a perfect idea. Her mom saved me from that hell.

"No thanks." She tightened her grip on his arm. "Your father and I have a date with the TV tonight."

He snapped his gaze back to her. "That is until Mrs. Batterton calls with something she needs to discuss for one of her five committees at church."

Grace laughed. "Dad, you know she's just lonely since her husband passed away last year."

"And she has a crush on the pastor," her mom added with a laugh.

Grace got her sense of humor and small stature from her mom, but everything else came from her dad. I'd forgotten how much she looked like him. They shared the same reddish-blond hair and bright-green eyes. But gray peppered his hair, and fine lines surrounded his eyes. In contrast, her mom's eyes were a deep rich mahogany, her hair a dark chestnut with caramel highlights. The whole family could've gone into modeling if God hadn't gotten them first.

Her dad rolled his eyes. "You two are hilarious."

"Come on, Asher." Grace turned and stumbled slightly, winced, then rubbed a spot above her knee. "Let's go. I'm ready for sugar."

Yeah, and to get away from your dad. Pretty sure a root canal would be more fun. "It sure beats running hills."

Before I turned to follow Grace, I caught her dad's worried gaze and the falter in her mom's smile. Only this time, their concern wasn't directed at me. They both watched Grace. *Damn.* It wasn't like I would turn her into a drug addict while we ate ice cream. I quickly looked away and fell in step behind her.

They followed us to the door. Did they do this for all her dates or just the ones with alcoholic potheads who used to be a part of the family?

"Be careful driving." Her mom patted my shoulder. "You have precious cargo, you know."

"I agree, Mrs. King." I glanced at Grace, my heart pounding in my throat and heat filling my face.

She blushed, and her mom smiled, but the faintest hint of a frown ghosted across her dad's face. He covered it with a polite smile, but his warning rang loud in my head. *Be careful, or else.*

****

Tucked in a grove of trees on the side of the road, Southside Dairy looked like a dive. The little building screamed for a makeover—or a bulldozer. Tired picnic tables covered with peeling paint rested in front of the building. To the left, a dumpster overflowing with empty boxes and full trash bags swarmed with flies. But if someone wanted hot greasy food and the perfect ice cream cone, this was the place to be.

Grace and I sat on a bench outside the walk-up window, eating our ice cream. Chocolate dripped on my jeans from the huge cone I held. "Shit, I'm making a mess." I licked the cone, spinning it in my hand to lick the rest of the drips before they fell, too.

She rolled her eyes and licked her huge pink scoop. "And you cuss a lot."

"Really? You never swear?"

She shook her head. "Only on accident. And not like you do." She laughed. "I had one too many bars of soap growing up. Now swear words make me taste bubbles."

"Whatever. I don't remember you ever saying a cuss word." I used my napkin to wipe a drip of pink from her chin.

She grinned and took a huge bite, coating herself with a pink mustache and beard. "Got a problem with a little mess?"

I laughed at the ice cream dripping from her chin. I copied her, my chocolate beard surely much more impressive. "Nope, I thought you did. Glad to know I can be my sloppy self around you still."

She threw her head back and laughed. "Remember when we were ten and made the mud pies at the church picnic?"

"And we tried to tell people they were chocolate? And old Mr. Peters believed us and ate a big spoonful?" I laughed with her. "He was so mad."

"My dad, too. He had to hear about that every year they planned the picnic until Mr. Peters could finally laugh about it." She shook her head and wiped her chin with a wad of napkins. Her smile faded. "He passed away last year. Cancer."

I wiped my face, too. "That's too bad. He was a nice man."

"You missed some." Grace wiped my cheek with a clean napkin, her hand lingering on my face. Her gaze lingering on my lips.

My heart thumped in my throat. I almost dropped the ice cream and pulled her to my chest. Instead, I held my cone out to her. "Want a lick?"

She wrapped her hand around mine to hold the cone steady, her tongue slowly licking the chocolate. My hand shook under hers, and I prayed she couldn't feel the tremors.

"That's good. But I still like strawberry better." She held out her cone.

I licked a path on the cone, pushing away the thought of her tongue licking the same spot. Who knew eating ice cream could be so exciting? "Nope, chocolate's the best."

She giggled, returning to her ice cream.

We sat in a comfortable silence as the cars cruised past on the busy main road. From a nearby table, laughter drifted on the cool, late-afternoon air. A young couple smiled as they watched their three small children run around playing tag, their sugar-induced squeals echoing off the little ice cream shop. Grace licked her cone, and I watched her tongue slip across her lips, catching the drips. I fought the urge to help her.

She caught me staring and blushed. Her free hand rested on her leg, and she rubbed it.

"How's your leg? Is the ice-cream therapy working?"

"Yes, I'm fine. Just a little sore." She rolled her

127

eyes. "I'll never make fun of you again when we run."

"I didn't mind." If I could be with her, she could laugh at me all she wanted. She still rubbed her leg. I frowned but didn't want to bug her about it.

"How are *you* doing?" she asked, then licked her cone.

I shrugged and took another lick of my ice cream. "I'm okay. If I'm with you."

She nodded and echoed Kali's words. "You know I'll be here to help, but you need to do this on your own, too."

"I'm trying." But I lied. This would be impossible alone.

She squeezed my hand. "You can do it. One day at a time. Maybe if you make a plan, that will help."

"What do you mean?"

"Well, like tomorrow at school. Think about the things that might influence you to drink or get high. Then make a plan to avoid them."

"You mean the people." She sounded like my mom, only more polite. "Just say it. I need to stay away from Connor and my friends."

"I can't tell you to do that, but if they tempt you, then yes, you need to stay away from them. Or tell them you're trying to change and ask them to support your decision."

I took a bite of ice cream and grimaced at the sweetness. "I tried telling Connor. He told me I was crazy and offered me weed. I'm sure the rest would do the same."

She smiled sadly. "Then they aren't your friends. They're your enablers."

I tossed the rest of my ice cream in the trash next to

the bench. She was right, but dumping him felt shitty. "Connor is the only one I consider my friend. I can't just ignore him. I did that to you, and you didn't like it either. Besides, his family life is worse than mine."

She shook her head. "But if he can't respect your attempt to change, then he shouldn't be your main concern. You need to think about what's good for *you*, what will make you happy and healthy."

What would make me happy? A no-brainer. I only wanted one thing—her. I looked at Grace, her long hair pulled back behind her shoulders, her skin glowing in the afternoon sunshine, and her lips wearing a small smile and strawberry ice cream.

Only she could make me happy.

I leaned in, hesitating, giving her time to pull away if she wanted to. My heart flew when she didn't, and memories of our inferior first kiss came flooding back. My nervousness and overly eager need for her had ruined that moment, but not this time.

I lightly touched her lips with mine, testing her reaction. Then our lips fully met, and it was the sweetest kiss but not because of the ice cream. Her warm fingers caressed my cheek, and I held them closer to my skin. My heart melted like the ice cream.

I never wanted this kiss to end.

But she sat back, and her lips curved up into a smile that stole what was left of my breath.

"That was the stickiest kiss in history." Then she leaned back toward me. "And here's the second."

She reached behind my neck and wove her fingers in my hair. Her lips pressed against mine again, warm and sticky, just like she said.

And I was stuck forever.

Chapter Ten

I picked Connor up the next morning for school. He fell into the passenger seat and pulled the car door closed, glaring. "Turn the music down. Why you got it so fucking loud? And since when do you listen to country?"

I reached for the knob, laughing. Grace'd had control of my radio last night, and I'd left it on her favorite station, a small piece of her to hold on to. "Sorry, guess you should have laid off the beer yesterday."

He smirked. "Hell no. That's what weekends are for, getting wasted and having fun. I save responsibility for the weekdays."

"I've never seen you be responsible."

He punched my arm, and I pulled away from his house.

"See, if you were responsible and worked out a little, that might have hurt me."

He laughed. "So what did you do all weekend, Mr. Responsible?"

"I sat in my room like a good boy and did my homework." I didn't want to tell him about Grace yet.

"That sounds fascinating." He yawned.

Remembering the ice-cream kiss, I agreed. "How're things at your house?"

"Well, Mom got fired yesterday. Dad loved that." His joking mood vanished, and he stared out the window at the passing houses. "She left. Went to stay with my aunt in Waukegan."

My stomach tightened. His mom knew his dad was an asshole. Why hadn't she taken Connor with her? I didn't want to ask. "So now what?"

"It's just me and the old man." He pounded a fist onto the door. "Damn, I wish I could get the hell out of there. But I don't have any fucking money."

"Sorry." The help wanted sign at the pizza place pulled at the edge of my memory. Maybe it was a stupid idea, but I wanted to help him. "Ever thought about getting a job? I saw a help wanted sign the other day."

I expected him to smirk, but he didn't. He pursed his lips. "That depends. Where?"

"The Other Place."

Connor groaned. "A restaurant? No way."

"Why not?" Even though I'd said I'd never work there, Connor was desperate.

"Because it would suck."

I laughed. "Well, it's just an idea. And you don't have many choices."

He frowned, looking out the window again. "If I apply, you do, too. At least we'll be in misery together."

"I don't need a job."

"Then you can give me your paycheck, and I'll get out of my house faster."

Well, I guessed Mom would be happy. Picturing Grace's response to me being responsible convinced me, too. I looked at him and raised my eyebrow. "Fine, but I'm keeping my money."

"Yeah, so you can spend it on Grace?" He wiggled his eyebrows. "Did you get anywhere with her?"

"No, dick for brain. We did homework." That

wasn't a total lie.

"Yeah, she's too uptight to have any fun. Don't worry, you still have Vikki to fall back on. She talked about you all weekend." He rolled his eyes. "She's hooked on you."

"Well, she can get unhooked. I don't need a stalker."

He cocked his eyebrow. "Why? She's easy. Just bang her when you need it and don't worry about it."

I cringed, gritting my teeth. "Maybe I don't want to just have sex. Don't you ever want something more?"

"More than sex? What else is there?" He chortled. "Don't tell me you want long walks on the beach and deep conversation."

I ignored him, clenching my hands on the steering wheel.

"Relax, I'm kidding." He pulled out his phone and scrolled across the screen. "I guess hanging out with Grace ruined your sense of humor."

I narrowed my eyes. "Leave her out of it."

"Damn, Asher." He looked up from his phone. "What's eating you?"

I turned at a corner. "Sorry, I'm just tense I guess."

Maybe Grace was right. If I wanted him to understand, I needed to tell him about my choice. Hoping I wasn't about to ruin our friendship, I drew a deep breath and dove in headfirst. "I've quit drinking and smoking."

I waited for the laughing, for Connor to tell me I was an idiot. He didn't disappoint me. I never knew *guffawed* was more than a word in a book.

"Stop, I'm too hungover to laugh this hard."

I glared at him. "You're an asshole."

His laughter died. "Wait, are you *serious*?"

"I can't keep partying all the time. And you

shouldn't either. At some point, we need to say no." I glanced at him. "I want to change because I want something more for my life than partying." Grace's face floated across my mind.

"Man, I thought you were joking." He shook his head and stared out the window for a moment, frowning. "I don't see it. What's the problem with having fun?"

"That's just it. It's not fun to lose control. It's not fun when I do stupid things because I'm drunk or high. I'm surprised I haven't died already from driving drunk or gotten a fucking disease from having sex with girls at parties."

I'm lucky I didn't die a few days ago on the damn cliff.

"It's not like you're an alcoholic. Why would you swear off it completely?" He exhaled. "There's no way I would. I don't have a problem, and I like to have fun."

"Well, I'm done. So if you can't handle that..." Laying this on him so soon after his mom abandoned him was shitty, but like Grace said, I had to think about what I needed to get through this.

He stared at me, a deep crease between his eyes. "I'm your friend, and I'll back you up if that's what you want. I'll get a job so I can leave my house. But don't expect me to change, too."

I relaxed in my seat. "Thanks. I wish you would think about it, though."

"Like I said, I don't see a problem with having fun. Let me know when you get tired of responsibility."

I pulled into the student lot, thinking about my day with Grace and ice-cream kisses. "I know how to have fun without partying."

"Sure, homework with Grace. Lots of fun." He

slipped his phone into his pocket.

I parked, and we got out to head into the building. The bipolar weather couldn't decide if it was spring or winter. I zipped my fleece jacket against the cold. "Have you and Vikki worked on your project at all?"

"Right. She spent the weekend wasted and looking for you." He pointed with his chin. "Look out. She found you."

I glanced to my left. Vikki walked toward me with a huge smile on her face. My stomach clenched.

"Asher, where the hell have you been?" She wrapped her arms around my waist. "You missed all the parties."

Connor smirked. "He was busy doing *homework* with Grace. I'll see you later." He patted my shoulder and walked away, shaking his head. She glared at his back.

Way to throw me under the bus.

I unwrapped her arms and stepped back. "I had better things to do."

She drew a breath and tried again, her eyes pleading with hope. "So you want to hang out after school today?"

For crying out loud. What would it take for her to get the picture? Either she was stubborn, or she'd killed way too many brain cells. Obviously, I needed to be more direct.

"Vikki, I don't want to hang out with you." I ignored the hurt on her face. "There's nothing between us. I don't want to be with you."

Direct enough?

Her palm connected with my cheek, leaving a sharp sting and the answer to my question.

"Fuck you, Asher." She glared at me, her eyes filling

with tears. "I know why you're doing this. I heard about you and Grace."

"What the hell are you talking about?"

She sneered. "Trina saw you kissing her at Southside yesterday."

Shit, where had Trina been? Not that I cared if people knew, but Grace would. So would her dad. I glared back at Vikki. "So?"

"You think she'll go out with you? Is that what you're hoping for?" She wiped her eyes. "Grace King thinks you're trash. And she's right. She'd never go out with you, and I don't want to either."

Heat filled my face, and my pulse throbbed in my ears. She was wrong. Grace had feelings for me. I wasn't trash.

"Whatever." I shrugged to hide my anger. "See ya around."

I walked away, my hands clenched, lying to myself, saying I didn't agree with Vikki. But I did, one hundred percent. I didn't deserve Grace. Not even the mint drifting past my nose could convince me of that.

By the time I got to senior seminar, I'd thought of a million reasons to back out of my attempts to change. Grace shouldn't have anything to do with me. I'd only drag her into the gutter, and she was too good for that.

I slouched in my seat, glaring out the window. Grace poked my shoulder, and I jumped.

"Hey, hubby. How's your day been?"

I'd never be good enough for her.

Hating myself, I glared at her. "It's been everything I expected it to be."

"What's wrong?" She rubbed my shoulder.

I jerked away, avoiding her gaze. Her touch made

me want more, and that was something I shouldn't have. "Nothing."

I glanced at Vikki. She smirked, and I shot her a fuck-off look for being right about me.

Grace followed my gaze and narrowed her eyes. "What did she say to you?"

"It was dumb to think I could do this. And even more stupid to think you could help. Forget it. Get a new partner."

She shifted on her feet for a moment, then walked away, ripping my heart from my chest.

Connor shook his head. He pinched his fingers to his lips like he was taking a toke, and my craving for weed skyrocketed.

I turned away, and my gaze went right to Grace. She spoke to Mrs. Kumar in a quiet voice. They looked at me, whispering things I couldn't hear.

I pinched the bridge of my nose and closed my eyes. *Fuck, fuck, fuck.* I wanted a beer and weed and anything else that would make this pain go away.

"Asher?"

I jerked my head up.

Grace stood next to me, holding a slip of paper. She held out her hand. "Come on."

"What?"

She took my hand and pulled me toward the door. "You and I need to go to the library to discuss our...project."

I turned back to Mrs. Kumar. She nodded, a concerned frown on her face. Connor grinned, and Vikki shot daggers at Grace with her eyes.

In the hall, I pulled Grace to a stop. The warmth from her hand in mine crept up my arm. "What are you doing?"

"I told you. We need to talk about our project. And I don't mean the marriage. I told Mrs. Kumar I was helping you get through a hard time." She pulled me by the hand again toward the library.

I followed, trying to keep myself from hoping too much. "Do you always get your way with teachers?"

"I'm a good girl, the preacher's kid. They never expect me to break the rules. Sometimes I get extra privileges."

We sat in a corner of the library away from the other students in a pair of chairs by the wall of windows. Sunlight fell on Grace's hair, setting the red on fire. I ached to feel its heat.

"Talk to me." She sat in the chair next to mine and held my hands. "Tell me what's wrong."

"I can't do this. I can't change." I slumped my shoulders and blew out a shaky sigh.

"I know this isn't you talking. What did Vikki say?"

I shook my head. "It's not her fault. She's right."

"But what did she say? Tell me so I can help you."

It was impossible to meet her gaze, so I closed my eyes. "She said what I already know."

"Tell me," she whispered.

I opened my eyes and forced myself to meet her gaze. "She said I was trash and that you knew it. She's right. I don't deserve you. Not after what I've done."

Her tear-filled green eyes glittered in the sun. "No, she's wrong. I don't think you're trash. I think you're kind of wonderful."

I squashed down the hope her words created. "If I was so wonderful, would I be thinking about sneaking out and getting high? Because that's what I want to do right now." Embarrassed, I dropped my gaze.

"Look at me."

How could she look at me like she wanted to be with me? Like she saw me as an equal? Couldn't she see that the damage I'd done wasn't something she could fix?

"You don't need it." She rubbed her thumbs across the backs of my hands. "Aren't there other things you want more?"

I just want you. You're the only thing that matters. But I shouldn't want you.

"You should stay away from me." My voice shook from fear that she'd listen to me. If she did, I'd self-destruct, but at least she would survive.

"I can't, Asher." Her tears spilled over onto her pink cheeks. "And I won't."

She grabbed my shirt and yanked me closer. The passion in this kiss would melt the ice-cream kiss. Her lips moved forcefully, demanding an answer from mine.

My heart ached to give her what she wanted, but my mind held me back because I wasn't what she deserved.

She leaned closer and slid her hands to my shoulders. Her quick breaths fanned my face. "You're the one *I* want. Doesn't that matter?"

"But I'm not what you n—"

"Yes." She placed her hand on my lips. "You're all I need."

She fell back into my arms, her mouth replacing the hand she'd held on my lips.

My heart raced, and as wrong as it was, I kissed her back, caressing her silky hair. The sun-warmed strands slipped through my shaky fingers. I hesitantly touched her tongue with mine, curious. She responded with a small gasp, her tongue answering my unspoken question with a definitive *yes*.

She rubbed her hand on my neck, right where my blood pulsed, pushed by the frantic beating of my heart. She pressed her lips closer, and the truth in her actions erased everything Vikki had said.

I wanted her more than weed. More than any burning alcohol. More than the minty air floating around us. I moved my hands to her back, pulling her closer, though I should push her away for her own good.

She slipped her arms around my neck and leaned into me, pressing her body against mine. A quiet moan escaped her throat, and I hugged her tiny waist, imagining what I'd do if we were alone.

"Ahem!"

We jumped apart, panting, staring up into the disapproving gaze of the librarian, Mr. Jackson.

"Well, I can't say I'm surprised to see you breaking the rules, Mr. Jacobs, but Ms. King?" He shook his head and handed us a referral to the office. "Grace, you should be more careful who you hang out with."

He glared at me like I had corrupted her. He had a point, but fuck him.

Grace blushed but lifted her chin high in defiance. "No, Mr. Jackson. There's nothing wrong with who I'm hanging out with. The problem is people are too judgmental."

Mr. Jackson's jaw fell open, and I bit back a laugh that would earn me extra detention.

She grabbed my hand again, and we walked toward the door. I opened it and held it while she stepped into the hall.

"I'm sorry. Your dad's going to kill me."

"No, he's going to kill me. I started it." She

squeezed my hand. "And I'm not ashamed to admit I'd do it again."

A few people moved in the hall, rushing to and from wherever they belonged. Ignoring them, I pulled her to a stop and gazed at her pink face. "Well, we're already in trouble. We might as well make it worth it." I kissed her eager lips, holding her close.

She wrapped her arms around my neck. If we weren't at school, I would have let my hands roam. But I respected her. She wasn't like the other girls I'd been with. I'd never loved them. I held her by the hips and dove into her eyes.

"I…" The words caught in my throat. No, it'd be crazy to think she'd want to hear them from me.

She whispered, "I know. Me, too."

I smiled, daring to hope it was true but afraid for the same thing.

"Come on, let's go face the consequences of our actions." She laughed, walking toward the office. "We'll be the talk of the school tomorrow. The preacher's daughter caught kissing the school bad boy."

"Maybe we'll earn some extra credit for our project. It takes a lot of dedication to get detention for taking your homework so seriously." We reached the office, and I opened the door.

"Maybe but getting busted for making out in the library at school is bound to have fatal consequences when I get home. I won't need the extra credit." She kissed me on the cheek as she passed, waving at the shocked face of the secretary behind the desk. "But it's okay, because you're worth it."

I laughed at her comment and the irony of our situation. Here I was again, in the place I struggled to avoid, this time with the preacher's daughter. Who was corrupting whom? My spirits soared because this time, I wasn't the one committing the crime. It was Grace, and I was her victim. And I wouldn't have it any other way.

Chapter Eleven

After school, Grace went to a student council meeting, and Connor and I stopped by the restaurant to fill out applications for two busboy positions. It was better than waiting tables. How hard could clearing off dirty dishes and wiping off crumbs be? Mr. Simmons, the owner, said he'd call to let us know if we got the jobs.

Yeah, can't wait.

I returned to an empty house. At least Mom wasn't here to lecture me about getting Grace busted for making out in the library. Then again, Mom would just be happy *I* didn't get busted for smoking weed on school property.

I threw my bag on the chair in my room, then texted Grace. I didn't want her to get in trouble with her parents, especially when it was my fault. She'd started the kissing, but I knew her dad would blame me. And he should. If I hadn't been whining about what Vikki said, we wouldn't have even been alone in the library.

—Is your meeting over yet?—

While I waited for her to respond, I reached for my bag and took out my statistics homework. The numbers jumbled in my mind, and I rubbed my eyes. My phone buzzed, and I grabbed it to see her response.

—Yes. Leaving school now.—

—Do you want me to come to your house so your dad can yell at me instead?—

Getting yelled at was nothing new for me.

—LOL. No, it'll be okay. I've got it covered.—
—I'm sorry.—
—Again, not your fault. I'll call you later...if I survive. :)—

I smirked. She'd survive, but I'd bet her dad wouldn't let her come over here again.

—I hope you do. I'd hate to never see you again.—

Wow. When had I turned into a fourteen-year-old girl?

—Don't worry, you will. Gotta drive. Call you later. <3—

I tossed my phone on the bed and tried to work, but concentrating on statistics was impossible. Memories of Grace's body in the library consumed my thoughts. Even though sex wasn't the biggest way I thought of Grace, I'd be lying if I said I didn't want her. She had my respect, but if she offered, I wouldn't say no. That fell under the idiot-response category.

I groaned, dropping my pencil on my notebook. Taking a deep breath, I lay back on the bed. Maybe a cold shower would help.

My phone buzzed, and I jumped. Connor's smirking face and middle finger greeted me. I tapped the screen, and he yelled in my ear.

"What the hell, Asher? You are the sex god of the world. How did you get Grace King to make out with you in the library?" He laughed, not even waiting for me to respond. "You have half the school pissed, you know. Mostly the stu-co kids. They think you're trying to use her. Which, I might add, is brilliant."

"I'm not using her." My stomach rolled. How many ways would I ruin things?

"Not yet but give it time. I'm sure she'll give it to

you." He moaned. "Man, I'll bet she's hiding a wild side. I've heard about preachers' kids."

I gritted my teeth. "Don't talk about her that way. I'm not using her. I *like* her. And the stu-co kids can piss off. It's none of their business."

"Who *doesn't* like Grace King? I'd kill for ten minutes alone with her. You know that's all it would take because it'd be hard to wait any longer. Damn, she's hot."

"What the hell? Did you not hear me say I liked her? Shut the hell up before I come and kick your ass."

"Jeez, man." He laughed. "I'm just kidding. Go smoke some bud. Abstaining is making you all uptight. Come over. Dan sold me some today. I'll share with you because I can tell you need it."

Why had I answered the phone? I'd known Connor would act like this, and I'd known what he'd offer. Talking to him was like talking to my own addictions.

"I have to go. I have homework to do."

"Man, I'm telling you. I know you said you want to quit, but you sound stressed out. Just give it up. Everyone needs to relax."

"I'm not coming over. I'll talk to you later." I ended the call and tossed my phone into the corner. "Dammit!"

My heart pounded, and my fingers itched to fill a bowl and puff away. Connor was right. I needed to relax. The news of what people were saying about me and Grace pissed me off. And Connor talking about hooking up with her himself—I could literally kill him.

Yeah, I need to relax. Now.

With Grace's face in my mind, I jumped off the bed. I crossed the room and yanked shorts and a T-shirt from my dresser, changed, and ran down the stairs and out the front door. I returned to more trouble.

"Where the hell have you been?" Mom greeted me at the door, frowning. "You're grounded, you know? You can't just leave whenever you want to."

I held up one hand and gripped the stitch in my side with the other. "Before you start, can I take a shower and get a drink?"

She crossed her arms. "Let me smell your breath."

I'd run five miles, trying to pound out my anger and frustration. My lungs were on fire, and I was close to puking on the marble entry, and she thought I was drunk?

"Mom, I was running, not drinking. Smell my armpits instead of my breath." I bent over and grabbed my knees. "If you don't let me go, I'm barfing right here."

She relaxed her shoulders. "Sorry, I told you you'd have to earn back trust."

"I get it, Mom. But really, I need to get to the bathroom." The run eased my stress, but I didn't feel better. Only a missed text or call from Grace would help.

"Go ahead. But once you're clean, come down so we can talk about what happened at school today. And your punishment."

"Right." I was already grounded. What else would she do? I trudged up the stairs, holding my side.

Normally, I didn't get in much trouble at home for breaking school rules. Not that I caused trouble in class. I just didn't go. Connor and I would skip and go to his house to drink and smoke instead. Mom probably figured her impassiveness had caused my current mess and wanted to make up for it by overreacting now.

I retrieved my phone from the floor where I had thrown it, expecting to see a missed call from Grace. I scrolled through the five calls from Vikki and two from Connor but none from Grace.

Maybe she was still getting a lecture from her parents. Her dad could preach for hours. I could only imagine how long his lecture against public displays of affection at school with the resident bad boy would take.

I turned on the shower. I hoped she didn't tell them it was her fault. That would be worse. Her dad would expect that behavior from me. His opinion of me couldn't get any lower. I didn't want him to lose faith in his daughter, too—not because of me.

After I had showered and dressed, I checked my phone again. Nothing. Hoping I might interrupt the lecture with a well-timed phone call, I brought up her number and tapped the screen. I waited for three rings, then a voice answered.

"Hello, Asher."

My heart raced in my chest, and my throat went dry. "Hello, Pastor. H-how are you?"

"Not so great. I'm sure you know why."

Fuck. Me.

I rubbed my eyes and sank to the edge of my bed. "Yes, sir. I do."

He drew a deep breath and exhaled into the phone. "I'm disappointed. I had hoped I could trust you with my daughter. But I see I was wrong."

With his reprimand, I was twelve years old again, getting in trouble for running through the narthex with Grace at the church lock-in when we should've been asleep. Just like that time, I listened, mute with shame.

The pastor continued. "Can you explain what happened today? Tell me why you performed an inappropriate act with my daughter at school."

I rolled my eyes, pulling up one corner of my lip. "It was just a kiss, Pastor King."

"Just a kiss? And you think that's okay at school? That I would approve?"

The nausea returned, and my hands shook. "No...I mean I didn't plan it... It just sort of... We were talking, and one thing led to another and...I kissed her. Honest, I wasn't trying to do anything else. It's just, I like her, and she's such a good person and—"

"Asher, I've known you for a long time, and I know you two used to be close." His harsh sigh created static. "When you left her, *we* had to clean up the mess you made. Had to listen to her cry herself to sleep every night. Watch her fall apart every time she heard a song that reminded her of you. Console her when she screamed at God for taking you away from her."

I tried to swallow the boulder blocking my throat, to defend myself, but his words added layers of guilt that I couldn't blast away with a nuke.

"There was a time I would have done anything to help you, to bring you back. But you've changed and not for the better. Drinking, drugs, inappropriate relations with other girls, I don't know who you are anymore. That's not someone I want to associate with my daughter."

I skipped from twelve at church to sixteen in Connor's shed. My stomach churned. His assessment of me fit. All true. Still, a spark of fight remained, and I fanned it with my desperate breaths. "Pastor King, I know I've made mistakes, and I'm trying to fix them."

"Yes, Grace told me. While I commend your attempt, and I wish you success, I can't allow her to help you. I can't watch her go through that again." His breath in the phone blew like a wind through my tomb.

"I'm sorry about the kiss, sir. I won't do it again, and I am trying to change. Please, isn't there some way you'll believe me?" I struggled to breathe and scramble on top of the landslide of panic.

Pastor King's silence stretched on for minutes, days, an eternity. Finally, he replied. "We have a group that meets on Tuesday nights at my church, for people with…your issues. Come to the group. The first step is admitting you have a problem. Until you can do that, I'm afraid I don't want you doing anything with Grace."

"If I come to the group, you'll let me see her?" How bad could the group be? I could always sit there and listen.

"No, you need to come to the group and participate. Sincerely."

My shoulders sagged. Of course it wouldn't be that easy. "What time is the group?"

"It starts at six in the basement of the church."

I swallowed to wet my throat. "I'll be there. But, sir?"

"What is it, Asher?"

"I want you to know Grace is important and I'm not doing this to hurt her or to use her. I respect her, and I would never hurt her on purpose."

"God forgive me for being blunt, but I'll believe that when I see it. You've already hurt her once, and she suffered greatly. You have a long way to go before you earn my trust back." His voice was a hoarse whisper. "And I don't think you have it in you."

I closed my eyes, biting my lip to keep it still. I'd known his opinion of me was low, but I hadn't known it had reached rock bottom like in the quarry.

The quiet click of him disconnecting tore like the final bullet through my heart.

A man of God, a father-like figure from my life, had told me I was hopeless. That must be a record somewhere—like in Hell. I rubbed my head, trying to get it together enough to go face the next interrogation. Mom waited for me in the kitchen. If her lecture took over five minutes, I would lose it.

I entered the kitchen and began round two.

Mom looked up from her files. "Well? What happened at school today?"

The best kiss ever. Grace showed me she still loves me, despite the way I hurt her and the monster I turned into. "I got busted for PDA."

And told by a pastor I was hopeless.

She glared at me, crossing her arms. "Yes, your principal told me. Why would you do something like that at school? And with Grace of all people. She deserves respect. She's not a plaything."

I met her furious stare with my heart in my throat. Her opinion of me must've been hovering near Pastor King's. But she was my mom. Surely it was a few notches higher.

"Asher, girls are not toys you can just use until they break and then throw away for a new one. And you already broke Grace once. Now you're trying again?"

Nope, hers was even lower. Did she really believe I viewed Grace as a *plaything*? My already dragging spirit crashed to the ground and splattered in a bloody heap and got trampled by elephants and caught on fire. I opened my mouth to argue, but what was the use? My mom had already chosen her side—against her son.

"Fine, I won't do it again. Can I go now?" I looked

at the door, biting my tongue. My hands hurt from clenching them.

She glared, huffing a frustrated breath. "Is that all you have to say? Aren't you even sorry at all?"

Sorry? Hell yes, I was sorry. Sorry I thought I could change. Sorry I'd hoped my mom would back me up and help me become a better person. All the anger, all the pain and embarrassment and guilt converged on my fractured heart and poisoned my tongue. I glared at her and let it all fly.

"No, I have plenty to say. For starters, go to hell, Mom."

She opened her mouth, her eyes widening so much her surgically tightened forehead wrinkled.

I curled my lip and yelled, "All my life, you've ignored me and pushed me aside, for work, for strangers, for all the men you didn't know I'd seen you screwing around with behind Dad's back, including Terry." Her gasp of surprise was perfect revenge. "Yes, I know all about how you used those men as *playthings*. Or maybe they used you, and that's why you think I'm doing the same to Grace."

She sank into her chair and covered her mouth with her hand, eyes filling with tears. "How did you…"

"I heard your phone calls. I saw the men who brought you home from parties you organized, weddings you planned for other normal people, all while Dad was at work, probably fucking one of his co-workers or his secretary."

She shook her head, tears flowing.

My rant continued. "I'm tired of being blamed for everything wrong in *your* life. For everything wrong with you and Dad. You want someone to blame? Blame yourself for causing your son's problems. Yes, I drank and smoked weed and had sex with girls just for the fun of it. But I learned it from the best. So if you want to judge someone, go look in the goddamn mirror and leave me alone!"

Grabbing my keys, I stalked past her, ignoring her tears and any guilt they made me feel. She deserved it.

I climbed into my car and slammed the door. The one person I wanted to see, I couldn't. I only had one place to go, only one other person who could make me feel better. I squealed my tires on my way out to announce my exit and drove to the only place anyone ever accepted me for who I was.

Chapter Twelve

Connor sat on the stained couch, swiping his phone with his index finger. He looked up when I slammed the shed door.

" 'Sup?" he asked, raising his eyebrows.

Falling into the chair across from him, I threw my hands up. "Hell if I know."

He tossed his phone on the seat next to him and kicked his feet on the rickety, beat-up coffee table. "I hope you didn't come here to figure it out. I don't have any answers for you. Especially if this is about Grace."

Pain shot through my chest. "No, it's my mom. She got pissed and lectured me 'cause she thinks I'm using Grace."

"Getting busted for PDA'll do that."

"I told her to go to hell." My neck grew hot.

He whistled. "I'm sure that pissed her off. At least your mom's still around."

"I guess."

"Did Grace get in trouble with her parents?"

"I don't know. But her dad isn't happy with me." I sighed, his words ringing in my ears. "He hates me."

"Dads always hate the guys their daughters like. I think it's part of the dad playbook." He dropped his feet from the table and stretched his arms above his head.

"Grace's dad told me I couldn't see her anymore. Basically told me I was too fucked up for his daughter."

Rubbing my head, I groaned. "Even my own mom thinks I don't deserve Grace. Dammit. Maybe she's right. Maybe everyone's right."

The cooler next to the couch captured my gaze. My throat grew dry, but I swallowed the saliva pooling in my mouth to wet it. Inhaling deep, I caught the faint scent of pot clinging to the furniture.

My heart raced. My shoulders tensed. I rolled my head from side to side, trying to look away from the red-and-white box filled with my demons.

"What do they know?" Connor asked. "If she likes you, fuck them. See her anyway."

"How? Her dad took her phone, so I can't call her."

Shrugging, he flipped open the cooler and reached inside. "Talk to her at school."

"Her dad said I had to go to meetings at their church before I could be with her."

"Meetings?" He smirked. "Like Bible studies or something?"

"No." I stared at the ice in the cooler. "AA meetings."

He laughed. "Seriously? What, he thinks you're an alcoholic?" He pulled two cans out and tossed one to me. "That's stupid."

I caught the beer, the cold metal greeting my hand like an old friend. Connor popped the tab on his, and my heart rose to my throat. One beer. That's all it was. I stared at the shiny silver top, remembering the way that first, icy swallow would bite into the back of my throat.

"Yeah." I spun the can in between my hands.

"You know." He took a sip and pointed his finger at me. "You could just go so he thinks you mean it. Then do whatever the hell you want. You aren't an alcoholic."

Nodding, I picked a piece of ice off the top of my can and flicked it away.

"Alcoholics are messed up. They do all kinds of weird shit to get drunk." He tilted his can again. "Now Vikki is definitely an alcoholic. That girl will do anything to get wasted."

Yeah, Vikki. She said I was like her. I didn't buy it but... I set the beer on the table. "I don't want to talk about Vikki."

"Whatever." He took another sip. "I'm just saying not everyone who drinks is an alcoholic."

Condensation collected on the outside of the can. I traced a drop as it slid toward the bottom, then picked up the beer and rubbed a finger over the tab. Just one beer didn't mean anything. It wasn't like I would be downing a twelve-pack, losing control, robbing stores to get more.

One beer didn't make me an alcoholic.

I popped the tab and took a long sip. The familiar zing eased the tension in my shoulders. I controlled this, not the other way around. I took another swallow.

"Cheers." Connor held his can up in a toast and took a drink. "Grace obviously likes you, or she wouldn't have made out with you in the library. She knows you party. What's the big deal?"

"She doesn't like it." Her green-eyed glare floated through my mind. I drowned it with another gulp.

"Eh, just don't tell her, then." He emptied his can and squeezed it with his hand. He tossed it aside and grabbed another from the cooler.

"Yeah, I guess." The last drops trickled on my tongue. *Huh. That went quick.*

"One more?" Connor asked, holding out a new beer.

Instead of Grace, I pictured her dad's raised

eyebrows and I-told-you-so glare. Then my mom's. Fire burned in my gut. They could kiss my ass. If one beer didn't make me an alcoholic, neither would two. I grabbed the can and pulled the tab. I had this under control, not them.

I pulled into the quarry as the sun set and drove right to the giant hole, my front wheels stopping inches from the edge.

I leaned back on the headrest and closed my eyes. Grace appeared in an instant, and my heart ached. How could the kiss we shared in the library have led to this chaos? What I had thought was a turning point turned out to be a disaster.

Then the first thing I did was run off to Connor's to drink. I told myself I had it under control, that I needed to relax. But one beer had turned into seven or eight, then a few hits on the pipe. I didn't need to relax—I needed Grace. And Kali.

I waited for mint. Emotional strength had never been my strong point, and the strength this disaster required was beyond anything I would ever hope to have.

"Kali, I need you." My whispered plea did what my ranting couldn't. The tears flowed from my eyes, burning my throat and scalding my cheeks.

Minty perfume filled my car, and her hand wiped away my tears. "I'm here, Asher. It's okay."

I opened my eyes. She opened her arms, then rubbed my back while I cried on her shoulder again.

"What am I going to do? I'm not strong enough."

Kali shoved me back by my shoulders and glared. "You are strong enough. You have to be. Grace needs *you*, and you can't let her down."

"Her dad is right. I *am* hopeless. I let everyone

155

down. At the first sign of stress, I run off and get drunk and high. I lashed out at my mom, wanting her to hurt like me. I'm no better than she is, pushing the blame for everything on her shoulders when really it's all my fault."

She sat back in her seat and rubbed her forehead. "Asher, your mother's mistakes don't define you. Her guilt is not yours to bear."

I nodded. "Maybe not, but there's plenty of guilt to go around. I've done such shitty, terrible things. I thought I could be different, and Grace made me believe I could. Without her—"

"You haven't lost her. Just because her dad doesn't want you to be with her doesn't mean that's what *she* wants."

"But she won't go against her dad's rules."

She smirked. "You don't understand teenaged girls. She's not about to let her dad stop her from seeing you."

"I may not know other girls, but I know Grace." I banged my head on the seat. "God, I hate this."

"God already knows. And hello, smart aleck, you know what you need to do. I shouldn't have to repeat it."

I looked at her from the corner of my eye. "What? What do I need to do?"

She shook her head. "Go to the meetings. Her dad laid the path right in front of you. All you have to do is take the first step."

I groaned. "I'm not an alcoholic. Those meetings are for other people, people with real addictions they can't control. Everyone telling me I have an alcohol problem is getting old. Alcohol doesn't control me."

"Then why did you go to Connor's?"

Heat burned my cheeks. "It was only a couple beers.

I'm not wasted. Alcoholics drink to get drunk."

"Alcoholics drink because they need to."

"Then see, I'm fine." I glared at her. "I don't need to drink. I just want to."

"Right." She caressed my arm, raising goose bumps on my skin. "You don't need it. It never crosses your mind. When someone else talks about it, you don't crave it. When things get hard, you feel stressed out, but the thought of alcohol doesn't make your mouth parched, your throat dry. You don't imagine the taste, quenching your burning thirst."

A black fire lit her eyes, the blue surrounding her pupils scorched away by the flames.

I squirmed in my seat, trapped by her eyes, their darkness pulling me in. She moved closer, laying her hands on my chest, rubbing my tense muscles. Her mint enveloped me, and I inhaled deeply. My heart reacted to her touch, speeding like it had when I ran.

"When Connor tells you about the parties you've missed, the drugs you could have had, the girls that were there, willing to do just about anything, you don't want any of it." She leaned even closer, her minty lips just a breath away from mine. "You don't want to feel their skin, taste their kisses. They don't make you feel wanted, special."

I couldn't breathe. The picture she painted in my mind pushed my desire for Grace away and left blackness in her place. The warmth of Kali's body leaning on mine eased my loneliness.

She breathed the next words in a sultry whisper. "None of that controls you. Wanting and needing aren't the same thing. You don't need it. But you know what you want." Hearing the promise in her words, feeling it in her touch while she caressed my chest, tasting it in her breath with her lips so close to mine, I wanted it all—and her.

I pulled her lips to mine, and the taste was everything I expected. She was mint and sugar, seasoned with guilt and pain. Like the best drugs I knew I shouldn't take yet wanted all the same. Her hair, smooth as silk, tickled my face and neck, like the soft caress of a lover.

But it didn't last. Her kiss brought with it a vision, black and oily, that seeped into my brain, like the ice from her laugh only hotter. Much hotter, with pain like nothing I'd ever experienced. Kali and my car faded, and I opened my eyes. I stood in Connor's shed, watching myself smoke weed with him.

My heart pounded. I knew what this was. Living this scene was bad enough, and I didn't want to watch it play out again. Connor's voice pulled my attention back to us, sitting on the worn-out couch.

"Asher, I'm telling you. Fucking forget her. She's not worth it."

I covered my ears to block out the words I'd said. But my memory voice came from within myself, doubling the pain in my head.

"I know. She's a pain in the ass. I don't need her." Smoke curled around my head.

I'd believed those words then, but I wanted to punch my past self in the face before he could do what came next. I pulled my hands away and looked at the door. My heart throbbed as I waited for her to enter. Grace walked in, tears on her cheeks, her wholesome face looking out of place in the dirty shed, a light in the darkness. One I'd been too blind and stupid to see.

"Asher, can we talk?"

My past self sneered, and Connor laughed. I wanted to scream at her to leave, to ignore what the old me was about to say. But I knew I couldn't change the past. I closed my eyes so I didn't have to see the look on her face again.

"There's nothing to talk about. Connor's right. You're not worth the hassle."

Her voice shook. "Please talk to me. We can work this out."

"No, there's nothing to work out. You want me to be something I'm not. This is what I am, and if you can't accept that, then just get the hell away from me."

I cringed, holding my head as pain exploded around me. Grace's sobs faded, and a new scene took the place of the shed.

I opened my eyes, blinded by the bright light surrounding me. I blinked away my tears and turned to the sobs behind me. My knees almost buckled at the new nightmare.

Grace's parents sat next to a hospital bed. Mrs. King covered her face, and Pastor King held her, one arm around her trembling shoulders and his other hand on the person in the bed. I couldn't move, and I didn't want to see who it was.

Look, Kali commanded. Her voice snarled in my brain, an ice pick driving deep. I grabbed my head and closed my eyes. The injury of only two people would have this devastating of an effect on the Kings, and the person in the bed was too big to be their young son.

"No, I can't." I shook my head, but Kali's voice grew louder, the pain increasing until I thought my skull would split open from the pressure.

I said look.

Shaking, I shuffled toward the Kings, wearing shoes of lead, the cold air laced with the coppery scent of blood. The supernaturally loud beeping of machines pounded out the rhythm of my speeding heart. I reached the bed, and the beeping stopped.

I looked down on Grace, white and still, her green eyes almost black, staring blankly at nothing. Bruises and scratches covered her beautiful face and the perfect skin of her neck. Her mother wailed as the doctor pulled a sheet over her head.

The scream lodged in my throat. I couldn't erase the vision as it expanded, swallowing me, squeezing the air from my lungs. I placed my hand on hers, the coldness of her skin contrasting with the heat of my tears. I closed my eyes and turned away from Grace.

"Stop, please! I don't want to see this." My heart ached, ready to explode from pain. But Kali wasn't finished.

A cold breeze blew across my face as the next scene unfolded. I was at the quarry, standing next to another me. I watched, helpless, as the other me sat on the edge of the cliff and downed gulp after gulp from a bottle in one hand, staring at a picture of Grace in the other.

I knew how this would end, like it almost had when I'd sat there the other day. Because I knew what happened to Grace, this scene made perfect sense. I welcomed the end to the pain.

My dream self stood, wiping his eyes. Then, holding her picture, he jumped.

This time the vision changed. I blinked, and I sailed through the air, headed for the bottom of the quarry. The scream finally left my lungs. It echoed off the jagged rocks, and I closed my eyes as the ground raced to meet me.

I landed in the front seat of my car, panting, sweating, shaking. Kali still lay on my chest. Her eyes were black, no white left at all, like ink had replaced the fluid and swirled behind her lenses. They were the eyes of Death. At last, I saw the demon inside her.

Frantic with fear, I shoved her away and gripped my head in my hands. She fell against the door, panting.

"Stop!" My scream echoed off the windows of my car. "That's enough!"

I tried to forget the coldness of Grace's skin. Dead. Gone. Tried to push away the memory of diving off the cliff, waiting for death to take me. This time, Kali offered no comfort, and I bore the sobs alone.

She sagged into the seat. Her eyes, normal again, were narrow slits, and she moaned, holding her stomach.

I glared at her. "What was that? Was that the future? If it was, push this fucking car right over the edge and let me go where I should've gone days ago." I wiped my eyes. "Please tell me that won't happen."

"Yes, Asher. That's what your denial, your selfishness, *your cowardice*, will cause." She sat a little straighter and glared at me. "I told you Grace needs you. Go to the damn meeting. It's for people with *problems* who need help, and you, without a doubt, fall into that category."

I opened my mouth, and Kali disappeared. My ears popped with the vacuum her sudden absence left behind. I leaned my head on the steering wheel, gulping air, squeezing my eyes closed until stars exploded behind my lids.

Denial was no longer an option. I was a fucked-up

mess, and I needed help. Alcohol, drugs, sex, they'd all become crutches for my biggest problem—fear, fear of taking responsibility for my own actions. I blamed everything on others and expected them to make up for what I thought they owed me. I was too scared to admit I had a problem, because it would mean *I* had to change, and if I did, I had to do it alone.

For whatever reason, if I didn't accept responsibility or own up to my problems and the fact I alone deserved the blame, Grace would die. And it would be my fault.

Grace wanted to help me fight these crazy addictions of mine, and I would fight for her. The image of her limp, lifeless body was something I'd never forget and something I vowed I'd never see, not if I could stop it.

All night I tossed and turned. After the fifth nightmare featuring Grace's rotting corpse yelling at me for letting her die while Kali said, "I told you so," I gave up on getting any sleep. At school, I waited by her locker. Even though her dad told me to stay away, I had to see her, had to touch her, to know she was alive and would still be there when I fixed myself. Each time the door to the parking lot opened, I looked for her.

The first bell rang.

"Dammit." I ran to my class and swallowed my disappointment.

I slid into my desk in stats and gritted my teeth. What was her dad doing, homeschooling her to keep her away from me?

Could her leg have gotten worse? Was she avoiding me? Had she changed her mind? So many questions and I had no way to get answers. I'm sure her dad still had her phone. And it's not like I could drive over there to check on her.

Even though he was a pastor, I'd bet her dad would shoot first and ask questions later. Getting killed by a gun-toting man of God because I defiled his daughter wasn't the way I wanted to go.

Maybe she would be at the meeting tonight. I cringed, picturing her there, listening to me admit I had a problem. She wouldn't judge me, but my stomach burned as I thought about her witnessing my confession.

The day passed slowly. The bell rang for my lunch period, and I faced a new dilemma. I always sat with Connor and our group of friends where the conversation revolved around one topic—partying. When was the next party? Where was the next party? Who would bring the beer and weed to the next party? Who would hook up at the next party?

After the trip to the quarry with Kali, and my nightmares, I had no desire to talk about the next party.

I bought my lunch and headed to the courtyard outside the cafeteria doors. It wasn't warm outside, but the bright sun made the chilly air bearable. I sat alone on a bench made from recycled milk-gallon caps, dedicated to a man I'd never heard of who made contributions to the school I didn't know or care about.

I was halfway through eating my pizza as Connor sat beside me. He frowned and crossed his arms, huddling against the chill. "What the hell are you doing out here? It's freezing."

I shrugged and took another bite of pizza. "It's not that cold. I needed fresh air."

"I thought maybe you found a way to sneak a toke at lunch." He leaned back on the bench and stuffed his hands in his jacket pockets. "Let's go in. I almost have

Dan convinced to have the party Friday night. His parents are taking his little brother on a soccer trip, and they'll be gone all weekend. We can hang there and not have to worry about parents for a couple days."

No parents and a weekend of getting wasted was my old idea of perfect. "I'm not partying this weekend. Remember?"

Or ever again if I succeed.

"Right." He rolled his eyes. "Then just come hang out."

"Why would I come watch you guys get wasted when I'm avoiding that?" I shook my head. "I'm not going."

"Whatever." He stood and jerked his head toward the door. "Let's go inside. I'm fucking cold."

"You go in. I'm staying out here."

He raised an eyebrow. "Why?"

"All they do is talk about partying. I can't sit with them anymore. Not if I want to change."

His gaze met mine, and the back of my neck went cold and not from the breeze blowing through the courtyard.

"Them?"

The hurt behind his glare brought instant guilt.

"Don't you mean me? I'm part of *them*. You used to be, too. Now what, you're too good for us?"

I swallowed my pizza, looking for the words to fix my friend's feelings. "No, I'm not too *good*. I'm too *bad*. Sitting with people who want what I'm trying to quit won't make it any easier. I'm still your friend. I just don't want to do the same old thing anymore."

"Really? 'Cause it feels like you're blowing me off. I guess I'll go back inside and sit with the bad kids." He took a few steps but turned back to face me. "I hope you get what you want. But like I said, I'm not interested in changing when I don't think there's a problem." He pushed open the door and went inside, leaving me alone once again.

The hollowness returned, but the pain from hurting him didn't even fit in the same universe as the pain from seeing Grace dead in my dreams. I knew who I couldn't live without.

Sucked wasn't a strong enough word to describe the rest of my day. I kept hoping Grace would appear and make everything better. Her absence made the day seem a hundred times longer and a million times darker.

I drove home scowling, a headache forming behind my eyes. The house was empty again, so at least I didn't have to face Mom. She hadn't spoken to me last night after I came home. I wasn't sure if she was embarrassed or hated me. Maybe a little of both.

I wanted to apologize, but she needed time to deal first, and I had enough on my mind to worry about. Mom's feelings scored way lower on my give-a-shit-o-meter than Grace's.

With a couple of hours to kill before the meeting, I sat at the dining room table to do my homework. Mrs. Kumar had handed out assignments for our marriages today—devise a family budget. Since Grace had our notes, I improvised. We hadn't chosen a house yet either, so I went shopping alone.

Using my tablet, I surfed the real estate sites and found a nice little three-bedroom brick home I thought she would like. I could have chosen a mansion since I was a surgeon, but no sense in making us house poor.

Besides, worrying about appearances was my

parents' thing, not mine. I had no desire to be like them. After factoring in the house payment for our new little home-sweet-home, I finished writing a budget, including utilities and taxes. With two business-minded parents, I guessed some of their skills rubbed off. It must have been through osmosis. They'd never thought to share anything with me.

"Dammit, Grace. This would be a lot more fun if you were here." I threw my pen on the notebook and leaned back in my chair, glancing at my phone. Did her dad have hers? Did she not want to talk? Believing she cared was easy when she sat right next to me or kissed me with her soft, perfect lips. But sitting by myself in an empty house with nothing to do but plan a pretend life I wished would come true, my doubt spread like a weed.

My wandering gaze fell on the stocked liquor cabinet, and my chest muscles tightened. I wanted to close my eyes, turn my head, run out the door screaming. Instead, the wood floor creaked under my feet as I approached the cherrywood hutch with the double glass doors.

In less than an hour, I would be at church with her dad who hated me, admitting my drinking problem to a room full of strangers. Why was I staring at this glass case like it held the answer to all my needs?

Oh. Right. My drinking problem. I flicked the door handle. The pendulum-style pull-chain knob knocked against the wood like the ticking of a bomb.

"Get out of here." I whispered the words to myself. But I didn't listen, so I said them louder. "Get the hell away."

I closed my eyes and leaned my head on the cool glass of the door. I tried to pull up a word, a command, anything to make myself walk away. But my mind tricked me, reliving memories of drinking with Connor at the shed, partying with Dan at his house across town while his parents were out. Like Mom was now. Gone.

"Dammit. Dammit. Dammit." I tapped my head on the glass with each frustrated exhalation. "Now would be a great time for you to lend a hand, Kali." I didn't expect her to show up. Could this be a test?

"Of course, idiot," I chided myself. Every day was a test to see how badly I could fuck things up. So far, I'd failed. I hadn't even been to my first meeting, and already I was falling off the wagon.

I grasped the door pull and eased open the glass. I cleared the tingle from my throat and reached for the green bottle of schnapps. The cut crystal sparkled under the LED lights that illuminated the cabinet. Using my fingertips, I caressed the side, then the stopper at the top. I hated schnapps, but even that would quench the sudden burning thirst that squeezed the sides of my throat together. I lifted it from the shelf and opened it, raising the bottle to my nose and breathing deep the sweet, minty scent.

My heart tried to escape my chest through my ribs. I sniffed again, bringing the bottle a little closer to my lips. My hands shook, and I spilled a little of the liquid on the collar of my shirt. Why had I picked up the bottle? Why wasn't Kali here yelling at me to stop? Why was I so damn weak?

I groaned. "God, *please* cut me some slack."

But I already knew I couldn't trust God to help me.

Then slack came with the buzzing of my phone on the table and Grace's face lighting up the screen. I glanced from it to the bottle in my hands, like I'd fallen into some twisted game created just for me by the Fates. Tilt back the bottle or pick up the phone? Take a sip or answer? Alcohol or Grace?

To hell with the damn Fates.

Slamming the bottle back onto the shelf, I ran to the table. I picked up the phone, fumbled it between my hands, and finally settled it to answer. "Hello?"

"Hey, Asher."

Her voice filled the empty hollow space in my chest, and I walked away from the cabinet. "Are you okay? Where were you today? Why haven't you called? Does your dad know you called? I thought he had your phone, or I would have called you sooner."

She laughed. "Are you finished, or do you want to add a few more questions to the list?"

Her laugh eased my fear. "No, you can answer."

"Well, I'm fine. I wasn't feeling well enough for school today. He told me not to call you, and my dad is at church and doesn't know I am talking to you." She giggled. "Mom left my phone on the counter, and I grabbed it when she wasn't looking."

"You bad girl. You're breaking all the rules, aren't you?" I exhaled a deep sigh, the doubts melting away. "Maybe your dad's right. I'm not a good influence on you."

"What do you mean? What did my dad say to you?" Her voice took on a hard edge.

"Nothing." *That you need to know.*

"Aaa-sher?"

I smiled at the motherly tone. "Graaa-ce?" My laugh ruined my attempt to mimic it.

"Ugh. If the church knew how my father was treating you, they'd ask for a new pastor."

"He has every right to not trust me." I glanced at the cabinet and walked away into the living room. "He doesn't want me to hurt you again. That's the only reason he thinks I'm wrong for you."

"You're not wrong for me. He doesn't know what he's talking about."

"The idiot me is definitely wrong for you. But I know I can change. I'm going to his meeting tonight. He said if I made the effort, he'd let me hang out with you. If nothing else, I'll prove him wrong out of spite."

She giggled. "I'll be there to help you."

"No, I need to do this alone, to prove to myself that I can." Taking that first step alone felt like jumping off a cliff, but it was time.

"Are you sure?"

I thought about the cabinet in the other room and how close I'd come to drinking from the green bottle. But I hadn't. That had to mean something. I could do this, for myself—and for Grace. Somehow, going to that meeting and owning up to my problem would save her life. Of course I would go.

"Yes," I said. "I can do it."

"I'm proud of you." She was quiet for a long moment, her steady breath the only sound.

"Are you still there?" I checked the phone. The time stamp still showed a running clock. "Grace? Hello?"

She giggled again. "Sorry, I think I nodded off."

"Uhm, am I *boring* you?"

"No, silly. I'm just tired. I went to the doctor today for my leg, and he gave me some medicine to help with the pain."

"Medicine?" The giggling, bad-mouthing her dad, it all came together, and I chuckled. "Grace, are you high?"

She giggled again, longer this time. "No, I'm taking medicine, not smoking weed."

I shook my head, laughing with her. How many pills had she taken? "What kind of medicine?"

"I don't know. A painkiller. It started with an O. My leg hurt bad today, but I feel good now."

She chuckled again, and I laughed. Getting to see her stoned on narcotics was a once-in-a-lifetime opportunity, I'd bet. I hated to miss it.

"Maybe you should go to sleep. You can tell me about this tomorrow, and I'll tell you about my first meeting." A painkiller that started with an O—oxycodone? Her doctor had pulled out the big guns. But why would he prescribe a narcotic for a pulled muscle? At least she wasn't tossing back a six-pack with her pills like I did.

"I won't be at school tomorrow either. The doctor told me to take a couple days off." Her voice became breathless. I was losing her to the drugs.

I frowned. Damn, I wanted to see her face-to-face to get a straight answer. In the back of my mind, warning bells went off. I'd never heard of someone missing school for a pulled muscle. She wasn't making sense, though. "Can I talk to your mom?"

"I haft go, Asher. I'm 'sausted."

I struggled to understand her slurring. *Dammit.* "Grace, please get your mom." Was this how I sounded when I was stoned? No wonder conversations with Connor were confusing when we partied.

"I'll talk tomorrow." She giggled one last time. "Hey, Asher?"

My heart beat a little faster when she whispered my name. "What, Grace?" I answered just as quiet, like we were playing sardines at the church lock-in, lying under the pews in the dark sanctuary to hide from the others. Pressing my fingers into my eyes, I sighed. I'd give anything to be lying there next to her again, because this time I wouldn't let her go.

Her next words were barely a whisper. Soft, like a warm breeze off the ocean in the middle of a dream. "I love you."

My breath caught in my throat. She ended the call before I could respond.

Chapter Thirteen

I pulled into the church parking lot and parked near the back door but stayed in my car and stared at the building. The setting sun cast long shadows on the light brown brick and reflected off the glass of the windows. Memories flooded my mind, drowning me, sucking the air from my lungs until I hunched in pain.

I looked at the line of windows leading to the classrooms in the education wing to my right. I blinked, and Grace's five-year-old face smiled back at me. Then she and I, eight, ran through the grass near the building, hunting for Easter eggs. Next came eleven, vacation Bible school, and I chased her with a water gun around the bench by the door. Finally, fourteen, Grace holding my hand under the maple tree in the church yard to my left, trying to convince me my parents' divorce wasn't my fault.

That was the last time I'd come here with her. Not long after that day, I'd met Connor and begun my headfirst spiral into Hell on Earth.

I closed my eyes, inhaling the familiar leathery smell of my car. "Damn." Why was I here? To fix my future or to relive my past? Both seemed impossible. I imagined Grace's lips on mine in the library, remembered her soft, whispered *I love you* on the phone, and found the strength to get out of the car.

I took a deep breath and walked into the building.

Her dad didn't think I'd be here. Honestly, I hadn't either, but seeing the girl I adored dead because of my choices changed my perspective on things.

I froze just inside the door. The narthex was unrecognizable. I took a moment to acclimate to the changes, my head spinning from the unfamiliar surroundings of a place I'd grown up in. Cream-colored tiles had replaced the old dingy brown ones on the floor. They gleamed in the light filtering through the multicolored stained-glass windows. The pale yellow on the walls soothed better than the seemingly ancient gray paint from years ago. Just the right touch for a sinner seeking redemption or a doomed alcoholic pothead who wanted to change his life.

I walked down the stairs on my right, which led to the basement of the church. Here nothing had changed, and the familiarity calmed my nerves. The narrow stairs, painted a dark brown, were depressing after the bright upstairs remodel. Maybe the money had run out before they could get down here. I smirked. *Time for another chili cook-off fundraiser.*

I turned left at the foot of the stairs, and the wide hallway opened to a large room that looked exactly as I remembered.

Dingy tan linoleum flooring ran the whole length of the basement. The small windows, set high by the ceiling in the wall across from me, didn't let in enough light to illuminate the room, but the fluorescent lighting exposed the walls, covered with a mixture of leftover beige and white paint mixed through the years to conserve resources.

This room had all the ambiance of a 1960s prison. Perfect place for an AA meeting—if someone wanted to encourage the alcoholics to drink.

People mingled around the room. Some sat in chairs facing a podium. Others stood in various spots, talking. Several people milled about around the coffee pot on the long counter by the kitchen to my left. Their loud laughter, echoing off the acoustic tiled ceiling, fit more with a potluck than a meeting about battling addictions. Instead of putting me at ease, their laughter knotted my stomach, made me feel even more like an outsider. I didn't have much to laugh about lately.

Pastor King stood among them, sipping from his cup. He glanced at me, and his eyes widened before he hid his surprise.

Jeez, doubt me much?

He patted the shoulder of the man he'd been speaking with and walked my way. His smile wasn't overly warm, but it wasn't icy either. "You came."

I cleared my throat. "Well, I told you I was serious. Grace is important."

"She is. But you should be here for yourself."

"Yeah, I am."

He nodded. "You came on a good night."

"Why is that?"

"It's a speaker meeting. We have a gentleman here to give his testimony. Usually, everyone who wants to share has a chance, but tonight only he will. It gives you the opportunity to acclimate before you share your story."

The knots in my stomach squeezed tighter. I didn't want to share anything, so listening to someone else share sounded perfect. "Do you run the meeting?"

He shook his head. "Only the members do that. Someone from the church is always here to get things ready. And to turn on the lights."

"Is there anything I need to do before the meeting starts?"

He pointed to the coffee. "Well, if you want any coffee, grab it and take a seat. The meeting starts in five minutes, and we always start and end on time." He turned to walk away, but I tapped his arm.

"Excuse me, sir. I have a question." I cleared my throat, and he frowned.

"What is it?"

"Well, Grace and I have a project to do for school. Did she tell you?"

His eye twitched, and he nodded. "The senior seminar project."

"Yes. Today Mrs. Kumar assigned another component, and I wondered if you would allow me to meet with her after school tomorrow to work on it?"

Any pretense of politeness evaporated, and he narrowed his eyes. "We've already had this discussion. I don't want you near Grace. Not until you get yourself under control."

Ignoring the burning in my face, I shrugged. "I know. But I don't want to fail the project. Or have Grace fail…because of me."

And I had to see her, to find out what was really wrong with her.

His frown deepened until his eyebrows made one straight reddish-blond line across his forehead. "I don't know. She wasn't feeling well today, and I don't think she'll be at school tomorrow either."

I already knew this, but I hoped he would let me come over to their house. I craved her more than beer. "The assignment is due Thursday. Could I stop by tomorrow on my way home?"

He rubbed his chin. "I suppose she'll have plenty of homework to do after missing two days. But I won't be home. I have a missions meeting before Bible study."

My heart sped, and I bit back a grin. Visiting her without her dad breathing down my neck? Perfect. I pushed away the images created by the thought of being alone with Grace while she was high on painkillers. God probably wasn't against shooting me with a bolt to remind me to behave.

"I don't want you to think this means I approve of you being with Grace." Pastor King pursed his lips for a moment. "But Ann will be there to keep an eye on you. Wouldn't want a repeat of the PDA in the library."

I cocked my eyebrow as he tilted the cup to his lips to hide his smirk. *Like I need a freaking babysitter.* Well, he didn't own the market on sarcasm.

"Thanks. We have a lot left to do for the project. I've already bought a house for us and made a budget, but I think Grace should be involved in the process, too, especially for the next assignment. She'll want a say in how many grandkids we give you."

He coughed, covering his mouth with his hand to stop the spray of coffee.

I didn't hide my smirk while I feigned concern. "You okay, Pastor King?"

He nodded, wiping his mouth. "I'm fine." He coughed again, and the hint of a real smile filled his lips. "You always were quick witted, Asher. Glad to see that hasn't changed."

The sincerity in his comment loosened the tension in my chest. I grinned, remembering the sarcasm wars we used to have before I lost myself. For a moment, those days felt like yesterday. Movement caught my attention, and I glanced toward it. At some unspoken signal, the others took their seats. My gut twisted.

"You'd better find a seat. We're about to begin." Pastor King patted my shoulder. "Relax and enjoy the meeting. These people are friendly and supportive. They'll never judge you."

I took a deep breath and nodded, but inside I knew everybody judged—and I'd always come up short.

"Just be yourself." He frowned. "Your old self, the one with potential."

He walked toward the front of the room, and I sat in the back row, picturing Grace's face. I pushed away memories from the past and waited for my future to begin.

Pastor King sat in the front of the crowded room, and it struck me again how much he looked like Grace. I pulled her picture up on my phone and held it in my hand.

A woman stood in front of us on the stage at the end of the room. She shuffled some papers on the ancient podium and raised her smiling face to us. "Good evening, everyone. I'm Jeannette, and I'm an alcoholic."

"Hello, Jeanette," the room said in unison.

I was the only one left out of the synchronized answer. *Great, I already messed up.*

"Let's open with the prayer of serenity." She closed her eyes.

Some bowed their heads, and others raised their faces. Still others raised their hands or just stared at Jeanette. I pressed my lips together and stared at my phone screen.

When the prayer ended, she raised her head. "Welcome. Do we have any first-time visitors who

177

would like to introduce themselves?"

My heart pounded in my throat. Pastor King said I wouldn't have to share, and I'd hold him to that.

An older woman in the second row stood, visibly shaking, her long dark hair rippling down her back. She looked like I felt—scared shitless.

"My name is Suzanne. This is my first time here." Her voice shook, too.

"Hello, Suzanne."

Jeez, I missed it again.

"Is there anyone else?" Jeanette's gaze fell on me, and she gave a slight nod.

Damn. I looked at Grace's picture, swallowing the lump of fear from my throat. *Do this for her.* I only had to say my name. I stood, and every eye turned my way. My churning stomach reminded me why I'd never joined the theater kids.

"Hi, I'm Asher. This is my first time here, too."

"Hello, Asher."

Falling into my seat, I clutched my phone in my hand like a lifeline, raising my gaze to Pastor King.

He lifted an eyebrow and nodded.

Jeanette continued. "Welcome to our visitors. Now we will all introduce ourselves, and then we will read 'How it Works' from the Big Book and complete the twelve traditions."

Names were given, readings completed, and the collections for self-support taken. Jeanette again took the podium. I'd lost track of the names for every "I'm an alcoholic," but by the end I could hang with them on the response. At least I had gotten one thing right.

"This evening, our meeting is an open meeting with a speaker. We will not be sharing tonight, but if you have a burning need, you can take one of the phone lists and contact someone who will listen."

Her eyes scanned the room, stopping on me. I slid down in my seat a little and bit my bottom lip.

"Please welcome our speaker, Dave."

I lifted my hands and clapped but stopped after one when nobody else did. A few gazes turned my way, and I slouched even more.

An older man walked to the podium and shook Jeanette's hand. His gray hair and tanned, leathery face betrayed his age, but his trim body looked strong and healthy. His brilliant smile shaved years off his face.

"Good evening. My name is Dave, and I'm an alcoholic."

"Hello, Dave."

Nailed it that time. I smiled at Grace's picture.

"My mother died giving birth to me. My father, stricken with grief, dumped me on a relative because he couldn't handle the loss of my mother and blamed me for her death."

I squirmed in my seat. *Shit just got real. No wonder he started drinking.*

"When I was ten, my father died from cirrhosis of the liver, and I became a ward of the state. That's where my story begins."

I glanced around at the others. Most nodded. Had they heard this story?

Dave continued with the same happy tone, like he told us a fairy tale instead of a nightmare.

"After bouncing around from one foster home to another, I landed in this little town with a family of five. My foster parents and their three children welcomed me into their home and took care of me. But that didn't matter. I was angry, hurt, and rejected, unwanted by my real family. Unimportant. Unloved."

He described his life, but I nodded with the others. Even though I'd lived with my parents until the divorce, I'd felt the same way most of my life.

"At eleven, I entered junior high and made new friends or enablers as we call them now." He chuckled, and the others joined him. "One friend made me feel extra welcome. She always included me, made sure I knew where to go and who to hang out with."

He took a deep breath and blew it out. "She introduced me to alcohol when we were twelve with a bottle of whiskey she'd found in her foster dad's garage. We drank it at the park while we sat on the swings.

"We drank our way through junior high and well into high school. It was the sixties, though, and we found other ways to…expand our minds." He laughed again with the others.

I frowned.

"When the alcohol wasn't enough, she and I discovered weed, heroin, cocaine. You name it, we did it. The pain from my past haunted me every night, and drugs and alcohol helped me to forget who I was."

Heat spread from my face to my neck. Dave told his story, but it was mine, too.

"She and I grew close. We understood each other, accepted each other. Loved each other." He grabbed a tissue from the box on the podium where he spoke, the soft *puff* loud as thunder in the silent room.

He wiped his eyes. "This is my story, so I won't share hers with you. But her path and mine intertwine, and parts of her story will forever be a part of my soul."

His smile faded, and his creased face aged ten years.

"We drank every night. It was the only way to ease our mutual pain. Soon, nothing else mattered. The only thing that mattered was where we would get our next high. Who would we steal from? Where would we get the money to buy our drink? What could we sell to get the cash?"

He spoke of his life, and I tasted mint. A flash of red to my left caught my eye, and I turned my head. Kali sat in the chair next to me and stared at Dave. I glanced around, but, as usual, nobody else seemed to notice her.

She ignored me and stared straight ahead. I followed her gaze and returned my attention to Dave.

"One night, we needed a fix. I had ten dollars in my pocket I had stolen from my foster sister. We used it to buy a fifth of vodka, but it wasn't enough. We had no money, nothing to sell. Or so I thought."

He cleared his throat. Nobody moved or spoke. Pastor King and several others cried openly now. Clenching my hands on my phone, I glanced at Grace's beautiful face. Her clean beauty couldn't ease my apprehension for what Dave would say next.

"We went to an area of town where people could find what they wanted and make trades for the things they needed. I had nothing but the clothes on my back and a burning need for something to relieve my pain. No matter the cost. If you've attended meetings for long enough, you know what rock bottom is. I found mine that night."

Tears fell from his eyes, little rivers of pain that washed through the lines on his face. The hum of the refrigerator in the nearby kitchen blended with the sniffles of those around me.

"I was so desperate for alcohol and drugs I sold the

one thing I valued most. The single most important part of my shitty existence." He glanced around at the faces staring back at him, but he settled his gaze on me.

I almost couldn't hear him over the beating of my heart in my ears.

"I sold my girl's body so I could have a drink and a hit of cocaine. I let other men take her so I could get high one more time. They shot her up with heroin and forced her to do things I won't repeat."

I swallowed the vomit in the back of my throat and closed my eyes. A cloud of mint enveloped me, burning my eyes with its strength. I turned to Kali, and the mint soured like rotting flesh.

Gone was the beautiful girl I'd met that day outside Connor's. Instead, her red hair was greasy and knotted. Bruises covered her arms, her face, her neck, blue and purple and green. Blood and dirt stained her torn pink tank top, her flare leg jeans covered with the same. Sweat and alcohol overpowered the mint, filling my nose and turning my stomach.

But her eyes sent the most pain to my heart, made me want to scream. The confidence, wisdom, kindness, and love she had shown me disappeared. Her soulless eyes full of tears found mine, hers shadowed by deep black circles in her sunken, yellow-tinged face. Blood leaked from the corner of her cracked lips and trickled onto her chin.

I shook my head, blinking away the hot stinging tears. *Kali* was Dave's girl? The one he loved, the one he helped ruin? She placed her cold clammy hand on my cheek and nodded.

At the podium, Dave blew his nose. I looked away from Kali and glared at him, the bitter taste of bile in the back of my throat. How could he have done this to her, all for a little booze and drugs? Hadn't he even thought about her before he sold her out? Considered her feelings?

Searing shame washed through me, remembering what I had done—to Vikki. To Grace. Were my choices any better? Wasn't I just as selfish? Nobody had died because of me. Yet. But the pain I'd inflicted had hurt them, too.

"When it was over, my girl died. Not her body, but her spirit. Her drug use got worse. She tried to cope with the pain I'd created for her. I was too drunk to help her, so I watched her fade away. I watched her slowly kill herself with drugs. I even helped by getting high with her."

Dave stopped and held his head in his hands. Beside me, Kali stood and walked toward him, clean and whole once again. Her Hollywood smile lit her beautiful face. She stepped up to the podium and caressed his hair. He lifted his head, and she kissed him on the cheek.

Wide-eyed, I glanced around, but everyone stared at Dave, crying and nodding.

Kali rubbed her hand down Dave's back. He stood straight again. Only I could see her whisper in his ear, but he stood taller with her by his side.

"I loved my girl. My Kali. And I know she loved me. When she died a few months later, I rightfully blamed myself and would have joined her except for one thing." He rubbed the kiss on his cheek. "She loved life, despite the shit hand Fate dealt and the choices she'd made. She used to tell me, 'We choose to make our life what we want, and we should grab the things we want before they slip away.' But most of all, she told me never avoid the things important for your future because you fear repeating the past."

Kali smiled at me from the front of the room, her hand resting on Dave's, and I finally understood why she'd given me a second chance at life.

Part of me wanted to tell him his love stood by his side, but I'd probably end up in the psych ward.

"I changed because of her, for her, but most of all, I changed for myself. I wanted to be a man she would be proud of. The kind of man she could love. I've not led a perfect life. I've slipped a few times over the years. Dove headfirst off the wagon."

His chuckle unlocked the frozen room, and they laughed.

"Each day is a struggle, but when I think I can't take another step and I want to quit trying, I think of Kali, and I remember life is worth the struggle. I've learned to forgive myself for the things in the past I can't change and move ahead, one step at a time. These meetings— the people I've met, the steps in the program—they've all helped me to stay strong."

His gaze landed on me again. His smile seemed brighter with Kali beside him, and I saw what they could have been.

"I couldn't have made it without the AA program. And I encourage anyone new to try it. If it works for you, then please keep coming back."

He stepped away from the podium, and Jeanette hugged him. He walked to the chairs, and others stood to hug him, too. A buzz of conversation filled the room.

Jeanette took Dave's spot at the podium. She cleared her throat, bringing the group's attention back to her. "Thank you, Dave, for sharing your story. As always, it was inspirational." Everyone clapped in agreement, including me. "Let's close with the Lord's prayer."

After the prayer, everyone stood, conversations springing up all around. I searched for Kali. She stood near Dave as he spoke with Pastor King. Neither man indicated they saw her, but Dave had the same peaceful look as he had when she joined him during his speech. His face glowed like a kid on Christmas.

Kali waved me over, and I smirked. *What is she going to do, introduce me?* I joined their small group.

Pastor King gestured to Dave. "Asher, this is Dave."

Dave shook my hand. "Hello, Asher. It's good to meet you. Although I wish we were meeting at a different venue."

I nodded. "Nice to meet you, too." I glanced at Kali beside Dave, her hand on his shoulder. What was the polite thing to say at an AA meeting? "Thanks for sharing your story."

"You're welcome. I've been doing this every year for the last forty years. It never gets easier to admit my part in ruining my girl, but it's worth it if it gives somcone else hope to change."

Kali's eyes filled with tears, and she gave him a loving gaze.

I raised my eyebrows. "Forty years is a long time. And I'm sorry about Kali."

She nodded to me but turned her attention back to him. She caressed his arm, wiping a tear from her cheek with the back of her other hand.

He sighed. "Me, too. She didn't deserve what I did to her, but I can't change the past. I hope someday I'll be able to tell her I'm sorry."

She blinked away her tears and kissed him on his

cheek. He raised a hand to rub the spot.

I grinned at Kali and then Dave. "I'm sure she already knows."

She scrunched her face, and her tears thickened, but she mouthed, "Thank you."

"Maybe, but I'd still like the chance. That's part of the program, righting your wrongs and telling the ones you hurt you're sorry for the pain you caused. I'll just have to wait until I'm gone to make my amends to her." A thick silence fell, and he stared into nothing for a moment. He shook his head and focused on me. "So Paul tells me he's known you for a long time."

"Yeah, since I was five." I met Pastor King's gaze, remembering that first Sunday we met, coming to church with my still-married parents. When he still liked me.

"Yes," Pastor King said. "Asher and Grace became fast friends and had many adventures together in our backyards. Not to mention the shenanigans they had here at church. I think we still have a few traces on the floors and walls from your games."

I followed his gesture as he pointed to a cracked ceiling tile.

"I seem to remember you broke this tile during a lock-in, playing kickball inside the basement."

The years faded, and I laughed at the memory. "Well, Grace was the one who kicked the ball. I just rolled it to her. She had on cowboy boots and blamed her bad aim on them."

My stomach twisted, and I put my hands in my pockets.

He and Dave laughed, but I glanced at the floor, my heart in my throat. I'd let Pastor King down, too. Big time. But like Dave had said, I couldn't change the past.

"I need to go wrap up a few conversations." Pastor King lifted his chin. "See you next week?"

I thought of all I'd done, the people I'd hurt, the wrongs I'd committed all for the sake of drinking and pot. I looked at Kali, still behind Dave, longing clear on her beautiful face, unable to talk to her love, to grow old with him.

Was that where I'd be right now if she hadn't helped me? Watching Grace live her life without me, watching her move on, watching her get married, watching her fall in love with another?

My chest burned at the thought of her with someone else. I'd made the choice to change, to live—and to save her from the death in my vision. If these meetings could prevent that, then I'd live in the church basement.

I smiled back at them. My answer strong and sure. "Yes, I'll be here."

Chapter Fourteen

After picking up a phone tree, I grabbed a couple of cookies and went out to my car. I wasn't surprised to see Kali waiting for me inside.

"Hey." I held out a cookie. "Want one?"

She laughed, the icy sound filling my head, like at The Cliffs, but a quick touch of her hand on my cheek ended the freeze. She grabbed the cookie and bit into it.

We ate in silence for a moment, and then I asked the question. "Why, Kali?"

She leaned her head back against the seat. "Why did I die? Because I chose to. My life was hard. I never had a family. I grew up bouncing between foster homes." She snorted. "Some barely fit the description. I was abused, molested, ignored, but never loved. Back then the system looked the other way. There weren't so many rules and standards in place. Not that they're much better now."

"Didn't you tell anyone?"

She shrugged. "There was nobody to tell. After I met Dave, he was the only one I talked to about it. He wanted to help me, but what could we do? He had his own problems with his foster family, though they were nicer to him. But we were just a couple of kids with no power to change things."

Leaning my head back, I nodded. "I know the feeling." How many times had Connor and I wished we could move out and get away from our parents? His dad was crazy, and mine, well, crazy came in different flavors. Avoiding pain by getting high was easier than reaching out to make things different.

"When I turned eighteen, Dave and I found a small apartment and tried to live our lives. But the drugs and alcohol had taken control long before that. He told the basics of our story."

I frowned. "Probably shouldn't say this, but how could he do it?"

She nodded, closing her eyes for a moment. "When you and I met, you still had time. Your vices hadn't controlled you completely. Dave and I were long past rock bottom. We were already six feet under, walking dead. That night was terrible but not even close to being the worst."

"It wasn't?" I shook my head. "It's hard to believe that."

"The worst thing I did was take away Dave's hope. I don't blame him for my death. I did that to myself when I overdosed." She let out a slow breath and wiped her eyes. "I gave up and hurt the only one I ever loved because I thought there was no hope for me. When I met you, you reminded me of myself before I reached rock bottom. I helped you because you still had that small bit of hope, and I didn't want my fate to happen to you."

I looked away from her loving gaze. Compared to Kali's and Dave's lives, I didn't have the right to feel sorry for myself. But my life wasn't easy either. Growing up with parents who ignored me and then tried to buy me back with money was its own form of abuse. I ended up the same as Kali—unloved, drunk, and stupid.

Dave chose to give away everything for booze and cocaine. Kali chose to let herself waste away. I'd chosen to drink and smoke weed. But that was the key, the defining factor—we'd made our choices. Like Dave, I wanted to make a better one. And I needed Grace to do it.

"I haven't given up hope. And I should have told you sooner." I laced my fingers with hers and kissed her on the cheek, like she'd done so many times tonight to her love. "Thank you. Thank you for giving me a second chance."

"You're welcome." She rubbed her cheek.

I followed the movement of her hand with my gaze. "Does Dave know you were there tonight?"

She shook her head. "Dave reacts because our hearts are connected, forever. I'm there each time he tells this story, to give him strength. He doesn't know I'm there, but I give him peace, nonetheless."

"Don't take this the wrong way, but that sucks. I'm sorry you don't get to be with him. You guys must have really loved each other."

A tear danced down her cheek. "Well, maybe someday we can be together. Until then, I'll keep plugging along, saving one goofy teenaged boy at a time."

"You're better than a guardian angel." I stuffed the rest of my cookie into my mouth. "You're my personal superhero."

"I don't know about the super, but I'm good with the hero. It's the least I can do to make up for the way I hurt Dave. AA isn't the only organization that wants their members to atone for their sins." She patted my knee, then clapped her hands together. "So what's a girl have to do to get dinner in this town?"

"Hmm, well, saving the messed-up ass of this goofy

teen is a great start." I turned the key and revved the engine. "I didn't realize you needed to eat."

Kali laughed, holding her hand on my leg to keep me warm. "I don't, but the best cure for sadness and regret is food and comedy."

"Comedy?" I raised an eyebrow.

"Yeah, come on. Let's get a pizza, then see a movie. I'm in the mood to laugh."

"Okay, but we're eating in the car. I don't want people to think I'm crazy when it looks like I'm talking to myself in a restaurant. Oh, and promise me one thing."

She raised an eyebrow. "What?"

I laughed and turned onto the street in front of the church. "Promise me you'll hold my hand so I don't end up as an Asher icicle in the theater."

She answered with an icy laugh and her hand on my leg.

****

The next morning, I laid on the horn, glancing at the clock. "Dammit. Come on, Connor. We're going to be late." I waited a minute, then honked again.

I'd overslept, tired from my date with Kali, and if he didn't hurry up, we'd never make it on time.

The front door crashed against the house. Connor stormed out, dragging his backpack with his jacket slapping against his leg as he ran. The burly form of his dad followed, wearing the stereotypical dirty white wifebeater and jeans, like he shopped at Assholes-R-Us. He stopped on the porch, but Connor ran to my car.

His dad yelled, "You'd better get your ass home right after school today! I'm not through with you!" He jabbed a finger at Connor, then glared at me.

Connor yanked the door open and fell into my car.

"Fuck!" He slammed the door shut and leaned his elbow on the door, his head resting on his hand.

Tires squealing against the pavement, I got away fast in case his crazy dad decided to come after my car with a crowbar. I frowned at Connor shaking in the seat beside me.

"What the *hell* happened?" His hair was a mess, and he wore the same clothes as yesterday. His shirt had a tear at the neck and a stain on his chest that looked like blood. I reached into the back seat and grabbed a shirt I had discarded on a warmer day.

I tossed it into his lap. "Here."

He pulled his shirt off and threw it out the window. He yanked mine over his head, covering the fresh red welts across his chest and back. My stomach churned. *Dammit.* This was out of control.

"Are you okay?"

He answered through clenched teeth. "I'm fine." He rubbed his hands through his hair, wincing. More blood stained his fingers, and he wiped them on his holey jeans.

"You don't look fine."

"It's nothing."

I'd been so focused on myself I hadn't noticed the escalation of shit Connor took from his dad. Some loyal friend I was. Time to change that. I pulled the car over to the shoulder.

"Don't say it, Asher." He rubbed his fingers across his forehead.

"You *need* to get out of there. Before he kills you."

He laid his head back on the seat and closed his eyes. "And where am I supposed to go?"

I opened my mouth, then closed it. "I don't know. Maybe you should go to the counselor at school. That's why we have them, right?"

"Sure. So I can end up in a foster home or something?"

I thought of Kali and the things she'd said about her foster families. I didn't want that for him. "What about your mom?"

"My mom doesn't want me. She made that clear when she left me with that bastard to save herself."

"Maybe if you called her, she'd—"

"I already did. She told me she couldn't help."

The hopelessness in his voice brought visions of the junkie Kali to mind.

My parents were shitty most of the time. But at least they didn't abandon me completely. One more solution popped into my head. One that could make my goal impossible to accomplish, but how could I ignore my friend?

I looked at him and made an offer I hoped I wouldn't regret. "Come to my house. I'll talk to my mom and Terry. Once I tell them what's up, they won't turn you away." If she did, I could always try my dad. He'd say yes for sure, just to one-up her.

"Really?" Connor smirked, but it didn't hide the hope in his eyes. "You want me and my bad habits to come live with you?"

I laughed. "Well, if you're under my roof, you'll have to live by my rules, son." I expected him to laugh and tell me to piss off. But instead, he stared at me, his half-healed black eye watering with a new redness surrounding it.

His shoulders hunched forward, and he scooted deeper into the seat, wincing and rubbing his back.

Then he grinned, the uninjured eye wet like the

other. "Thanks, Asher." His head bobbed with his swallow, and I knew, if he was okay with giving up weed, if he was near tears, he had been near his own rock bottom. I hoped I'd caught him before he hit.

****

"Asher, I don't know. That's a big commitment, letting him move in." Mom rattled off her fifth excuse for why my idea sucked. "What if his dad gets angry and causes trouble?"

I groaned and leaned up against the wall outside the student entrance to the school, shielding my eyes from the bright sunlight. Connor had gone in before the bell, but I had to settle this with my mom before I could go to class.

"Mom, he has nowhere to go. His own mother turned him away. His dad will kill him if he stays in his house. He's already beaten him." I exhaled a frustrated breath, playing my final card. "I don't want to see my friend dead, Mom. If you won't help, I'll call Dad. We'll go live with him instead."

Her car engine hummed through the phone while she considered my latest threat. The live-with-Dad card had always worked. But she didn't bite as fast as I had hoped. Maybe I shouldn't have told her to go to hell.

"I'll talk to Terry," she finally said. "But if he says yes, Connor will follow the same rules you do."

"I already told him that. He said he'd deal." I massaged my forehead. "Thanks, Mom."

"Don't thank me yet. If Terry doesn't agree, I can't help."

Knowing Mom, she would get him to agree. He'd do anything to make her happy. He'd *been* the other man and didn't want to be in my dad's shoes someday.

194

"Okay. I'm going to Grace's after school to work on our project. I'll call when I leave there." I squirmed against the bricks, frowning at the unfinished conversation. "Mom?"

"Was there something else you need?"

Understatement. "No, I just... I'm sorry. About what I said."

I couldn't say I didn't mean it, the part about the men anyway. But that didn't mean I couldn't regret telling her to go to hell.

She breathed into the phone speaker, and I could picture her chewing her lip, trying to decide if she should accept my apology. I wasn't sure she would, but I felt better for offering.

"Thanks," she said. "Maybe we both have things to apologize for. We'll talk later."

"Okay. Bye, Mom."

"Bye, Ash."

I hung up, knowing that "later" usually never came. Still, I went inside the school with less knots in my stomach. At least, unlike my friend's mom, mine still cared enough to be around me.

****

At lunchtime, I looked for Connor. He sat at our normal table with my old crowd, watching everyone eat. His smiling face hid any trace of his earlier trauma, but he was good at faking. He laughed at something Dan said and shoved him in the shoulder, no pain registering from the movement.

I bought my lunch—with an extra burger for Connor—and walked toward the courtyard door. I caught his eye, and he nodded. I went to the bench and ate my cheeseburger, waiting for him. At least today was warmer.

He approached, his left leg dragging slightly and slowing his gait. He lowered himself to the bench beside me, holding his side and leaning forward to keep from pressing his bruised back into the bench. He grimaced, then blew out a breath between his teeth.

I'd done the right thing. He had to get away from his psycho dad.

"Hey." He snagged a french fry off my tray and popped it into his mouth. I tossed him the burger and he caught it, giving me a sloppy salute.

"I called my mom. She's talking to Terry, but I'm sure he'll say yes. He kisses her ass, so we should be good."

He nodded. "Was she pissed?"

"Yes." I took a bite of my burger. "But only because she thinks you'll try to corrupt her little boy again."

"Can't promise I won't." He glared at the ground. "Dad always says I'm only good at getting in trouble."

He sounded a lot like me. Well, me before I'd made my choice. I wanted to help him, but I hadn't even fixed my own problem yet. "Maybe we can get a deal on group therapy."

"Maybe, or a really big bag of weed."

I lifted an eyebrow in warning.

"Just kidding."

"I have to go to Grace's after school. You got somewhere to hang besides your house?"

"Yeah, I'll be at the police station."

My burger froze halfway to my mouth. "What?"

He smirked. "My counselor saw me in the hall and asked about the bruises. Mandated reporter, you know. She called whoever, and they called the cops. I told them

I'd stay with a friend, and they want to take me home to be sure my dad doesn't blow when I go get my stuff. They said I had to go to the station after school."

Shit. What if Terry said no? "Okay. Then I guess I'll pick you up there."

"If your mom's asshole husband says no, we'll just tell the cops he said yes and figure something out."

I nodded. "He won't say no, and if he does, there's always plan B."

"B?" He raised his eyebrows.

"Yeah, my dad." I wadded my napkin onto my tray. "He'd love to tell Terry to go fuck himself and look like the good guy."

He laughed, then winced and stood with exaggerated slow movements from the bench. "Asher, our families are both totally whacked, you know?"

I laughed and walked slowly toward the door with Connor limping beside me.

"Yeah, I can't argue with that."

Chapter Fifteen

Good thing the cops were helping Connor, because after school, I ran to the student lot, hopped in my car, and sped to Grace's house like I held first place of the Indy 500. The weather was nice again today, sunny and warm, with a clean breeze to make things interesting. If Grace wasn't sick, it would be the perfect day for a run. I smirked. I'd only been sober for a few days, and already I sounded like a jock.

In front of Grace's house, I parked behind a small SUV. I read the license plate and grimaced. *Britt 2.* Great, the worst possible stu-co kid that could be here.

After climbing the steps two at a time, I knocked, bouncing on the balls of my feet. Mrs. King answered and greeted me with a smile.

"Hello, Asher. Come in." She stepped back and pulled the door open.

"How is she today?"

"She's better. She might be able to go to school tomorrow. Paul told me you were coming to work on the senior seminar project. She's in her room. You can go on in. I need to finish making dinner."

Alone with Grace in her bedroom? Pretty sure that's not what Pastor King had in mind. My heart, already beating fast, sped even more. Heat spread up my neck, and I snapped my jaw closed. "Uh…okay. Sure."

Mrs. King laughed. "She's more comfortable in

there because of the pain in her leg. Besides, she has company already. Just leave the door open."

The heat spread to my cheeks. "Thanks, Mrs. King."

She nodded and returned to the kitchen. I crossed the tidy living room and stepped into the hall. Grace's bedroom door stood open, and laughter floated out.

I paused in the doorway. Grace met my gaze with wide eyes and a smile that lit up her face, the sparks stoking the inferno in my gut. I drew in a sharp breath. It only fanned the flames.

"Hey." She patted the bed next to her, and the flames engulfed my heart—and a few other body parts.

I swallowed, hard. Britt, our senior class secretary, sat in the chair next to the bed. She glared at me, probably reading every emotion on my face—and sharing every one of them.

Ignoring her scowl, I sat at the foot of the bed and tickled Grace's foot. "How's your leg, faker? Skipping because you're afraid to run with me again?"

She giggled and jerked her foot away. "Yes, that's why I'm sitting here with a crap ton of homework. I skipped two days of school to avoid having you *try* to keep up with me." She held out her hand, and I laced my fingers into hers.

Britt cleared her throat and waved at our joined hands. "So? What? Are you two a couple now? You know the senior seminar assignment isn't real, don't you?"

"Well, we are married." Grace winked at me and giggled. "Kids are next, right?"

My heart leapt to my throat. She didn't answer Britt's question, but she didn't have to. It wasn't a yes, but it definitely wasn't a no.

"Yep. Maybe we can work on that tonight." I wiggled my eyebrows suggestively.

Grace blushed and bit her lip. She dropped her gaze to our hands.

Britt rolled her eyes. "Whatever. I'll go so you guys can work. Call me if I need to pick you up in the morning, Grace." She stood and curled her lip slightly in my direction. She had never liked me. Of course, that's because she wanted Grace to herself. I wondered if Grace had figured out yet that Britt was hot for her.

"Okay, Britt, thanks for bringing my homework." She waved at the stack of books on her nightstand. "I hope I can catch up."

Britt laughed. "Let me know if you need any help." She leaned in and folded Grace in a gentle hug. I smirked at the longing on her face, and she flipped me off behind Grace's back. Not that I blamed her for wanting Grace.

Britt frowned at me. "See you later."

"Bye." I tried not to be rude, because I knew it would upset Grace. Britt huffed and walked away, pushing the door open farther as she left the room.

I turned back to Grace, and blood pounded through my body. Her hair fell over her left shoulder, and the skin on the right side of her neck gleamed in the soft light from her bedside lamp.

The fire inside my body flared red hot. I clasped both her hands with mine to keep from touching her somewhere else and studied the country music posters on the wall behind her bed.

"Hey, Asher?" Her soft voice kissed my ears.

I pulled my gaze back to her twinkling eyes. "Yeah?" *Breathe. Breathe. Don't think of her smooth skin.*

"You can come closer." She tugged on my hands. "I won't bite, I promise."

"Not even if I want you to?"

I expected her to laugh, but she scooted closer.

I kept my distance, trying to be good and earn the little bit of trust her dad had shown by allowing me to come here.

She came closer still and caressed my cheek with the soft palm of her hand. "Come *here*," she breathed.

I looked down into her bright-green eyes and lifted an eyebrow. "Are you high again?"

"No." She giggled. "Well, maybe a little. Now c'mere."

I leaned in and touched my lips to hers, praying her mom stayed in the kitchen. For at least an hour. Or two.

The small moan that escaped her chest added more fuel to the inferno. She pressed her lips closer, and I knew I'd taste strawberries in my dreams. Her hand moved from my cheek to my shoulder, and she scooted closer to me on the bed.

I pressed one hand against her lower back and gently brushed the hair from her shoulder. Craving a taste, I placed a kiss on her neck, and she shivered, slipping her hands to my chest. I returned to her soft lips, and they moved in perfect rhythm with mine. She leaned closer, and her hands traveled lower, past my stomach. Then lower, touching me softly and easing a moan from *my* lips. The faint crash of something dropped in the kitchen snapped me back to reality.

I captured her hands with my own and held them to my chest, my breath coming in fast, shallow pants. "What are you doing?"

She wet her lips with her tongue. "Nothing."

"I thought preachers' kids weren't supposed to lie."

"Sorry." She closed her eyes. "I didn't mean to offend you."

"Grace?"

She kept her eyes closed.

I lifted her hands to my lips and kissed her fingers. "Look at me."

Her cheeks reddened, and she met my gaze.

"Believe me, I'm nowhere near offended. I want you more than anything in this world. But we can't—not yet, not like this, and especially not when your mom is in the next room." I leaned my forehead against hers. "Ask me again when you're not under the influence."

She laughed, but a tear slipped out of her closed eye.

My lungs deflated. "I'm sorry. Did I say something wrong?"

"No, it's…it's nothing." She opened her eyes. "It's just these pills."

I frowned, wiping the tears from her cheeks with my thumbs. "Are you sure?"

"I'm okay." She leaned back on her pillow and rubbed her thigh. "Maybe we should work on the project."

I scooted Britt's vacated chair closer and sat next to Grace. Pushing her hand away, I massaged above her knee.

"Thanks. That feels good." She relaxed her head back against the pillows piled up behind her. After a moment, she picked up her pen and placed our project notebook onto her other leg.

I told her about the house I'd picked and the budget I'd set. She added my work to the notes she'd kept for us.

"Why did you pick such a small house? I thought you would want a bigger one, you know, like you have now."

I shrugged. "The house doesn't matter. It's what's inside that counts. And I didn't want all our money to go to a house payment."

She tilted her head and raised her eyebrows. "Very logical but still oddly romantic."

I laughed. "We'll get an A for sure. Our kids will go to good colleges with all the money we save, and if you are a good girl, I'll allow a little extra for us to go on a vacation."

She cocked her eyebrow. "Excuse me? Allow?" She set the notebook on the bed and laid her hands on top of mine.

I flipped them over and twisted my fingers with hers. "I am the man of the house, so I'm in charge, right?"

She hit me on the shoulder.

"Sorry, kidding."

"You better be. I won't stand for chauvinism."

"I'm not a chauvinist. I want to take care of you."

She smiled, and I leaned my face toward hers, touching her lips once more with mine. I pulled back and stared into her emerald gaze. Heart in my throat and my breath shaking, I whispered, "Because I love you."

Her eyes filled with tears again, and her bottom lip trembled. Then she squeezed her eyes closed, and a sob tore from her chest.

"Grace?"

She wrapped her arms around my neck, and I held her. Her body shook in my arms. I stared wildly at the wall behind her. "Please don't cry. Whatever I did, I'm sorry."

Her sobs grew louder, and she tightened her hold on my neck.

Had I misread everything? My heart fell. My *I love you* had caused this.

"Asher?"

I looked toward her mom standing in the doorway, a sad smile on her face.

"Maybe she shouldn't take those pills, Mrs. King."

"It's better if you go, Asher. Grace can explain later."

"No!" Grace clung tighter to my neck. "I don't want him to leave."

Yeah, what she said. I held her closer to my chest. Kali's vision crept into my head—Grace dead, cold. I mentally shoved it away.

"What's wrong, Grace? Please tell me."

"Asher, you need to leave." Tears gathered in her mom's eyes. "I promise she'll be fine."

Grace leaned back and yelled, "You don't know that! And *I* should get to decide what happens in my life, and I want him to stay!" She broke off with another sob and covered her face with her hands.

I reached for her and pulled her back into my arms. She buried her face on my shoulder.

Staring at her mom, I tried to swallow, tried to talk, but my throat threatened to close.

Mrs. King covered her mouth with her hand, her body shaking, too. She switched her gaze to me, pleading with her eyes, then ran from the room.

"What is it?" I held Grace by the shoulders and stared into her teary eyes. "I can't help you if you don't tell me what's wrong."

She clutched the front of my shirt, her bottom lip still quivered, and her fingers shook against my chest. "I love you, too."

"I'm here for you." I caressed her hair, then lifted her chin with my fingertips. "But you need to tell me how to help."

"Asher…" She shook her head, and the fear in her eyes sent chills along my spine.

The front door slammed. Mrs. King spoke to someone, though I couldn't hear the words over Grace's sobs. Seconds later, her dad stood in the doorway.

Leaning against the doorframe, he wiped a hand down his face. "I knew this wasn't a good idea. You shouldn't have come, Asher. Go. Ann and I need to talk to Grace alone."

My gut clenched, and I glanced between her and her dad. She didn't argue with him, but I turned back to her and held her face between my hands. "Do you need me to stay?"

"It's okay." She leaned her forehead on mine. "I'll call you later." But she slid her arms around my neck and held tight for a moment.

Ignoring her dad, I held her face again and pressed my lips to hers—another ice-cream kiss with her hand on my cheek.

"Okay." I stood from the chair and faced her dad. The pain on his face took my breath away. I couldn't move. I'd expected him to be angry. I'd just done what I told him I wouldn't, kissed her—in her bed no less. He glared at me but pressed his lips together. If whatever was wrong with Grace was bad enough to make *that* acceptable in his eyes, what did it mean for Grace? For me?

Pastor King shook his head, dropping his gaze to the floor. "Thank you."

I moved again with his dismissal, then stopped in front of him. "Please," I whispered. "Tell me what's going on."

"Grace can tell you later." He gripped my shoulder. "Everything will be fine."

If Grace weren't sobbing behind me, and Kali's vision hadn't filled my head, I would have believed him. I turned to her one last time. "Call me."

She nodded, pressing her lips together.

I walked away from her on rubber legs, past her mom crying in the kitchen, and outside into the mocking sunshine. Hollowness filled my chest because I'd left my heart in the room with Grace. All I wanted was to hold her and demand to know what the problem was. Because I knew, without a doubt, the vision unfolded—and I had to stop it before it was too late.

With my heart hammering, I sat in my car in front of Grace's house, staring at nothing. When Kali showed me the vision, I'd thought maybe Grace would die from an accident or something I caused. After watching her verbally attack her mom and hearing the things she said, I could see there was more to the story, and it had something to do with her recent illness.

How could a sore leg cause her death? People didn't die from pulling a muscle.

Shaking my head, I turned the key, and my engine roared to life. I glanced in the rearview mirror as I pulled away to go find Connor.

The police station was across town, closer to where Connor lived in the more rundown section. A dirty brick building with barred windows, it looked more like an actual prison than a police station. Instead of saying, "Come here for help," it screamed, "Run while you still can."

I parked in the visitor lot next to the building and jogged to the door, passing several men in suits and a tired-looking officer carrying a cup of coffee toward the patrol car parked at the curb. Connor had better be ready. I wanted to be available when Grace called.

I checked my phone, tapping the icon for the missed call and message from Mom. I listened to her okay for Connor to stay with us. At least I had that.

Inside, I approached the help desk. The gray-haired man behind the counter raised his droopy eyes and favored me with a deep frown. His bushy mustache twitched, and he mumbled something under his breath like the crotchety old neighbor everyone avoided.

"Can I help you?" He even had the growly voice they always used on cartoon police.

"I'm looking for my friend, Connor Martin. I'm supposed to meet him here."

The man looked at his computer screen, tapping on the keyboard. "He's in with Sergeant Winne. Room 156, down the hall on the left." He picked up a newspaper folded to the crossword puzzle.

I followed the dingy hall to the correct room. Connor sat on one side of the desk, a single duffel bag at his feet. All his stuff fit in one bag? My stomach clenched.

And I felt sorry for myself?

The sergeant behind the desk stood. My mouth fell open, and I lifted my chin to gaze wide-eyed into hers. I was six feet tall, and she had a couple of inches on me. Blonde hair, blue eyes, strong, and lean, she didn't belong behind a desk. She would fit better on the runway in Paris.

She smirked at me and pointed to a chair next to Connor. "Sit down, please. And close your mouth. You're drooling."

Connor snorted and shifted in his seat. I glanced at him. He held an ice pack to his eye.

"Did he hit you again?"

Officer Winne pressed her lips together.

He laughed. "Yes, but it was worth it to see him taken down by Sergeant Winne." He gestured to the blonde goddess behind the desk. "I guess he thought she would cower like my mom. Now his ass is in jail."

"Your dad has balls to hit you in front of a cop. Or he's just an idiot."

"You know Dad." He shifted the ice pack higher on his eye. "He thinks he can do whatever the hell he wants. To everyone."

I turned to Sergeant Winne. "So can we go? My mom said it was okay for him to stay with us."

She leaned back in her chair and steepled her fingers. She pursed her lips as she gave me a long blue stare, and I squirmed in my seat like I'd done something wrong.

"I'll need to call your mother to be sure this is legit." She nodded to Connor. "Taking in someone with his background is a big responsibility."

I gave her Mom's number, and she stepped out of the room, closing the door behind her.

"She'd better hurry. I need to get home." I rubbed my neck, but the muscles wouldn't give.

"What's up?"

"It's Grace." I glanced out the door. Sergeant Winne

paced back and forth, talking on the phone in the office across the hall. I hoped Mom was on the other line and not Terry.

Connor laughed. "She got you worked up this afternoon? Don't worry, I'm sure Vikki would come relieve you."

I glared at him. "Jeez. Can't you ever be serious?"

His gaze fell to the floor.

I bit my lip. *God, I'm a dick.* He'd had the worst day of his life, and I added to it. "Sorry, I know you were making a joke."

He shrugged and picked up his bag. "Yeah, you're an idiot. But thanks for helping me. You're the only one who has."

"That's what friends are for." I slapped him on the back.

"If you start singing or try to hug me, I'll punch you in the face."

"Don't worry, I'm not in the mood to sing, and Grace is the only one I want to hug." The smile left my face. "Something's wrong."

"What do you mean?"

I pressed my fingers into my eyes. "I don't know. Her leg has been hurting since we ran Saturday, and her doctor gave her oxycodone. But who does that for a sore muscle?"

"Maybe her doc is a pill pusher. You know, like the docs that get a kickback from the pharm companies if they promote their medicine."

"There's more to it than that." I told him about the scene this afternoon. "Something is wrong, but they won't tell me what it is." I stood and paced the tiny office, smirking. "Not like I have any right to know. Her dad still hates me."

He stood, too. "Yeah, girls sure like you, but you piss off most dudes. Except me. But then I need a place to stay, so I can't afford to hate you."

"Yeah, I know."

"Don't worry too much until you talk to her. Sometimes girls overreact. I'm sure she's fine."

Him trying to make me feel better was so out of the norm it almost worked. Then the image of Grace dead blasted in my mind. No, she wasn't fine. But maybe I could find a way to make that true.

The door opened, and Sergeant Winne returned. "Your mom said it's a go. You can leave. But, Connor, I'll be in touch with you about your dad. And I've notified your mother of the situation."

He raised his eyebrows and glanced at me. "Is she coming back?"

Sergeant Winne's blue eyes softened. "No, she said to have you call her later if you want to talk."

I glanced at Connor's face, my stomach knotting for him.

He pressed his lips in a line, and a muscle in his jaw flexed. "No, I don't think I will."

The sergeant dipped her head at me, then patted Connor's shoulder. "You have a good friend here. Focus on the positive."

"Right."

She ignored his curt reply and opened the door, gesturing to the hall. I followed him out of the building. Once we got to my car, he reverted to his usual, sarcastic self.

"Man, I need to stop back by my house. I forgot something."

"What is it?" I frowned.

He jerked his thumb back toward the jail. "With the Amazon watching me pack and my dad beating on me again, I didn't get to grab any provisions."

I blew out a hard breath. "Connor—"

He groaned. "Fine, never mind."

"Look, I can't tell you what to do. But this might be a good time for you to cut back. Besides, my mom would kill you faster than your dad if she caught you with drugs in her house."

"Maybe. And since we have work tomorrow, I guess I should hold off. Don't want to be hungover my first day on the job."

Work? "What are you talking about?"

"Didn't you get a call? I have training after school tomorrow." He frowned. "No way, if I got the job, you better be there, too."

I stopped at a red light and pulled my phone from my pocket to check my voicemail. I listened to the message and shrugged. "You're right. Looks like we're both working men now. Be there after school tomorrow."

Connor slouched in his seat. "Thank God. There's no way I'll go to work alone. I need you to help me learn responsibility."

I barked out a laugh. "Yeah. That's like the blind leading the blind."

Chapter Sixteen

Once we got home, Terry and Mom waited in the living room. Connor followed a few steps behind me, then we stood together facing them.

Connor cleared his throat and shifted his bag on his shoulder. "Thanks, Mr. and Mrs. Andrews, for letting me stay."

Mom's eyebrows pulled together, and she patted his shoulder. "You're welcome. I know things are hard for you right now."

"Thanks, Mom." I lifted my chin at Terry's smirk. "And thank you, too."

He lifted his head to peer down his big nose at Connor and me. "This isn't an easy arrangement for any of us. Asher is trying to get his life straightened out and stay sober. We expect the same from you. If you stay here, there's no drinking or drugs."

I held back my eye roll. "He knows that."

Mom laid a hand on Terry's arm, her eyebrows raised in warning. "I think we all know the stakes here."

He ignored her, glaring at Connor. "Then he knows about paying rent?"

Connor and I glanced at each other with raised eyebrows. Surrounded by his expensive Italian leather furniture and six-thousand-dollar imported throw rugs, Terry had the balls to tell Connor he had to pay rent? I looked at Mom, but she stared at the floor, biting her lip.

"Are you kidding me? You want my friend to pay rent to escape his abusive father?"

Terry crossed his arms. "Watch your language. This is my house, and these are my conditions. Take it or leave it."

"Mom?" I glared at her.

"Asher, we're trying to help. I don't think Terry's request is unreasonable."

He grinned maliciously behind her, conveniently out of reach. I narrowed my eyes.

"But," she continued, "it's ridiculous for us to take money from a boy who needs help." She frowned at Terry. "So we will only save the money Connor pays and keep it until he has enough to get out on his own. Consider it a savings plan."

Terry's face turned red, but I knew he wouldn't argue. "The other man" syndrome scared him to death. Score one for Mom.

"Thanks, Mom. Is that cool with you, Connor?"

He nodded. "I can live with that. How much do I need to pay?"

She waved a hand. "Well, first you need to find a job. We can figure out the rest after that." She smiled at him. "I need help from time to time with my party business if you're interested in making some extra money."

Who the hell is this, and where is my mom?

I raised my eyebrows, and she winked at me.

Connor cocked his eyebrow. "I won't have to try on dresses, will I?"

"No." She laughed. "I need help hauling things and setting up for parties."

"Since Asher and I already have jobs, I'll have to

work around that schedule."

Her gaze flew to me. "You have a job?"

"Yeah." I rubbed the back of my neck. "I guess I forgot to tell you. We're bussing tables at The Other Place. We start tomorrow."

She raised her eyebrows at Terry's wide-eyed gaze. "Well, it looks like you don't need to complain about that anymore."

He swallowed, a muscle flexing in his cheek. "That's great."

"Yeah, it sure is." *Asshole*. I turned to Connor. "I guess we don't need plan B after all."

He slapped my shoulder. "Nope. This plan should help keep me in line."

Mom squeezed my shoulder and pointed to the stairs. "Show Connor the guest rooms. He can use whichever one he wants. Terry and I are meeting friends for dinner. You two can find something to eat on your own."

Terry curled his lip and left the room, huffing out a breath as he passed.

She stood to follow, but I intercepted her and wrapped my arms around her shoulders. "Really, thanks."

"Everyone needs a little help now and then." She squeezed me tight and stepped back, lifted the corners of her lips, then followed Terry out of the room.

Upstairs, Connor picked the room next to mine. He threw his bag on the giant bed and fell across the mattress. "Ahh, just like going to a hotel. Too bad there's no maid service or wet bar."

I dropped into the brown leather side chair in the corner of the large room. "Sorry, you'll have to make your own bed and drink milk." I glanced at my phone and frowned.

He pointed with his chin. "Nothing from Grace yet?"

I shook my head.

"Text her." He rose from the bed and lifted his bag, unzipped it, and reached in to transfer his clothes to the small dresser, cramming them into the drawers.

"I don't want to bug her."

He snorted. "Dude, just text her. I'm sure everything's fine. If she's taking painkillers, she's probably overreacting, like I said."

"Maybe." I tapped a quick text to Grace.

—*Can you talk yet?*—

I bounced my knee and tapped my phone against the side of my leg. Staring at it, I willed her to text me back. Several minutes passed and still nothing. I tossed it onto the bed. "C'mon. Let's see what we can find in the kitchen."

"Thank God. I'm starving." Connor stood, then paused by the door. "Think I have to pay for food here, too?"

"I'm sorry. I didn't know Terry would be such a dick to you."

"Whatever, he's nothing compared to my dad. And your mom's idea of saving money for me is cool." He leaned against the doorjamb and picked at his fingernails. "I'm not good at doing the right thing, so maybe this will help."

"I hope so. God knows we both need it." I stood and walked to the door. "Come on, I need to stop checking my phone. Let's go make a pizza. After that, maybe I can paint your nails."

Connor laughed and followed me to the hall. "Only if I get to pick the color."

****

I waited hours for Grace to answer my text—and the five others I sent. Sleeping was out of the question. My churning stomach wouldn't allow it. I lay in bed, letting my thoughts run wild. The longer I waited, the wilder the thoughts got.

She'd said she loved me, but my *I love you* made her sob. Maybe it was too much for her. Maybe *I* was too much for her. Maybe the combination of me and whatever was wrong was too much for her. Maybe…maybe…maybe…maybe I needed a drink.

"Dammit." I rolled on my back in bed and threw my arm over my eyes. "Come on, Grace. Talk to me."

I looked at my phone for the millionth time. Nothing. Unable to stand it, I rolled out of bed and plodded into the bathroom. The drink of water didn't help. I fell back into my bed and bounced my fist on the mattress.

I pictured Grace's smiling face covered with pink ice cream, her flushed cheeks when I kissed her on her bed, her gut-wrenching sobs when I left her with her dad. At what point my thoughts became dreams, I wasn't sure. But I found no relief in sleep. Grace haunted me.

****

Grace wasn't at school the next day. Or the day after that. And she never texted me. By Friday night, my nerves were so strained I considered not going to work. During training the previous day, the owner had told us we weren't old enough to serve the beer. But I knew it was there, and I might skip the cup and stand with my head under the tap.

Since it was my first official full shift and I didn't want to be a total fuckup yet, I dressed in my jeans and black T-shirt uniform and went downstairs to wait for Connor.

Mom sat in the living room waiting for Terry. Going out. Again. At least he kept her busy. Dad never had. Which was probably why Mom had found other ways to entertain herself.

"Come here a second, Asher."

I stepped around the corner and frowned. "What?"

She raised her eyebrows. "Having a bad day?"

"You could say that."

"Still no word from Grace?" She smiled gently.

"No."

Mom's mixed drink on the end table drew my gaze. Tiny droplets of condensation gathered on the outside of the glass, running down the sides in little rivers that reflected the orange of the juice inside. I swallowed the saliva forming in my mouth.

Connor and I drank screwdrivers at Dan's parties. I missed the sweet flavor of the juice and the bite of the vodka. One drink was all it would take to quench the burning thirst in my throat.

Mom cleared her throat and pushed the glass behind the lamp. She stood and crossed the room to hug me. "I'm sorry. I shouldn't have that in front of you."

"It's okay." But I glanced at the glass once more before looking away.

"No, it isn't." She nodded her head like I'd asked her a question. Or maybe she had asked herself one. "Tomorrow, I'm emptying the liquor cabinet. Terry never wanted it anyway. And I don't need it either."

"You don't have to do that." But as soon as the

words left my lips, I searched for her glass again.

Mom touched my cheek with her hand, and I met her gaze.

"I want to help you. It's not a problem, really."

Maybe she was right. If Grace kept ignoring me, I might... I dropped onto the couch, leaning my head into my hands. "Dammit. Why won't she call me?"

She sat next to me and rubbed my back. "I don't know. Maybe she needs time to figure things out."

"Time to figure out how to get rid of me." I squeezed my head and groaned. "I knew it was too good to be true. Why did I think I could get a second chance with her?"

"Give her some space."

"Yeah, she'll figure out she's better off without me."

She opened her mouth as Connor walked in and clapped his hands together.

"I'm ready. Let's go clean some tables." He glanced between Mom and me. "Uh, sorry. I'll wait out in the car."

"I'm ready." I stood and rolled my shoulders. "Let's get this over with."

Mom patted my shoulder. "She'll call."

"I hope so. See you later, Mom."

"Have a good time." She grinned at us. "Remember to smile. You'll get more tips that way."

****

Connor and I got to the restaurant five minutes early. We checked in and waited for the dinner crowd to arrive. Filling water glasses, delivering bread, and taking dirty dishes was mind-numbing physical work, but it took my mind off Grace.

I had one half of the store to serve, and Connor had the other. We passed each other a lot but had little chance to talk.

I'd always thought this dingy place didn't get much business, but I was wrong. Time after time the bell above the door rang, and family after family entered, many with small children who left huge messes for us to clean up.

After one particularly sloppy toddler left a cracker explosion on the carpet, Connor groaned in passing. "If they don't keep that kid contained, I'm going to shove those crackers up his dad's—"

"Connor." Mr. Stone, our boss, tapped him from behind. "Bring a broom to table sixteen. They've had another spill."

I laughed at Connor's groan.

"Fuck me." He headed to the utility closet for a broom.

The bell above the front door jingled, signaling another customer. I turned and froze. Grace and her parents stood in the doorway, waiting for a seat.

My eyes drank her in, the careful way she held onto her dad's arm, the way she stood, slightly hunched, the almost translucent quality of her already pale skin. Yes, she *was* sick.

Her gaze found me across the room, her emotions playing like a movie across her face. Surprise, the hint of a loving smile, then pain. She flashed a glance at her mom and bit her lip.

"Get over there, Asher." Connor pushed me from behind. "Don't let her do it."

"It?" I scrunched my eyebrows in confusion. "Do what?"

"That's the look my mom had before she left me. Don't. Let her. Do it." He glared at Grace and shoved me forward.

Taking shallow breaths, I moved toward Grace on legs like rubber. The heartbeat in my ears drowned out the static-filled music playing through the old speaker system in the ceiling. I stopped in front of her and focused on her face—the rings under her bright-green eyes, the curve of her soft pink lips, and the tears she tried to hide with a shaky smile.

Pastor King patted her hand. "Hello, Asher. I didn't know you worked here."

I nodded, but I couldn't look away from Grace. "Yeah, I just started."

"That's wonderful," Mrs. King said. "Joel will be sorry he missed seeing you. He's staying with a friend tonight."

I nodded again, but my eyes followed Grace's every move. She stared at the floor, a wrinkle forming on her forehead. My heart pumped like I'd fallen off the cliff again.

"Grace?" My voice sounded desperate to my own ears. "Are you okay?"

She raised her gaze to her parents and sniffled.

Mrs. King patted her cheek. "We'll be at the table."

Grace took a deep breath as they walked away. "Asher, we need to talk."

"That line has never in the history of the world been followed by *anything* good." I took hold of her icy hands, and she squeezed mine.

She glanced toward the kitchen. "Shouldn't you be working? I don't want to get you in trouble."

"I've spent the last two days considering every possibility for why you've ignored me from amnesia to zombie attack. I don't care about dirty dishes and empty water glasses." I gently traced the dark ring below her left eye with my finger. "Why didn't you call me?"

She squeezed my other hand. "What time does your shift end?"

"We close at ten, and I have to help clean. So ten thirty?"

"Okay. I'll meet you back here." She nodded at her parents. "I'd better go. I'll see you later."

"Ten thirty." My lips ached to kiss her.

"I'll be here."

My gaze followed her as she joined her parents at their table. Taking shallow breaths, I escaped to the kitchen.

Connor stood by the sink, refilling his water pitcher. He glanced over and raised his eyebrows. "Well?"

"She's meeting me back here after work."

"I'll get a ride home."

I followed his gaze through the kitchen door to a girl on the waitstaff, Chloe. She was cute—long dark hair, nice figure. Her dad was also the owner, and she went to private school. She laughed at something another server said, and her face glowed. Then she glanced our way and smiled at Connor.

He raised his eyebrows.

"Be nice to her. You have to work with her now." I nudged him with my elbow. "You know what they say about office romances."

He snorted. "No, but your dad sure does."

I shouldn't have, but I laughed. "Shut up."

Connor took one last look at Chloe and strutted into the dining room with his water pitcher.

I checked my phone. Two more hours.

Chapter Seventeen

Sometimes when we were kids, Grace and I had snuck out of our houses and sat in her backyard, staring at the stars. We talked about the possibility of life on other planets, convinced the scientists were wrong and kids just like us sat on their planet wondering if we were real.

Some nights we made plans to meet, but she never showed. Disappointment always sent me moping back inside until I'd see her the next day. She'd tell me her mom or dad had caught her trying to sneak out and sent her back to bed.

Waiting for her outside the restaurant felt the same. The disappointment of her absence tonight wouldn't evaporate in the morning with her smile. Our real future was at stake, and fear made me nauseous.

I leaned on my car, bouncing my knees and scanning the empty street for hints of Grace's approach. Connor had gotten his wish and climbed into Chloe's car. She was nice. He'd better not blow it with his usual bullshit.

Headlights shone in the distance, and I froze. Grace's yellow Bug came into view, and I blew out a breath. I couldn't relax, but at least she hadn't stood me up.

She eased into the spot next to me and rolled down her window. "Follow me." She closed the window before I could respond. Shrugging, I got into my car.

She drove through town, and I followed. She turned on a familiar route, and my heart sped.

The Cliffs were dark, lit only by the sliver of moon and our headlights. Grace parked away from the edge, near the grass, and turned off her car, leaving on the lights. I did the same.

I climbed out, glancing at the dark chasm. Without sunlight, the hole looked ominous. I half expected tentacles to reach out and grab me, finally claiming the life it should have taken.

She limped to my side and wrapped her arms around my waist, her head on my chest. I held her, allowing myself to believe in hope.

"I've missed you, Grace. Why haven't you called me?"

"I'm sorry." She released me and lifted a wool blanket from the back seat of her car. She grabbed my hand. "Come on. It's a warm night. Let's sit for a while."

I took the blanket from her and spread it on the grass next to her car. She leaned in through the open window and turned off her headlights. The stars, unhindered by the city lights, loomed so bright above us they looked close enough to touch.

I turned off my lights, too, and it increased the effect.

Grace sat on the blanket, her slender frame silhouetted against the grass. I sank next to her and stretched my legs, waiting for my eyes to adjust to the darkness.

She rested her chin on her knees, her gaze set on the night sky. "Remember when we used to look at the stars, Asher? When we were kids and never thought we'd get old?"

She reached for my hand, and I held hers. A brisk wind rustled the grass and left goose bumps on our skin, so I wrapped an arm around her and pulled her into my warmth. She leaned her head on my shoulder.

"I do remember." But I didn't want to talk about the past. I needed to know we had a future.

"I wonder what it's like to grow old."

"According to most old people, it sucks."

She turned her gaze on me. "I'd like to know."

"You will."

"Nothing's guaranteed," she whispered.

My heart pounded in my chest. "Tell me what's wrong."

Her eyes sparkled in the dark, reflecting the lone streetlight at the entrance to the quarry. Without answering my question, she reached behind my neck and pulled me in. She kissed my lips. I melted against her without a fight.

We'd had the sweet ice-cream kiss and the rule-breaking library kiss and even the drugged-out confused kiss. But this kiss was different. This kiss had one purpose—and it wasn't to behave.

Her hot breath filled my mouth with her pure desperate need. Because mine was just as great, I couldn't tell her no. Not this time.

Grace was my air, my life, she was my soul, and I'd die without her. I still craved alcohol. I still wanted that bliss that came from getting high. But neither of them compared to the way I wanted her. No twelve-step program could help me now. She was more than desire. She was my strongest addiction ever, and I had no hope to walk away.

"Please, Asher." She grabbed my shirt with her fists,

her voice thick with emotion. "I need you."

The cool night air filled my lungs. She was everything I ever wanted, all the love, all the acceptance I craved. With her, I belonged, mattered. Easing her back on the blanket, I kissed her neck, her jaw, her ear. She tugged on my shirt, and I let her lift it over my head. Her trembling fingertips caressed my chest, and a shudder of excitement shook me.

I tucked a loose strand of her hair behind the curve of her ear and gazed into her heated eyes. The flame inside answered before I asked the question. "Are you sure?"

"Yes." She smiled, her teeth flashing in the dark. "I'm sure."

I leaned in to kiss her again. My hand shook as I reached for her face. My heart beat hard, out of control. Each pulse echoed in my ears and danced with her sighs. I kissed her jaw, and goose bumps raced across her soft strawberry-scented skin.

She caressed my shoulders, her hands on my bare skin like an open flame, burning right to my core. I grasped the edge of her T-shirt and slowly pulled it up, only pausing my kiss long enough to slip it over her head. I brushed the soft skin on her stomach with my fingertips, expecting her to be shy, but she breathed harder, faster, and pulled off her bra before I could blink.

I raised my eyebrows, and she giggled at my surprise. Then her lips were on mine, and my bare chest was on hers, and laughing was the last thing I wanted to do.

Grace owned me, body and soul. Next to the edge of the chasm where I'd begged an angel of death for another chance at life, she and I made love under the glittering light of the stars and the moon. I never realized what a difference love could make. Love made it sweeter, better. Love made it perfect.

Her soft body moved against mine, around mine, and I tried to be gentle. This was new for her, but she wasn't hesitant. The feelings electrifying my body were so different, so new, it felt like my first time, too. No high had ever been so perfect. My doubts for our future and fears of her rejection burned away with the heat of her body.

She cried out, and I joined her, tasting her release with my lips, experiencing it with every smoldering inch of my skin against hers. I'd been falling into trouble for years, and it had almost killed me. Her body sent me over a different edge. I spiraled out of control while the waves crashed over me. But I'd die this kind of death forever and never complain.

Grace panted and wrapped me in her arms, our hearts pounding together, skin against skin. "Thank you," she whispered against my lips.

We held each other, the stars of our childhood twinkling like diamonds in the black sky above.

I kissed her again, soft and sweet. "I love you. I'm sorry I wasted so much time."

"Me, too." She smiled and pushed my hair back from my forehead. But tears gathered in her eyes, sparkling like the stars. She blinked, and they disappeared into the hair on her temples.

The pain in her eyes crushed me, like a mountain on my chest. "Please tell me what's wrong."

She bit back a sob.

I propped up on my elbow and kissed away her tears, then hugged her to my chest. I tickled her back, her skin hotter than normal. Too hot.

"Grace?" My heart sped again.

"I don't know how to tell you."

"Just tell me so I can help you."

It approached. The edge, the chasm I was so afraid of falling into. The vision. I lay on the brink, balancing on the breath I struggled to draw with my cement-filled lungs.

She shuddered, her tears hot and wet on my bare chest.

I closed my eyes and squeezed her tighter, trying to hold us together as she whispered our fate.

"Asher, I'm dying."

Chapter Eighteen

Breathe. Breathe. Exhale.

Chapter Nineteen

Grace's body shook from the earthquake of her confession, and my body trembled with the aftershocks. Pushing off the ground, I moved to a sitting position and brought her with me, holding her hands in mine.

"What do you mean...dying?"

"I'm sorry, Asher. I'm so sorry." She scrunched her eyebrows, and tears cascaded down her flushed cheeks.

I lifted her chin with my knuckle. "Grace, tell me."

"I h-have cancer."

Her sobs shredded my heart, tore apart everything that made me whole. Now the demon had a name. The killer had a voice. Now I knew what I was fighting, but helplessness washed through me. How would I save her from cancer? Anger at the unfairness seeped in, and its burning fire held me together with its heat.

Grace shivered, and I grabbed her shirt, slipping it over her head. We dressed quickly, silent and surrounded by a thick cloud of fear. Red spots filled her cheeks, and her eyes had a glassy feverish look. I wrapped the blanket around her. Using a kiss, I checked her forehead and found the heat I'd expected. I pulled the blanket tighter around her body.

"Why are you apologizing? This isn't your fault."

She sniffled. "I'm sorry. This is so unfair to you. I said I would help you, and now I can't."

"This isn't about me. And you have helped. Being

with you gives me a reason to change." I caressed her cheek with my finger.

She shook her head. "No, we can't be together."

"Don't say that." Ice filled my veins, worse than when Kali laughed. "I'll be there to help you through this."

"But I don't want you to be there. My doctor says starting treatment right away might give me a chance to cure it." She wrinkled her forehead. "Did you hear that? *Might*. I don't want you to watch me die."

Her words brought on the images from the vision I'd tried so hard to forget—her glassy eyes, the sobs, the smell of death. Anger burned away the memories. Dammit, Kali said I would save Grace.

"Listen to me." I grabbed her by the shoulders. "You are *not* going to die. I won't let you."

She closed her eyes. "It's not up to you."

"Yes, it is. And it's up to you, too." I gave her a gentle shake. "Fight, dammit. You've never given up before. Don't give up now when it matters the most."

She sniffed again, her chin on her chest. "I can't win, Asher, and I don't want you with me for this."

"Tough. Because I will be."

She rose unsteadily to her feet, and I stood with her, holding her hands.

She pulled away from my grasp. "This won't end well, and I don't want you to think it's your fault, to blame yourself, to abuse yourself again." She took a step toward her car.

Oh hell no.

I grabbed her arm and spun her back around to face me. "You're crazy if you think I'm going to let you walk away from me. We belong together. I need you, and like it or not, you need me."

She bit back a sob and shook her head. "No, I need to go." She opened her car door, and I slammed it shut.

"Please don't run away." I grasped her shoulders, my throat as dry as the desert.

"Asher—"

I cut her off with a kiss. No sweetness, no confusion, no passion, this kiss was fueled by sheer, hopeless, terror. She wanted to abandon me, and I couldn't let that happen. If she left, how would we save each other?

She pushed against my chest, but I held her tighter. My heart neared explosion, and I'd almost run out of arguments. This kiss was my last weapon in this battle.

She stopped pushing and slid her arms around my neck.

I kissed her for another moment, then leaned my forehead against hers. "Why did you want to make love if you don't want to be with me?"

"I wanted to experience it with you at least once before I..." She looked at the ground. "I have to go."

"I won't let you push me away."

"You should."

"When have I ever done what I should?"

The corner of her mouth lifted. "Goodbye, Asher."

"No, stay with me." I clenched my teeth.

"I can't."

My tight throat released the tears I'd struggled to suppress. "Grace, please."

She wiped away my tears with her fingers like I'd done so many times for her.

"Don't call me. I can't bear to have you watch this. If you love me, stay away, because that's what I want." Her lips touched mine one last time, soft as the feather of an angel's wing.

But as she slipped into her car and drove away, out of my life, the fire of Hell consumed me.

Watching her pull away felt like hanging from the rock in the quarry. Heart thumping, hands slipping, holding on to the last hope for redemption and survival. Only the rock wasn't a rock. It was a clump of mud that crumbled in my fingers and sent me plunging to the bottom hundreds of feet below.

The Fates weren't laughing anymore. They'd had enough of me and launched their final attack. And they would win. Without Grace, I wouldn't have the strength or the reason to fight.

"Dammit!" I pounded my fists on the hood of my car. I leaned against it, eyes closed, fists clenched. Kali's footsteps crunched on the dirt behind me.

"Liar!" I spun around and screamed at her beautiful face, the face I'd trusted. "You said I would save her. How the hell am I supposed to do that? Do I look like a goddamn doctor?"

I pushed away from my car and stomped toward the edge of the quarry, screaming, kicking rocks over the edge as I went.

Kali followed me.

"Asher, calm down. You can still save her." She moved between me and the edge, blocking my path. Maybe she thought I planned to jump again. Which didn't sound like such a bad idea. The Fates would be happy at least.

"No, I can't. I can't cure cancer." I pushed my hand through my hair. "She's dying, and I can't do anything to stop it."

She looked at the ground. Her silent confirmation

fueled my anger like oil on a flame.

"You gave me hope, but it was all a lie. You said I had a second chance. What for? What was the damn point? So I can end up like Dave? Watch the girl I love die and spend the rest of my life regretting how I didn't save her?"

Her head snapped up. She narrowed her eyes, and the black deepened. Smoke seeping from the ends of her hair, she spoke through clenched teeth. "I didn't lie. And leave Dave out of this. You're not like him."

I curled my lip. "No, I'm not. Because I'm not the one *helping* Grace die. I don't have a choice like he did."

Flames crawled over her shoulders, trailing down her arms to her fists. "That's enough, Asher. I know you're hurting, but you need to stop. Now."

"Get the hell away from me." I jabbed my finger at the gaping black hole behind her. "If you knew she was going to die, you should have let me fall into that quarry. If I can't be with her, then I don't want to be here. And I sure as hell don't want to be fucking sober."

The fire fizzled, hissing into nothing, and Kali frowned, reaching for my hand.

Curling my lip, I jogged back to my car and sped away, dirt and grass flying up from my tires. Pain obliterated any fight that remained. I craved release. Speeding through the darkest night of my life, I knew where I'd find what I needed, and nothing would stop me this time from getting it.

****

Light spilled from the windows of Dan's house, illuminating the front lawn like an airport runway, beckoning me with the promise of oblivion and relief from my soul-crushing pain. I jogged up to the door and pushed my way inside.

A wave of pot hit me in the face, and I winced. Not from distaste, but longing. Someone handed me a bowl, and I inhaled without a second thought. Grace's eyes drifted in front of me. I took another hit.

"Hey, look who's back!" Connor smacked my shoulder. "I told you you needed to relax."

"Yeah, you're fucking right. You been here long?"

"Nope, just got here." He handed me a beer. "You look like you need this more than I do."

I popped the top and drained the can in a few long gulps. Why was it so easy to just pick up where I left off? Doing the wrong thing took no effort at all.

I searched the room for more alcohol and spied a cooler near the kitchen door. I stalked across the room, pushing my way through the crowd.

Connor followed me, frowning. "What's up?"

"I don't want to talk about it."

He cocked an eyebrow. "Did something happen with Grace?"

I crushed the empty beer can with my fist and threw it against the wall, then grabbed a full one from the cooler.

"Yeah. Something happened." I popped the top and tipped the can to my lips. I chugged until it was gone, then took another toke. Instead of relaxing, my heart raced from the weed. I reached into the cooler and snagged a third can of beer.

"Man, slow down." Connor smirked and grabbed the beer. "What would Grace think?"

Her name was like a punch in the gut. I pushed his chest, and he stumbled backward, eyes wide.

"Fuck off, Connor. Spare me the lecture." I snagged

the beer and stormed into the empty hallway away from the crowded living room full of drunks.

Connor followed me. He gripped my shoulder and pulled me to a stop. I spun around to face him.

"Jesus Christ, Asher. What happened?"

"She told me…" My throat closed. Stabbing my own chest would be easier than saying the words out loud.

"She told you what?" he pressed.

I swallowed. "Grace has cancer."

He stared at me with his brows drawn together, like I'd spoken Chinese. "Cancer?"

"Yes, cancer. Fucking cancer." With every word, I hit the wall with the palm of my hand, shaking the picture frames that hung there.

He grabbed my wrist as I aimed for the wall again. "Asher, man, I'm sorry. That sucks." He shook his head. "What happens now?"

I barked out a laugh. "Now she dies. So I'm here to get fucked up." I popped the top on my beer and swallowed half of it in one gulp.

He grabbed it. "You need to go home. This won't help."

"Oh, it helps." I reached for my beer, and he tossed it away, spilling it on the carpet.

"Whatever, there's more where that came from." I tried pushing past him to return to the other room.

He sidestepped to block my way. "Stop. I know you don't want this."

"Fuck yeah, I do. Grace is dying. I can't be with her anymore because she told me to stay away. What's the point of changing when she was the reason?" I pushed him with my shoulder.

"Dude, come on. Let's go." He pressed his hands on my chest.

"No, I'm staying. Now get out of my way." I shoved him against the wall.

He shadowed my steps to the living room. "You're gonna regret this."

The party was in full swing. Everybody stumbled around, laughing, drinking, having fun. They didn't have the Fates after them, and their hearts weren't dying.

I hated them all.

I grabbed another beer from the cooler and opened it, falling onto the empty couch. I tipped the can to my mouth and took three long gulps.

Connor sat next to me, empty-handed.

I raised an eyebrow. "Aren't you drinking?"

"One of us needs to stay sober to sneak us into your house." He pointed to the fourth beer in my hand. "At the rate you're going, you'll be puking in about fifteen minutes."

"Whatever. Do what you want. I'll just sleep here."

Someone passed me a bowl, and I took another long drag.

Connor grabbed it and handed it off to the girl standing next to him. "No, your mom would blame me if we didn't come home tonight. Then we'll both be on the street. I got your back." He smirked at the can I held. "But when you blow chunks, I'm not cleaning it up."

"Great." I guzzled more beer.

He sat beside me, grabbing the pipes as they made their rounds to me and passing them on to the next person.

Three cans later, the couch became a demonic merry-go-round in the middle of Hell. I closed my eyes and leaned back. Grace's face tormented me. "Shit."

Connor groaned. "You can say that again."

I opened my eyes.

Vikki stumbled toward me and fell onto my lap. "I've missed you, Asher." She wrapped her arms around my neck, pulling my face to hers. She tasted like a joint. Grace had tasted like peppermint.

Was this all I'd have now? Drunk sex with girls who had even less self-esteem than I did? Only the best for me, compliments of the Fates. Heat spread from my chest to my face. *Fuck the Fates.*

"Get off me." I pushed her away, and she slid onto the coffee table. A few people nearby laughed.

Vikki's face turned red, and she fumbled her way to her feet. "What the hell is wrong with you?"

Connor laughed. "Looks like he's tired of banging a skanky ho. Why don't you go find a new guy to stalk, Vikki?"

Her face grew redder, and she glared at him. "I wasn't talking to you, loser. Why don't you find a new *family* to stalk?" She sneered. "Oh wait, you did. Asher's family."

I jumped off the couch, which, after the tokes and beer, wasn't a good idea. I stumbled toward her and caught my leg on the coffee table. Cursing, I grabbed the arm of the couch and righted myself.

"Shut up, Vikki." I looked at Connor, red-faced on the couch, lips pressed together. "Let's get out of here." He was right. Puking was imminent.

He stood from the couch slowly, his gaze never leaving Vikki's face.

She smirked back at him and flipped her hair. "What's the matter, Connor? Need your *boyfriend* to fight your battles? Is that why you moved into his house?"

Somehow, I made it between them in time to stop him from hitting her. His fist connected with my jaw instead, my head snapping back. She screamed, and the music cut off. Everyone froze, except Connor. I pushed with both hands on his chest, and he struggled to get around me—to get to Vikki.

"Stop. She's not worth going to jail. Come on, let's get out of here." He stopped fighting me, and I let go to rub my jaw.

He yelled at Vikki. "You're such a whore."

She crossed her arms and smirked.

Dan came and stood behind her. "You guys need to go." He narrowed his eyes and nodded at me. Nothing like this had ever happened at one of his parties before. He didn't allow violent wasteoids. We wouldn't be welcome back.

Vikki would, though. He always needed cheap easy girls for his parties.

I met his glare. "Right. Sorry."

He nodded again, and I pulled Connor toward the door. Outside, we walked to my car. Well, he walked. I sort of lurched.

"That bitch. I can't believe we both had sex with her."

He held out his hand, and I raised an eyebrow.

"Give me the keys," he said.

"I can drive." But I pulled the key out of my pocket and dropped it. As I bent to pick it up, my momentum carried me forward. I grabbed the car to hold myself steady.

"There's no way I'm letting you drive. You're

wasted." He still held out his hand.

"Right." I tried to click the lock button on the key fob, but it kept wiggling in my hands. Six beers and just as many tokes in less than an hour wasn't conducive to driving. Vomit burned the back of my throat, and I ran to the bush next to my car to water it with my stupidity.

In a way, I welcomed the burn of my stomach acid eating away at my throat. I sure as hell deserved it. After the last heave, I spit and wiped my mouth with my arm.

Glancing at Connor, I tossed him my keys. "Don't wreck it."

"Never thought we'd be in this situation. Me sober and you fucked up."

"Yeah, pretty pathetic."

I climbed into the passenger seat, and he drove us home. I leaned my elbow on the car door and rested my head. At least I had purged some of the poison from my system.

The night replayed in my mind. Work had been good. Making love to Grace had been perfect. I could still feel her body, still smell her hair, taste her lips. I tried to swallow, tried to inhale. My breath came in a gasp, and tears fell silently on my cheeks, each one burning a trail of shame on my skin.

Why was I such an asshole? I'd broken my promise to Grace, to Pastor King, to my parents, to Kali—to myself. I was drunk and high, two things I never wanted to be again. I was so weak without her. To make matters worse, I'd taken it all out on Vikki, the one person even more fucked up than I was. She had enough problems, even though I didn't know what they were, and I only added to them.

Connor had tried to help. I had just been too stupid

to listen. I swallowed as another wave of nausea hit. "Thanks, Connor."

He looked at me from the corner of his eye. "For what?"

"For helping me."

He shook his head. "Well, if by helping, you mean punching you in the face, then you're welcome."

"Yeah, that did kind of wake me up. And I'm pissed I had to take it for *Vikki.*" I rubbed my forehead. "By the way, don't do that again. You shouldn't hit a girl. You're not your dad."

The darkness couldn't hide the red on his face. His hands clenched the steering wheel. "I was tonight. And I wasn't even drunk. At least Dad had that excuse when he'd beat my mom."

I had no answer for that.

"Asher?"

"What?"

He squirmed in his seat. "When's the next...meeting?"

My heart thudded in my throat. "Tuesday."

He pursed his lips and stared at the road. I didn't push for more.

We pulled up to my house, and I hit the garage door opener. Connor parked in the garage, and we entered the quiet house. We stopped inside the doorway, and I held a finger to my lips.

"They're in bed." At least I could avoid her disappointment. We crossed the kitchen and took the stairs to my room. He followed me inside, and I closed the door.

Laughing, he sat on the foot of my bed. "Let's bust out the polish."

I wanted to laugh, but my head filled with memories of Grace, smothering the laugh before it escaped. I took my phone from my back pocket and dropped it on the nightstand, then sat and leaned against the headboard. My head spun in crazy circles as I closed my eyes. "What am I going to do?"

"I'm the wrong one to ask. My life is more messed up than yours. Or at least it was. I'm sorry about Grace."

Hot tears fell on my cheeks again. Now I laughed and glanced at him. "If anyone had told me a week ago that you and I would sit here having a heart-to-heart while I cried like a baby, I would have punched *them* in the face." I wiped away more tears.

He grabbed the box of tissues from the dresser behind him and tossed it in my lap. "Sorry, I kinda suck at deep emotional conversations. Wish I knew what to say to help you."

I plucked a tissue from the box and blew my nose. "Don't worry, I know someone who will."

I reached for my phone and scrolled through the contacts until I found his number. The only person who would know *exactly* how I felt. I tapped the number.

He answered on the third ring in the same friendly voice he'd used at the meeting. "Hello?"

I wiped more tears from my face. "Hey, Dave. This is Asher. Can you talk?"

Chapter Twenty

Bright, blinding sunlight blasted through my windows the next morning. I woke and pulled a pillow over my throbbing head. "Holy Mother of God."

My mouth felt like a spider's egg sac—dry, stringy, and sticky. I wiggled my tongue a few times, trying to wet it, but it was no use, and my head hurt too much to walk into the bathroom and get a drink. I rolled over onto my stomach, keeping the pillow over my eyes.

"Did you have a good time last night?"

Kali's quiet voice startled me, and I spun over onto my back. Big mistake. My stomach rolled, and I jumped out of bed to run to the toilet. Beer never tasted the same on its way out.

I flushed and grabbed the cup on my sink to fill it with water. I swished and spit a few times, took a long drink, and went back to my bed. I couldn't meet Kali's gaze. My mind rewound all the horrible things I'd said to her last night.

"I'm sorry."

She frowned, glancing at my messy hair and clothes, wrinkled from being slept in. They still smelled like weed and vomit.

"Well? Are you going to answer my question?"

I covered my eyes with my arm. "Let's see, I made love to Grace, which was great, then found out she has cancer and will die. Not great. Not that I'll know until it's over, because she doesn't want to hurt me, and she thinks never talking to me again is the best way to keep that from happening. Then I let everyone down and got shit-faced wasted and puked most of the night and this morning, and now I'm sitting here trying to apologize to an angel of death who I insulted by comparing my self-pitying hungover self to the stronger, sober love of her life who she can't be with but would trade anything, including my sorry ass, for the ability to spend one more day with." I pinched the bridge of my nose. "And I took a punch to the jaw from my best friend for the girl I used way too many times. So, no. I'd say I didn't have a good time last night."

She snorted, and I looked up at her.

"Asher, I wouldn't trade you for anything. You're way too entertaining." She sat on the bed and held out a hand.

I took it in mine. "You were right. I'm nothing like Dave. He's so much stronger than me."

"He's a different person." She squeezed my hand. "Don't compare yourself to him. Just one step at a time. Focus on making yourself better than the day before. You need to ask for forgiveness from those you've hurt, but first you need to forgive yourself."

"You sound like Dave. That's what he told me last night." I lifted the corner of my lip. "I'll have to start with the other-people part. I don't have it in me to forgive myself yet."

She patted my knee.

I picked up my phone and dialed the first number, expecting her not to answer. But she did on the fourth ring.

"Hello?" Her voice was gravelly with sleep.

I glanced at Kali and drew a deep breath. "Hey, Vikki. It's Asher."

After a beat of silence, she whispered, "What do you want?"

"I called to apologize for last night. I didn't mean to hurt you. You know, when I pushed you on the floor."

"Oh." She cleared her throat. "You kind of made up for it, blocking Connor's punch."

"Maybe. I…" I raised my gaze to Kali, and she nodded her encouragement. "Vikki, I'm sorry for the way I've treated you, and I'm trying to change. Not partying anymore. I won't be hanging out with you either. I love Grace, and she's the one I want to be with." *While I can.*

Vikki breathed into the phone, and my stomach twisted, but not from the hangover.

"Asher, you can go fuck yourself."

She laughed, and I closed my eyes.

"Which you'll have to do if Grace King is the girl you want. She's such a prude. You'll never get in her pants. And don't worry about hurting me. My feelings are fine. I have plenty of other options out there besides you. Good luck with *changing your life*. I saw how well that's going last night." She ended the call, cutting off her laughter.

I raised my eyebrows and stared at the phone. "That went well."

"Not everyone will forgive you. But you still have to try." Kali sighed. "Vikki is only one person. One who is uber jealous for you I might add. She may say you don't matter, but that's a lie."

I flipped my phone over and over in my hands. "What can I do?"

She stood and moved to my window. The sunlight set her hair on fire, the gold twinkling. "Nothing. She has her own path to choose."

"What will happen to her?"

She shook her head. "I can't tell you that. That's not why I'm here."

Connor threw open my bedroom door. I jumped, glancing between him and Kali. She smiled, but he didn't even acknowledge the hot redhead standing by my window. At least I knew if he couldn't see her, he wasn't about to bite it.

He sat in the chair next to the window. "How's the stomach this morning?"

I glanced at Kali's smirk and said, "A little choppy." Scooting back onto my bed, I moaned, rubbing my bruised jaw. "You should have hit me before I drank."

"Hey, I tried to get you to stop. You wouldn't listen."

"Yeah, it's my fault." I rubbed my temples. "I called Vikki to apologize."

"Why?" He looked at his feet. "You weren't the one who tried to punch her. I should be the one calling."

"I wouldn't. She's not in a very forgiving mood."

I told him about our phone conversation, and he shook his head.

"That girl's hopeless."

"Yeah, maybe." I met Kali's gaze, and she pursed her lips.

Connor clapped his hands together and stood. "Well, I'm going out for a while."

"Where to?" My stomach fell. "Going out" could mean a lot of different things to him.

"Oh, nowhere important." He glanced at the floor,

his face flaming red.

Kali covered her mouth, her shoulders shaking with silent laughter.

I pressed him. "Come on, tell me where."

"Fine, since you've gotta be all up in my business." He pulled his shoulders back. "I'm going to church with Chloe."

I gaped at him, taking in the unusually dressy clothes he wore—khakis and a button-down shirt. "Holy shit."

He narrowed his eyes. "Are you trying to be punny?"

"No." I laughed. "But admit it. It sounds odd coming from you. When did you decide to get godly?"

"When Chloe drove me home yesterday. We talked. She's cool." His face reddened again, and he cleared his throat. "Anyway, she asked me if I wanted to come, and I said sure."

The tightness in my chest eased. "I think it's a great idea."

Kali nodded in agreement.

"Whatever." He looked at his phone. "She's picking me up in five minutes. Do you want to go? She goes to the same church as Grace."

After the AA meeting and before my pity party last night, I had planned on going to church to show Pastor King I was serious about changing. Now I had to see Grace and convince her that we needed to help each other, not drift apart. Last night was a prime example of how I'd be without her. And I still had to find a way to save her, too.

I looked at my clothes, breathed into my hand, and sniffed. "I'm not going anywhere without a shower. I'll meet you there. Save me a seat."

Kali tapped an imaginary watch on her wrist. Heart racing, I hopped up, ripped off my dirty shirt, and ran into the bathroom.

****

I swallowed my fear and stepped into the church. Climbing the stairs, I squinted against the sunlight streaming in through the wall of windows next to me. I reached the door to the narthex and blew out a breath, running a hand through my damp hair. A well-dressed middle-aged couple greeted me.

The man shook my hand. "Good morning. Welcome to Nameoki Church."

"Thank you," I replied.

The woman by his side handed me a piece of paper. "Here's a bulletin. In case you want to know what's going on in the church."

"Thanks." I took the bulletin and headed across the narthex to the open double doors leading to the sanctuary. The red-carpeted aisle stretched a million miles long. I stared, remembering when Grace and I used to race back and forth down that aisle until we collapsed in a heap on the altar steps, laughing.

At the far end, a fifty-foot arched stone wall stood, adorned with only one thing—a giant wooden cross. A thousand memories flooded my mind, drowning me with emotions I didn't expect—or welcome.

Fear was the most powerful, followed by shame, and my stomach churned. I didn't belong here.

"Asher."

I turned my head to the right. Connor sat in the pew next to Chloe who waved me over. I sank next to him on the gray, cloth-covered seat. My head spun from stress and the hangover.

"Hi, Chloe," I said.

"I'm glad you could come."

"Yeah." I frowned. "I used to come here every Sunday."

"Really? That must have been before I moved here." She raised her eyebrows. "What made you stop?"

"Oh, you know." I glanced at Connor. "Things got in the way."

"Well, what matters is that you came back." She handed me the attendance booklet to sign. "All it takes is that first step."

I gazed around the sanctuary. The massive arched wood ceiling and walls swallowed the quiet hum of conversation. People smiled and laughed, some faces familiar, others new to me.

My gaze fell on Mrs. King and their son, Joel, sitting in the second pew on the left side of the church. My heart pounded, but Grace wasn't there. I swallowed my disappointment.

"Sorry, she's not here," Connor whispered.

"Yeah." I leaned back in the pew and closed my eyes. Maybe I should leave. Go to her house and make her talk.

The organist played, ending the quiet hum of conversation. Leaving now would be rude, so I stayed seated. Two young girls carried in long brass torches glowing with an orange flame, followed by Pastor King.

He glanced from side to side at his church members. His gaze landed on me, and his eyes widened. Then he smiled, a warm smile even. I guessed I scored a couple points.

I nodded back. Grace was dying. How could he act

like everything was fine? It must be a pastoral superpower.

He continued to the front of the sanctuary.

Connor leaned closer. "He looks like he's seen a ghost."

I smirked. "Shut up."

Not much had changed in the service. We sang, prayed, gave money, and heard announcements. The only difference was how I felt about it. I'd never given much thought to anything Pastor King said before. As I listened to his sermon this time, guilt settled like sludge in my gut. The words rang out—forgiven, redeemed, loved. None of them applied to me, though. If God had forgiven me, would Grace be dying from cancer? Shouldn't I be the one? Shouldn't I suffer for all the shit I'd done instead of her?

How could a loving, forgiving God let someone good like Grace suffer, and allow someone who'd made all the wrong choices, someone like me, to live a longer life? I clenched my fists and glared at Pastor King.

Connor nudged me with his elbow, and I jumped.

"What's wrong? You look like you want to kill the pastor."

I relaxed my fists. "Nothing."

He shrugged and looked away, holding Chloe's hand. At least he was having a good time.

The service ended, and the throng of people filed out down the center aisle to shake the pastor's hand as he stood by the exit. I didn't want to, but Connor and Chloe waited for me to move, and I had to go into the aisle to let them out of the pew. They stepped in front of me and joined the line. I got behind an elderly lady with hunched shoulders who had bathed in perfume. I covered my nose to help settle the rolling in my stomach.

"Asher?"

I turned toward the tap on my shoulder. Mrs. King pulled me into a hug.

I hugged her back. "Hi, Mrs. King." I looked at Joel standing on her left.

He smiled at me, his green eyes a replica of Grace's.

I rubbed his head. "Hey, squirt. How's it going?"

He hugged my waist, and I patted his back. I did the math in my head and realized he'd be eight in three months. Before I got stupid, he had looked up to me. I hoped he'd found a new role model.

"Where have you been?" he asked. "I haven't seen you in forever."

"I've been…" High and drunk wasn't something I wanted him to hear from me. I glanced at Mrs. King.

"Asher has been away, but now he's back." She ruffled Joel's blond hair. "Why don't you go downstairs and see if they need help in the kitchen?"

He groaned. "But I want to talk to Asher."

"I'll talk to you later. Maybe we can get ice cream sometime." His wide-eyed grin made me laugh. If only everyone were as easy to please.

"Okay, see ya later." He weaved through the crowd and headed for the basement.

"How are you, Asher?" Mrs. King asked. "I know you've talked to Grace."

I nodded, clenching my jaw. "I came here today to see her."

"She didn't feel well enough to come." She pressed her lips together, and a tear slipped down her cheek. She brushed it away with a quick swipe of her hand. "I know you have questions. Can you stay and talk with us after the potluck? You're welcome to eat, of course."

"I'd rather see Grace." I shifted on my feet and dropped my gaze to the floor. "But she told me she doesn't want me around."

"She doesn't mean it. She's hurting." She patted my hand. "Please stay and eat, then we can talk."

I nodded, then, bypassing the line, she slipped out the door.

Chloe and Connor were next to shake Pastor King's hand. I glanced at them and cut back through the pews to exit through the side door. Pastor King's stare followed me, burning holes into my back.

I hid outside on a bench in the prayer garden at the back of the church. The sun shone bright in the sky. The purple and white petunias lining the building glowed in the light. The warm wood of the bench heated my back. I eased on my sunglasses and crossed my arms over my chest.

I wouldn't eat at the potluck, but I could wait here for them to finish. Maybe I'd get the answers I needed from her parents. My stomach churned with guilt as I thought about my weakness last night. But I had to be strong for Grace. Kali had said there was still hope to save her, and what better place to find hope than church?

God didn't make any sense to me, but maybe Pastor King and his wife knew something I didn't. I fell asleep on the bench in the sunshine. Joel woke me by tickling my side.

I grabbed him and tickled back. "You asked for it, squirt."

He squealed and squirmed, trying to get away. I let go, and he sat next to me.

"My mom said to come and get you. She wants you

to come downstairs and eat."

"Tell her thanks, but I'm not hungry."

He stuck out his bottom lip, looking every bit like the little boy I remembered. "But they have fried chicken."

His pout reminded me of Grace. I poked his stomach. "Well, nobody said there would be fried chicken."

"There's always fried chicken at a Methodist potluck," he said, wise beyond his years. He grabbed my hand and yanked me toward the door. "Come on. I'm starving."

"Why haven't you eaten yet?" I checked my phone. Half an hour had passed while I napped.

"I waited for you." He bounced through the door and took the steps to the basement.

I added Joel to the list of amends I needed to make to the King family.

Downstairs, the fellowship hall looked different from the meeting night. Round tables filled the area instead of rows of chairs. People smiled and talked, ate or visited. Several ladies stood behind the open counter to the kitchen, refilling water pitchers or placing more food on the buffet.

The atmosphere was too happy for me. Did any of them know about Grace? If they did, why weren't they crying and falling on their knees to pray? How could they celebrate and laugh and eat?

Joel pushed me toward the counter. "Come on, Asher."

I picked up a plate and filled it with food I wouldn't eat. Joel and I sat at an empty table. I picked up the drumstick and took a bite, surprised when it tasted good.

The grease helped ease my hungover stomach, too. I took another bite.

"Hey, I thought you'd left." Connor slid into the chair on my right, setting his full plate on the table. Chloe sat next to him, her plate full, too.

I shifted my gaze between them. "I sat outside for a while until this intruder came and got me." I poked Joel in his side, and he laughed. "Where have you two been?"

Chloe blushed, and Connor shrugged. "Oh, just...talking."

"Never mind." I ate some potato salad. "None of my business."

Joel chewed on his chicken and eyed Connor. "Who is he?"

"That's my friend Connor." I nodded to Joel. "This is Grace's little brother, Joel."

Connor lifted his chin. "What's up, Joel?"

Joel glanced from Chloe to Connor. "Are you her boyfriend?"

Connor shook his head and winked at Chloe. "No, we're just friends."

Joel nodded. "Good, because girlfriends are gross."

Connor and I laughed, but Chloe gave Joel a mock-angry glare.

She licked the fried-chicken grease off her finger, then pointed it at Joel. "That's only because you don't have one yet. Give it a few years. You'll be as desperate to find one as Connor is."

Connor squeezed her side, and she giggled.

"Watch who you're calling desperate. You're the one I'm chasing."

She rolled her eyes, but her blush deepened.

I raised my eyebrows in surprise. Connor's usual

comments revolved around the size of girls' boobs or how easy they were. I'd never seen him try to flirt before either. He was surprisingly good at it.

"Whatever, I still think girls are gross." Joel grabbed his empty plate and looked toward the dessert table. "Asher, do you want dessert?"

"No, thanks. Why don't you eat mine? The chicken filled me up."

His eyes brightened. "Okay, double desserts for me." He threw his plate in the trash, then rushed to look at the treats.

Chloe followed him with her gaze. "You're good with him. Most of the time he bounces off the walls."

"Does he still? I thought maybe he outgrew it."

She shook her head. "I think Pastor and Mrs. King have a hard time with him. Lucky for them Grace doesn't cause any trouble." She took a sip of lemonade.

I scowled, and the chicken squawked in my stomach. I pushed my plate away and leaned back in my chair.

Connor glanced at me and cleared his throat. "Come on, let's check out the dessert table. If I'd known I could eat like this, I would have come to church more often."

He took Chloe by the hand and led her away. She laughed, and his smile grew. I liked to see him with someone normal, but their flirting made me miss Grace even more. I closed my eyes, imagining her next to me.

Someone sat next to me, and the seat creaked. "Hello, Asher."

Pastor King startled me from my daydream. I sat straighter in my chair. "Hello, sir."

He folded his hands on the table. "Did you enjoy the service today?"

He'd made eye contact with me as I glared at him during the service, so he had to already know the answer to that question. "Not too much."

He nodded, looking at the table. "This should wrap up in a few minutes. Ann and I would like to talk to you in my office if you don't mind."

"That's why I'm here. Though I'd rather talk to Grace."

He drew a deep breath. "We'll meet you upstairs in ten minutes."

"Okay."

He walked back to the kitchen where his wife helped with the cleanup. I watched them working together, smiling, visiting with the others. I knew they loved Grace. But they didn't look worried at all.

Must have been another superpower, acting like he didn't have a care in the world when really he had a hyper son and a dying daughter. *Yeah. And I used to think church was a place where people went to learn the truth.*

Chapter Twenty-One

Pastor King's office had made the cut on the renovation schedule. Pale gray walls, dark wood furniture, a huge mahogany desk on one side, and a small leather couch and matching chairs on the other. The cushiony carpet muffled the sound of my footsteps, lending a cozy feel to the room.

Perfect for telling the pothead boy who loved his dying daughter to leave her alone and let her die in peace.

Pastor King sat in one chair, and his wife sat in the other, more somber than at the potluck. I sat on the couch, clenching my fists in my lap and bouncing my leg.

Pastor King leaned forward to rest his elbows on his knees.

"How are you doing with your effort to change, Asher?" Mrs. King started off with the worst possible question.

I didn't want to lie to her, but I was too ashamed to let them know how spectacularly I had failed last night. Then I remembered what Dave had said. I needed to be honest with myself and others. So I described how I fell off the wagon. And why.

Pastor King listened, staring at the floor. He looked up frowning. "I'm sorry to hear you gave in, but I understand. You're new to this and haven't built up strength yet."

"I don't know why she pushed me away. I don't want her to…" I swallowed back the tears. I couldn't cry in front of her dad. He already thought I was weak. Not that dudes couldn't cry, but I needed all the help I could get with him.

Mrs. King slid next to me on the couch and placed her hand on mine. "There is hope for Grace."

"How? Tell me about her diagnosis. I don't understand."

Her dad cleared his throat. "She has acute lymphoblastic leukemia, or ALL. She's in the high-risk group, so her treatment will be aggressive. The first phase of treatment, remission induction, begins this week."

I wrinkled my forehead. "Remission induction? What does that mean? What will she have to do?"

Her mom patted my hand. "She'll begin chemotherapy and radiation. Once she's free from cancer cells, they'll add her to the list for a bone marrow transplant."

"So that's it? Then she'll be cured?" How the hell was I supposed to help? I frowned at the worried look they exchanged.

"It's not that simple." Her mom drew a breath and blew it out. "Killing the cancer cells could take weeks or months. And finding a marrow match isn't always easy. She's got a long road ahead of her, but yes, there is hope at the end of that road."

"What can I do to help?" I wasn't an idiot. I wouldn't be a part of the cure, but my stomach twisted at the thought of Grace dealing with her cancer treatments alone. I had to be there for her.

"I know you care for her, Asher." Pastor King

cleared his throat and glanced at the floor.

"No, I love her." I wanted them to know how I felt, so they wouldn't have any doubts about me. "She's only pushing me away because she thinks I won't be able to handle it, that I'll start drinking again. But that won't happen."

He squinted his eyes. "It already did."

Shit.

"I didn't get drunk because I found out she had cancer. When she left…" My face heated, and I glared at him. "Last night was a mistake I won't make again. And I won't give up on her. Not even if you want me to."

He gazed into my eyes with that same steady stare I had avoided before. I met it head-on. He'd already seen my failings. I had nothing left to hide.

"She doesn't want people to feel sorry for her, so we aren't allowed to tell anyone about the cancer. And she doesn't want you to see her during treatment, to see her sick. She thinks it will be too much for you." Her dad nodded. "And I think she's right. This is too much for you to handle while you fix your own life."

"Right." I glared at him. "And you don't want her to be with me."

He wrinkled his brow. "That's not it, Asher."

"Yes, it is." I lifted my hands in frustration. "When will you believe me? Believe that I love her and I would do anything to earn the right to have her? You know she loves me, too, and you can't handle it."

"Yes, she loves you." He spoke slowly through his teeth. "But that doesn't erase what you did. How badly you hurt her."

"She's forgiven me," I yelled. "Shouldn't you respect her choice?"

He leaned forward. "She's blinded by her feelings. *I* know better. I can remember the pain for her and try to protect her from feeling it again."

"Her or you?" The words slipped out before I could stop them, but they hit their mark.

He jerked like I'd slapped him. "This isn't about me," he said, pressing his fingertips into his eyes.

"Isn't it?"

"No," he growled.

He glared, but I jumped from the couch. Fighting back a scream, I pointed a finger at his chest. "You're lying. Grace and I have worked through our problem, but you still want to punish me for hurting *you*, not her. The least you could do is be honest with me. Especially here!"

I held my arms out, gesturing to the church.

"You're damn right!" He stood, too, waving a hand at me. "You have no idea how you ruined our lives. All of them! What it was like to bring Grace back from depression, the brink of *suicide*! You destroyed her hope, her faith, everything."

He paced as Mrs. King cried silently, hiding her face behind her shaky hands. Hiding from me but it should have been the other way around. I could barely breathe around the landslide in my throat. Grace had tried to kill herself? Over me?

He jabbed a finger at me. "And Joel, he worshiped you like a big brother. Imagine having to answer his questions about where you were with lies. I couldn't even tell him *why* you abandoned him, because I didn't want him to know what you were doing. Drinking, drugs, having sex with any girl stupid enough to trust you."

Heat scorched my face, and Joel's six-year-old

smiling face teased my memory, adding more rocks to the ones in my throat.

"She wasn't the only one who loved you, Asher. And she wasn't the only one you dumped for your selfish desires and self-pity. We all lost you." Pastor King slumped into his chair, tears dousing his anger. "So forgive me if I have a difficult time letting you back in her life when we aren't sure how much time she has left. For not believing you when you say you won't do it again."

Mrs. King wiped her eyes and went to him. She held him as he cried, and my stomach churned. Their pain was my fault. I had to make it right if I ever wanted to truly be with Grace. But more than that, my heart ached to mend this bridge I'd blown apart with drugs and alcohol, because I needed them just as much as I needed their daughter. I sat and rubbed a hand through my hair.

"You're right. You're absolutely right. All the blame is mine and…I'm sorry. I didn't come here to fight. And I'm sorry for disappointing you. For hurting all of you. For…everything." My tears joined theirs, and I held my head in my hands. "But I promise, if you give me another chance, I won't leave you again. I love you, too, and I need you."

Raising my head, I met their teary gazes. Mrs. King still had her arm around the pastor, and he held her other hand between his. They exchanged a glance, and she gave him a watery smile.

"Keeping them apart won't help either of them." She dabbed her eyes with a tissue. "Grace needs him. He's her hope for living."

Pastor King raised his head to look me in the eye. We stared at each other for a moment, and my throat constricted. Could he see the truth in my eyes? Did my rant and apology earn me that much trust at least? I'd never realized how much his understanding meant to me. As I sat here on the edge of this new cliff, my hands shaking, tears still flowing, I craved his forgiveness almost as much as I'd craved Grace's.

After another moment, he swallowed, then nodded. "You were right, too. I put my feelings ahead of Grace's. I know you're really trying to change, and I believe that you're sorry."

Nodding, I rubbed my eyes and restated my promise. "I messed up. Bad. Made dumb choices. I'm sorry. Sorrier than you could ever imagine. I won't ever hurt her again. Or you or Mrs. King or Joel, I just—"

"Asher?" He grinned. "Sometimes you still talk too much."

I half laughed, stood, and held out my hand.

He stood, too and took my hand. Then with a tug he pulled me to him and hugged me.

I hugged him back. The pressure on my chest eased, and I finally took a deep breath.

"Earn this," he said.

"I will. Thank you."

He patted my back and let go, then Mrs. King wrapped her arms around me, too.

"You can do this, Asher. Grace needs you to be there for her." She released me, and Pastor King held her hand.

"If I could just get her to talk to me…"

"She's at home now. I'd bet a little ice cream would soften her up," her dad suggested. "She's not able to eat much."

"Is the pain in her leg from the cancer?"

"The leukemia cells have built up by her thigh bone.

261

That's what's causing her pain." He bit his lip and rubbed his forehead with shaky hands.

Seeing his tears, I felt guilty for worrying about crying in front of him and for thinking they didn't show enough emotion during the service and potluck. I guessed they had to hide this because once they let this kind of pain show, it'd be hard to cover back up.

I shook my head. "How do you do it?"

He looked up, tears in his eyes. "Do what?"

"How do you serve a God who would do this to someone as good as Grace?" I thought having the Fates after me was bad, but at least they were known for their erratic behavior. Pastor King claimed God loved us. This wasn't how I envisioned love.

"God didn't do this." He shook his head. "He doesn't make bad things happen. We do."

I frowned. "You didn't give Grace cancer."

"No," he said. "I didn't. But cancer is of this world, not from God. He didn't give it to her either. But you can bet He'll use it to make something beautiful."

Something beautiful from cancer? Sounded like bullshit, but it seemed to give him peace, so I nodded like I believed him.

"I know you don't believe me. But it's already happened. The beautiful has already begun."

"How? What? Nothing good will come from cancer. Just a long road ahead filled with pain for all of us, most of all for Grace."

Pastor King nodded to his wife.

She squeezed my hand between hers. "Facing mortality can change a person's perspective. Make them see what is truly important to them. Grace was able to forgive you for the hurt because you *are* important to her.

Her cancer brought you back to her, Asher. To us. That's something we've all been praying for."

My breath caught in my throat. How could my broken messed-up life be the beauty they'd looked for?

I returned their loving gazes, heart racing. Love I'd thought they buried when I left Grace, left them. The final bits of the wall I'd built between us with drugs and alcohol crumbled into dust. I'd thought they hated me and never wanted me around again. But that was only because I was an idiot. I should have known they would pray for me. Pastor King had been more of a father than my own.

I cried again, feeling every bit like the prodigal son. Grace's mom held me again through my tears. We cried together—for Grace, for us, and for hope. Inside I laughed, though, remembering the fried chicken. The prodigal son got the feast after all.

****

I parked my car in front of Grace's house and jogged toward the door, holding a bag with a container of strawberry ice cream. Anticipating her smile and maybe a few kisses, I moved faster. But as I drew closer to the house, breaking glass and loud crashes resounded behind the door. Kali exploded into view on the porch and frantically waved me forward. My heart stopped.

Another crash and another shatter had me jumping up the steps. "What's going on?"

"Get in there. Before she hurts herself." Kali disappeared, and I grabbed the door handle.

Locked.

Remembering they kept a spare key hidden under a flowerpot, I grabbed it, opened the door, and rushed inside.

I ducked as a plate flew at me. It smashed against the door, and I covered my head to avoid the shattered pieces raining down around me. It ended, and I jerked my head up. Grace stood in the tiny kitchen, pulling another plate from the cabinet.

"Grace, stop!" I dropped the bag of ice cream and took a step toward her.

She glared with wide eyes, her face a deep blood red. I worried that some of it might *be* blood.

"Get out of here. I don't want you here!" She let loose with the plate, and I ducked again. It shattered against the door, the pieces tinkling to the floor.

I ran toward her before she could reload, then wrapped her in my arms from behind. She struggled, trying to pull away, bucking her head back and forth, kicking her feet into the air, screaming like a wild animal. I squeezed her tighter.

"Please stop. You'll hurt yourself."

She sobbed, but her struggling increased. Her hair whipped my face, and I closed my eyes. Afraid I would hurt her myself, I loosened my grip and lost my hold on her. Strong in her rage, she slapped me, and my head snapped to the side.

Kali stood in the living room, yelling at me. "Grab her, Asher! She's going for the knives!"

Grace screamed and reached for the knife block on the counter. I tackled her to the ground before her fingers touched the first handle.

Twisting so I could take the force of the fall, I held her, and we landed in a mess of utensils and broken dishes. The ceramic shards pressed sharply against my back. I rolled, holding her under me, and she screamed again. She struggled to free herself from the weight of my body on top of hers.

"Calm down. It's okay. It'll be okay." I panted with the effort to hold her down—and the effort to hold back my tears.

"It's not okay. I'm dying." She screamed again, shaking my eardrums. "Did you hear? *I'm fucking dying!*"

She threw her head back, and I caught it in the palms of my hands to keep her from cracking her skull on the floor. The suffocating weight of her words crushed the air from my lungs.

"Grace…" I choked, and tears fell, hot and wet on my face.

My tears triggered hers, and the fight drained from her writhing body. A wail escaped her lips, and she went limp on the floor beneath me.

"I don't want to die." Her body jerked with the force of her sobs.

I sat and lifted her with me until we were leaning against the refrigerator. I held her to my chest.

She hugged my neck, sobbing, repeating over and over, "I don't want to die. I don't want to die. I don't want to die."

"Shhh, shhh. You're not going to die. You're not. You're not." I rocked her side to side, repeating *my* refrain in our twisted song. Her sobs slowed to hiccups, and I stroked the back of her hair.

Around the kitchen, every drawer lay on the floor, their contents spilled. Broken dishes lay everywhere. A crack glittered in the window above the sink. Gouges covered the wall, and a broken chair lay in pieces on the floor below them.

The destruction didn't end there. Broken picture

frames littered the living room, and the end tables were overturned.

I glanced at Kali, and she shook her head, tears rolling down her cheeks.

"Are you alone here?" I asked Grace.

"Yes, my parents and brother are at church."

Relieved she couldn't see Kali, I held her by the shoulders and glared into her eyes. "You are not going to die. Understand?"

Her eyes were red, and blotches mottled her smooth skin. She had blood on the corner of her mouth, and I wiped it away with my thumb. The cut appeared minor, but I cringed seeing it on her perfect face.

"But, Asher, I—"

I didn't let her finish her excuse. Instead, I kissed her softly, holding her cheeks. The salt from her tears tingled on my tongue. "Trust me. I love you, and I'm not going to let you die."

"But this is cancer." She looked at the floor. "I wanted us to be together."

"We are together. This doesn't change anything." I hugged her to my chest. "I'll help you through this. And you can't tell me to go away because I won't listen."

"Tell me something I *don't* know."

"Okay." I laughed. "How about this? I went to church today."

Her back stiffened, and she pulled away. "You did?"

"Connor went with me."

"Now I know you're lying."

"Nope, he was the one who asked me to go. Because Chloe invited him, and he likes her."

"Too much." She rubbed her forehead and groaned. "You should have stopped with *I went to church today*."

I pulled her to her feet. "Oh, it gets better. I had a nice long talk with your parents, and they agree with me. I'm here to stay. You're stuck with me."

"This is a nice fantasy world you live in." She brushed the hair from my forehead with a gentle touch of her fingertips. "Can I visit it sometime?"

I tilted my head. "Why don't you believe me?"

"Because it's too good to be true. And those things never work out."

"I know this won't be easy. But I'm here for you. *Always*. And that's the truth." I sealed my promise with another kiss.

She pulled back and held my hands. "Well, I know how you can help me now."

"Oh?"

She waved a hand at the destruction she'd caused. "Got a broom?"

I laughed and kissed her cheek. "You sit. I'll clean up."

"I can help." She reached toward the broken cups on the floor.

"Nope." I scooped her up in my arms, and she giggled.

"Put me down."

I carried her to the couch and used my foot to move the overturned lamp. I set her gently on the cushion and knelt beside her.

"You stay here. Your face is bone white, and you're burning up." I brushed the hair away from her glassy eyes. "You need to rest after your Hulk impersonation."

She laughed and pulled me in for another kiss. Her lips trembled from her chills. I reached for the blanket she had thrown on the floor and tucked her in.

"Thank you," she whispered, her eyes already drooping shut. She laid her head back on the couch.

"You're welcome," I whispered back, though I knew she didn't hear me.

A soft snore left Grace's mouth, and I smiled. I walked into the kitchen to pick up the bag with the ice cream and put it in the freezer. Then I grabbed the broom from the closet. I'd only cleaned up a small portion when her parents pulled in the driveway. I took a deep breath and braced myself for their reaction.

The door opened, and her parents entered, freezing in place just inside the door. Joel bounced in behind them and froze, too.

Her mom covered her mouth, lifting a broken frame containing a family photo from some past beach vacation. "What…" She shook her head. Joel wrapped his little arms around her waist, his wide eyes darting from place to place in the trashed room.

Pastor King frowned, glancing into the kitchen. He rubbed his eyes and hunched his shoulders. "What happened?"

I explained how Grace had flipped out like the girl from *The Exorcist* and pointed to her sleeping form on the couch. "I stopped her before she could hurt herself, and I think she got it out of her system. She just needed to blow off steam."

Joel nodded. "Lots of steam." He looked at Grace, and his eyes filled with tears.

"She's okay, squirt. All right?"

He ran to me and squeezed my waist.

I hugged him back. "Don't worry, everything will be fine. She was just mad and had to let it out. Like the Hulk, you know?"

He giggled. "She's not the Hulk."

"I know." I rolled my eyes. "She didn't even turn green."

His laugh eased the tension. His parents moved from their frozen positions.

"Come on, let's get this mess cleaned up." Pastor King wrinkled his eyebrows and nodded to Grace. "Maybe I should move her."

"I'll do it." I reached one arm under her knees and the other behind her shoulders, lifting her from the couch. She snuggled into my chest, and I kissed the top of her head.

"Ewwww." Joel scrunched up his face. "Yuck."

I cocked my eyebrow. "Someday you won't mind so much." I glanced at her dad, worried I'd pissed him off, but he just shook his head.

"You're stronger than me. I haven't been able to lift her since she was ten." He bent to right the overturned end table.

I carried Grace to her room and laid her on the bed, then covered her with her blanket. I leaned in and kissed her forehead again, frowning at the excessive warmth. I crossed the little room and turned back to take another look. Grace smiled in her sleep. I smiled back.

I turned off the light, closed the door, and went to help with the mess.

Chapter Twenty-Two

Dad's car sat in the driveway at home. *Weird.* I parked and ran inside. Time to tick a few more amends off my to-do list.

My parents sat in the kitchen at the breakfast table, on opposite sides facing each other. It reminded me of the day they'd told me about the divorce. Arms crossed, angry scowls, neither looking at the other. Only two things had ever made them look that way. Since they were already divorced, I must be the reason.

I got the ball rolling. "What's up?"

"Do you want to explain where you've been?" Mom glared at me. "I've tried calling you all afternoon. I was just about to call the police and hospitals to see if they had you."

"Asher," Dad said. "You promised you would try to stay clean. What have you been doing?"

I raised my eyebrows. Did they have so little faith in me they thought I'd been out getting high or drinking all day and that's why I didn't answer my phone? It was a hard pill to swallow, but I had to admit it was my fault they didn't trust me.

"Sorry. It's been a rough day, and I had something important to do." Sitting in the chair next to Mom, I pulled my phone out of my pocket and saw the twenty-three missed calls.

No wonder she'd called Dad. I chuckled, imagining

that conversation.

Her face turned red. "There is nothing funny about this. For all I knew, you could have been dead on the side of the road."

I bit back my laugh and glanced at Dad, a permanent frown etched on his face.

"I wasn't drinking or getting high." I leaned my elbows on the table. "This morning, Connor and I went to church. Then I stayed there for a potluck and after that, to talk with Grace's parents."

I might as well have said I went to Mars.

Mom groaned. "Quit with the bullshit. Where were you?"

I ignored her and looked at Dad. "After I talked to her parents, I went to Grace's house to help her."

His face hadn't changed. He pursed his lips and stared at me. "I think he's telling the truth, Beth."

She narrowed her eyes. "What?"

"There's something else I need to tell you." I glanced at my hands folded on the table and cleared my throat. "I've joined an AA group, and I'd like you both to go with me to the next meeting."

Kali's minty perfume embraced my head, and her unseen hands squeezed my shoulders.

Dad continued his stare.

Mom shook her head, her eyes filling with tears. "How long has this been going on?"

"I've only gone to one meeting."

He sat straighter in his chair. "Why didn't you tell us?"

"Because I wasn't fully committed yet. I had a small relapse after I got some news I couldn't handle."

They exchanged a glance, and I swallowed, trying

to push away the boulder that blocked my throat.

"Grace has cancer."

She gasped. He cussed under his breath.

I bit my tongue, and the metallic taste of blood filled my mouth. The sweet strawberry scent from Grace's hair rose from my chest, calming my erratic heart.

"When she told me about the cancer, she said she didn't want to be with me. That she didn't want me to watch her die."

Mom's sob slipped through her fingers. "How bad is it?"

"It's cancer." I shrugged.

Dad leaned forward on the table. "There are a lot of factors that can increase her chances. She's young and strong, so there's hope, Asher."

"Thanks. Anyway, that's why I slipped up." My face burned. "She told me yesterday and pushed me away. She said she didn't want me with her, and I lost it. I went to a party last night and got wasted."

Mom asked, "How did you get home without killing yourself?"

I exhaled a breath. "Connor. He was at the party, too. He tried to get me to leave, but I didn't listen to him. So he stayed sober to take care of me. When we got home, I called a guy I met at AA, and he helped me work through it."

She shook her head. "And I thought Connor was a bad influence on you. Looks like I owe him an apology."

I laughed. "I don't know if I'd go that far. He's trying, but he still has issues, like me."

Dad rubbed his temples. "You said you went to Grace's house today. Is she talking to you again?"

I told them about the scene at her house. They

listened—Dad frowning, Mom crying. I rushed through, leaving out the details. I didn't want to relive it.

"I'm not letting her go through this alone. And I'm not letting her down." I met their gazes. "Or you."

"Oh, Asher." She scrunched her face and hugged me around the neck. "We'll be there for *you*."

He nodded. "When is the meeting?"

"Tuesday at six, at the church." Blinking away tears, I drew a deep breath, hope sprouting inside my chest. I thought of all the things they hadn't done for me. The ways they'd hurt each other. My relationship with my parents was still a long way from fixed, but maybe we'd finally stopped breaking and could begin repairing the cracks.

****

I drove to work right after school the next day, so I wouldn't see Grace and would only get a phone call later. The hollow pit in my chest deepened.

Mondays at the restaurant sucked. At least on the weekend, lots of customers alleviated the boredom. Most of the night I did busy work, which left my mind free to miss Grace. I restocked the freezer, scrubbed the bathrooms, and cleaned the soda machine. I wiped my forehead with my arm and rubbed the sticky syrup from the soda spout.

"Asher, when you finish the soda machine, my dad wants you to rotate the cheese in the freezer. Pull the old stuff forward and place the new in the back." Chloe held her hands up, palms out. "Sorry, don't shoot the messenger."

"Don't worry about it. At least it makes the time go faster. Better than sitting around doing nothing." I squatted, wiping the last of the splattered cleaning water from the floor in front of the machine.

"Yeah, Mondays are boring." She rolled her eyes and glanced around the dining area.

The one table of patrons boxed up their leftovers.

She leaned against the counter. "Asher, can I ask you something?"

I held back my groan. Girls almost always followed that question with another designed to make guys uncomfortable. "Maybe. It won't embarrass me, will it?"

"No, it's more likely to embarrass me." She dropped her gaze to the floor, cheeks already turning red. "Don't take this the wrong way, but does Connor like me, or is he…" She cleared her throat. "Is he just trying to get with me for sex?"

Yep, awkward. I set the bucket and rag I'd been using on the floor, then leaned back on the soda machine, trying to keep a poker face. "I've known him for a while, and he tries to get a girl to put out every time."

Her cheeks grew redder.

I chuckled. "Every time but this time."

She looked up at me, blue eyes sparkling. "Really?"

I raised my eyebrows and dropped my chin to my chest. "Chloe, you got him to go to freaking church for a first date. Trust me. He likes you."

"Sorry." She crossed her arms over her chest. "I shouldn't bring you into it. It's just some of my friends told me how Connor is, and they thought he was using me."

Her friends could shut the hell up and stay out of it. I cocked an eyebrow at her. "Do you like him?"

"Well, yes. And he's been respectful. Maybe a little too respectful." She bit her bottom lip. "He hasn't even tried to kiss me yet."

I bit back another laugh. *He must be serious.* "Then it doesn't matter what your friends think. Follow your own gut." I smirked. "Or maybe girls would say follow your heart."

"Gut works for me. I'm not prissy." She patted my arm. "Thanks."

"You're welcome." I hefted the bucket of soapy water and turned toward the kitchen for my date with the cheese.

"Asher?"

I turned back, questioning her with my eyes.

"I'm being nosy, but is everything okay with Grace? She never misses church, and her parents seemed a little stressed Sunday."

They hadn't told anyone about the cancer, and I wouldn't be the one to spread it around. I gave the truth as I saw it. "Yes, she's fine."

At least, she will be.

A wrinkle formed between her eyes, but she nodded. I could tell she didn't believe me but was astute enough to realize I couldn't tell her what was happening. I could see why Connor liked her—she was thoughtful.

"Okay, I'll say a few extra prayers for whatever burden is weighing them down."

The bell above the door jangled with a new group of diners.

Chloe winked and grabbed the menus. "Besides, God knows their needs, even if the rest of us don't."

She went to greet the customers, and I went to move the cheese. I didn't know if God was the right one to trust with Grace's needs. Making amends with God was still on my to-do list.

****

I quietly climbed the stairs to my room, trying not to wake my mom. The snores coming from Connor's room told me I'd have to wait until tomorrow to tease him about my conversation with Chloe.

After I showered, I lay in my bed and dialed Grace's number.

She picked up after one ring. "Hey. How was work?"

With her voice in my ear, I relaxed into the feather pillows behind my head. "Boring, and I don't want to talk about it. Living it was bad enough." A thousand pounds of rocks fell on my chest when I pictured her face. "I missed you today. How are you feeling?"

"Well, I don't make a good superhero. My Hulk episode wiped me out."

"Yeah, you kind of sucked at it. But I'll be your Black Widow. I'll sing you a lullaby and pet your hands."

"I miss you, too," she whispered. "Can you come over tomorrow after school?"

"Already in my planner."

"You have a planner?"

How was it possible to smile with her voice? "Yes, and you are on every single page for the rest of my life."

She grew quiet, her soft breath the only sound. "Hmmm. That sounds like Heaven."

"For me. You might have a harder time putting up with all my shit."

"You don't scare me. I know how to take care of you."

Yeah. Compared to cancer, I was a kindergartener on a bus full of prison inmates. "And how will you take care of me? What's your secret weapon to battle my bad choices and selfishness?"

She yawned. "Just love."

"I'll take it," I whispered. "But you know what?"

She whispered back, "What?"

"It's my secret weapon, too."

She laughed softly. "I'm really tired."

My stomach ached to be with her, and I wanted to keep talking. But she needed to rest. "I'll see you tomorrow after school, then."

"Okay," she whispered into the phone.

"I love you, Grace. Sleep well."

"I love you, Asher."

Damn. I clicked End, set my alarm, and tossed my phone on the nightstand. I sank deeper into the mattress and feathers, drifting off to sleep with Grace's *I love you* still sighing in my ears.

Chapter Twenty-Three

On Tuesday, I felt like a kid waiting for Christmas. I checked the clock every ten minutes, willing it to move faster. But somebody had placed a time warp on the school's clocks. Each minute lasted an eternity until I wanted to scream and run out of senior seminar.

The last bell blared over the intercom. I grabbed my bag and bolted out the door.

"Asher, wait up," Connor yelled from behind.

I slowed to wait for him. "I gotta go." I wove between the snails in the hall.

He smirked, falling into step beside me, walking out to the parking lot. "I know, you're going to see Grace. Just tell me what time the meeting starts tonight."

I jerked to a stop. "The meeting?" Damn, Chloe *was* a good influence on him.

"Well, I thought I would check it out. See what it's about." His face reddened, and he kicked a loose stone, bouncing it across the pavement.

"It starts as six. But if you come in late, they won't turn you away."

He nodded and raised his gaze. "I have to work until six, but maybe Chloe's dad will let me leave a few minutes early."

"How will you get there?"

"Chloe said she would take me. She goes sometimes to help get the snacks ready, so it's cool."

I bit back my laughter, watching him, his face red, hands in his pockets, then out, shifting on his feet. Connor's life was hard. He deserved someone like Chloe in it.

I remembered my conversation with her. "I like Chloe. But please kiss her already. I think she's ready."

He laughed and shook his head. "Not yet. I'm waiting for her to make the move. I don't want her to think I'm just after sex. Because this time I'm not." He glanced around. "But if she's up for it, I'm not against it either."

Laughing, I patted his back. "There's the Connor I know." I hit the remote for my lock, and my car beeped. "Need a ride to work?"

"Nope, my ride's here."

He waved, and I looked behind me. Chloe pulled up in her car and lifted a hand to us.

I waved back. "See you at the meeting?" My chest lightened as I imagined him getting sober, too.

"I'll be there. But then I have to meet Vikki to work on our project."

An anvil replaced the lightness, and I rubbed the back of my neck. "Oh, well, I guess you have to get it finished."

"Don't worry. I'm meeting her at the restaurant. Chloe will be there, too, to help close up." He grinned. "I'm not an idiot, Asher. And I won't let Vikki talk me into anything."

"Good, because she's an expert at that."

Chloe honked, and Connor waved again. "I'll see you later. Have fun with Grace."

He jogged to her car and got in. He caressed her hair but didn't kiss her. I shook my head as I got into my driver's seat, rooting for her to make a move. Then I laughed.

"Why am I watching them like a freaking movie?" Maybe something beautiful had happened from all of Connor's pain, too, but I still wasn't sure God was responsible. I started my car and sped toward my own romance story.

****

Grace greeted me at the door. I stepped in, and she squeezed her arms around my neck, raising up on her tiptoes. Her lips touched mine, soft at first, then firmer as her breath sped. My head spun from the heat in her kiss. Strawberries floated off her hair and skin. She even tasted like them.

She pulled away and drew a deep breath. "Hi."

I laughed at her anticlimactic greeting. "Hi." I wanted to pull her back for another taste, but my heart already beat marathon fast. And the rest of me sizzled. Sex was out of the question. She was too sick for that.

She took my hand and pulled me to the couch. "How was school?"

We sat, and she snuggled into my side. I rested my arm on her shoulder, trying to control my racing pulse.

"School sucked. But now it's over, so all is good."

She laid her hand on my leg, and I swallowed.

"Where is everyone?"

God, please let Joel be here so I don't do anything stupid.

She traced a pattern on my thigh with her fingers, and I tensed.

"Dad's at the church getting ready for the meeting, and Mom took Joel to dinner and to buy a new video game. He's been a little down, and she thought it would cheer him up."

Are her fingers on fire? I swear she'd branded my skin through the fabric. I squeezed her closer and held her hand. We were alone. Nobody here but us. For a while. The freaking Fates were taking another crack at me, trying to make me be an idiot.

Don't. Do. It.

She was sick, fragile, perfect. I struggled not to be a total douche and make a move on my cancer-ridden girlfriend. What kind of ass would that make me? I tried to focus on what she said about her brother.

"Joel's a sensitive kid. He's worried about you." *Like me.* "He sure didn't like when I kissed you the other night." I chuckled, remembering his reaction. I'd been the same way at eight.

"He tries to act mature, but girls still gross him out." She raised her hand to my face, tracing my lips with a featherlight touch. "I don't think it's gross."

She was the cat, and I was the mouse, helpless to escape. Not that I wanted to. I tried to swallow, but my throat was too dry. My heart beat so hard I'm surprised Grace didn't dance to the rhythm.

Instead, she leaned closer, sliding her hands up my chest. She stared into my eyes, then her gaze fell to my mouth. She ran the tip of her tongue along my bottom lip. Fates or not, cancer or not, she had a hunger in her eyes, and I wanted to feed it.

"Asher, will you make love to me?"

I exhaled, head spinning from holding my breath.

"The last time I was afraid of, well, everything. And now I'm not."

She spoke against my lips. I forgot how to inhale.

"I know everything will be fine. And I want to be

with you, forever." She pressed her lips on mine, and I gave up trying to be good.

The Fates can win this one. I'm okay with that.

I carried her to her room again, this time joining her on her bed. Unlike our first time at The Cliffs, she wasn't on fire, at least not from a fever. She kissed me like she was dying, and I was the one who would save her. Which was the absolute truth.

"Grace, I love y—"

She pulled my face back to hers, increasing the tempo of our kiss. She tugged off her shirt, and my breath stopped. I pulled off my shirt, too, then the rest of our clothes. Her soft skin touched my chest, and I forgot about talking.

I lost track of time after that. Not like at school where every new minute I wasn't with her made me want to stab my eyes with a pencil. This time, I lost track of the fear and pain, my addictions, her cancer, the horrors to come with her treatment. All I needed was the here and now. My beating heart, her soft body, and our love—and hope.

She was the only thing in this world worth living or dying for. And though my only purpose for being alive—for being here on this earth—was to help Grace live, as we twisted together in her bed, skin against skin, I'd already had a taste of Heaven.

****

Grace and I sat next to each other on the couch, our project notebook spread on the coffee table in front of us. I sat close to her, our thighs touching and my gaze glued to her flushed face. She wrote in the notebook, and I played with her hair, twisting her ponytail between my fingers, letting it slip away only to twist it again.

"You should scoot away. My mom and Joel will be back soon. She's more lenient than my dad, but even she would disapprove of…" Her cheeks grew redder. "Well, you know."

"We're just sitting together, but you're probably right." I placed a kiss behind her ear, smiling at the shiver that ran through her body. "One look at your face and she'll know what we did. Don't ever play poker."

She giggled and pushed my chest. "I'll remember that. But I must be okay at hiding things since my dad hasn't killed you yet for defiling his daughter."

"Me?" I widened my eyes. "It was your idea. Both times."

She rubbed her fingers along the inside of my thigh, and it was my turn to shiver.

"I didn't hear you complain."

I scooted away and put a few inches of space between us. "Maybe you're right. It might be safer to sit over here. I've been a bad influence on you."

She laughed, and the front door opened. Joel burst through like the Tasmanian Devil in the old cartoons, followed by Grace's mom.

Grace winked at me and gave me a sweet, innocent preacher's-daughter smile, like we hadn't just spent the last hour blissed out in her bed. "Hi. How was dinner?"

Joel ran over to the couch and squeezed between his sister and me. "Hi, Asher. I didn't know you'd be here. Want to see my new game?"

"Hey, what am I? Chopped liver?" Grace tickled Joel's sides, and he laughed.

"I see you all the time. I never get to see Asher. Want to play?" He held out the new video game and raised his eyebrows.

"I'll play next time. We have to leave for a meeting soon."

His forehead wrinkled.

I poked his stomach with my finger. "But I'll come over tomorrow and beat you. I mean, play."

His smile returned. "Okay, then I'll go practice so I can win."

He jumped off the couch and ran through the living room. Sliding on his stockinged feet across the wood floor in the hallway, he turned and dashed into his bedroom. Soon beeps and whistles from the TV floated out the open door.

Mrs. King shook her head. "I'm glad he's in a better mood, but it sure adds to the noise in here." She grabbed the paper shopping bag Joel had tossed onto the floor. "How's married life going? Is it everything you hoped it would be?"

We froze. Grace's face reddened, and I bit back a laugh. Her wide-eyed gaze fell on me.

I told her mom, "Got it under control."

"Yes, we're good." Grace cleared her throat. "Marriage should be a piece of cake."

Her mom glanced back and forth between us with raised eyebrows. Professional poker player was definitely out as a career choice for Grace.

I laughed. "I don't know about a piece of cake. But it will definitely be sweet."

"So long as it comes later down the road." Mrs. King glanced at the clock. "You two had better get going. The meeting starts in twenty minutes."

"Okay, Mom. Can I leave this stuff here?" Grace waved at the papers strewn across the coffee table. "I'll need to add a little more later when I get home."

"Yes, I'll tell Destructo to leave it alone." She gave Grace a hug. "I'll see you later."

"Bye, Mom. I love you."

"I love you, too, sweetie." Mrs. King smiled at me. "Good luck, Asher."

I squeezed Grace's hand and smiled at her mom. "Thanks."

On the way to the meeting, Grace turned to me in the car. "Are you ready for this?"

"For what?" I lifted her hand to my lips and kissed her knuckles.

"For sharing tonight?"

Am I ready? Admitting my problem in front of everyone. To utter those famous AA introduction words?

"Part of me is terrified. But another part of me knows it will be a relief. Once I do it, there's no going back. Everyone will know me for what I am. But maybe that's the only way for me to beat it. Owning up to it and tackling it head-on."

"I'm proud of you." She leaned over and kissed my cheek.

"Thanks."

We pulled into the parking lot, and I parked between my parents' cars. They waited inside the door.

Mom hugged us both. She didn't say anything about the cancer, but her eyes filled with tears.

Dad coughed. "Well, let's go. I think it's almost time to start."

Grace and I led them to the basement. The crowd looked the same as last time. People milled about, drinking coffee, talking, and laughing. I waved at Dave, and he ambled over to greet me.

"Hey, Asher. How are you? Everything going

okay?"

"I'm good. Thanks." I turned to my parents. "This is Dave, my sponsor. This is my mom, Beth, and my dad, Michael."

They shook hands.

"Thank you for coming to support Asher." Dave nodded to Grace. "And I know you, young lady. How are you doing? Keeping that little brother of yours out of trouble?"

She laughed, and we all smiled in response.

"That's not my job, Dave. I think he has a special angel for that."

He bobbed his head. "I have to agree with you. That boy is a ball of energy. Most of his trouble is of the collateral nature. He needs an angel to keep track of him."

I smirked. His sister obviously needed the same thing. The mint hit my nose, and then Kali appeared behind Dave. She placed a kiss on his cheek, and he absently rubbed it.

Grace grinned. "They say we all have our guardian angels, right?"

Kali winked, and I laughed in agreement.

Pastor King waved from across the room as he took a seat in the front again. Grace waved back, and we all found our seats. Kali followed Dave to his chair in the row ahead of me. Just before the leader began, Connor and Chloe rushed around the corner.

Faces flushed from running, they sat in the row behind us.

Connor patted me on the back. "I told you I'd make it."

Chloe snorted. "Well if you hadn't stopped to ki—"

"Shhh. It's about to start." He patted my shoulder. "By the way. You were right."

I glanced at Chloe's red face and snorted a soft laugh.

She tried to glare at me but ended up laughing herself. "Shut up, Asher."

"What did I miss?" Grace watched us with a confused smile.

I kissed her hand again and shrugged. "I'll tell you later."

The leader began with the usual routine—prayers, announcements, collections. Then it was time for the introductions. Others began, giving their names and years of sobriety. Of course, I nailed the responses.

Finally, it was my turn, and I stood on steady legs. Grace sat to my left, still holding my hand. My mom sat on my right next to my dad, Connor behind me. Surrounded by the most important people in my life, holding the hand of my true love, I introduced myself to the room of strangers who knew me better than the rest of the world.

"Hello. My name is Asher. And I'm an alcoholic."

Chapter Twenty-Four

After the meeting, I held Grace's hand. Connor and Chloe stood a few feet from us, talking quietly. His gaze never left her. He brushed her hair from her eyes, caressed her arm, and finally held her hands in his. She blushed, leaning into his touch.

"Wow," said Grace. "I've never seen Chloe embarrassed. Or act so interested in a guy."

"Really?" I raised my eyebrows and chuckled. "I won't tell Connor. It'll go to his head."

"Yeah." She giggled, turning her back to them. "And he can't afford to blow it with his ego."

I nodded, then pulled her toward me and wrapped my arms around her waist. She rested her hands on my chest. The rings had darkened under her eyes, and she stifled yet another yawn.

"Want me to take you home?"

She shook her head. "I'll ride home with Dad. He's almost finished."

I pulled her even closer and rested my cheek on her head. "Thanks for being here with me tonight."

She tilted her head back. "Anytime."

I kissed her softly.

"Watch out," she said. "Inappropriate behavior at church will get you in trouble."

I leaned in and whispered, "Then it's a good thing nobody saw us at your house."

Flirting with Death's Grace

She giggled and stepped back to hold my hand. "This might be safer."

"But not as much fun."

She rolled her eyes, and I laughed, glancing at Connor as he and Chloe joined us.

"I've gotta go meet Vikki." He curled his lip. "I can't wait for this project to be over. Think I can apply for a fake divorce?"

Grace laughed. "There are only a few assignments left. You can make it."

"Maybe." He shrugged. "With my luck, she'll kill me, and we'll fail the class."

Chloe hugged his arm. "Your luck is changing, though."

"True." He kissed her cheek. "Too bad you don't go to our school. Maybe we could have been partners instead."

"Good luck." I slapped him on the shoulder. "See you at home."

"See you guys later." Chloe pulled Connor toward the stairs, and they disappeared around the corner.

Mom and Dad shook hands with Dave, then joined me and Grace.

"You did good tonight." Mom rubbed my arm.

I shifted on my feet, glancing between them. "Thanks."

"I'm glad to see things turning around." Dad turned to Grace. "You'll keep him in line, won't you?"

She laughed. "Oh yeah, I'm sure I can get him to behave."

"I'm right here. I can hear you talking about me." I pinched her waist. "But you're right."

Mom and Dad smiled at each other. I could almost

see the pictures of weddings and grandbabies scrolling through their minds. No, wait, those were my thoughts. Grace had turned me into that guy from *The Notebook*.

Dad said, "I've got to go. Asher, I'll see you in a couple days. I have to go to Seattle and help train my replacement."

The old abandonment fear crept into my chest. "When will you be back?"

"I'll be home on Friday. I already have the return ticket." He clapped a hand on my shoulder. "We'll go for pizza."

I laughed. "Sounds great."

He hugged Grace. "Take care of yourself."

Mom hugged her, too. "Yes. We're here if you need anything."

"Thank you." Grace tightened her hold on my hand. "Everything will be fine."

I smiled my thanks to my parents, glad they didn't make a big deal out of the cancer. "See you at home, Mom."

She and Dad walked together toward the stairs, and for a moment, I got lost in the past. But I shook my head. Some things couldn't be fixed. As least they were civil to each other now. I couldn't expect more than that.

After they left, I hugged Grace again. "Let me walk you upstairs. I don't want you to fall."

She rolled her eyes. "I'm not quite that fragile."

But as I walked behind her on the stairs, I frowned at her slow careful steps and her heavy breathing.

In the hall at the top, I led her to a pair of padded armchairs set against the wall.

"Thanks." She leaned her head back and closed her eyes. "You don't have to stay. Dad will be ready soon."

I knelt in front of her and leaned my head on her lap, rubbing my cheek against the softness of the leggings she wore. She played with my hair, and I closed my eyes.

"Are you sure you don't want a ride home?" The thought of leaving her caused me physical pain. My heart strained against my ribs with every breath.

She yawned. "No, you need to go home. I'll fall asleep before Dad pulls out of the parking lot. It's not like riding with you would give us more time to talk."

I lifted my head and wiggled my eyebrows suggestively. "Maybe I thought we'd do something else."

"You got all that energy earlier." She caressed my face.

I kissed her, trying not to picture the way she looked in her room. On her bed. Footsteps echoed up the stairs, and I pulled away from her kiss.

"I don't want your dad to kill me tonight," I whispered. I sat in the other chair and held her hand.

"He wouldn't. He knows I need you."

Pastor King came around the corner and stopped. "Everything's cleaned up. You ready to go home?"

"Yes, I'm tired."

He frowned and glanced at me. "I have to make a quick stop. Do you want Asher to take you home now?"

Yes.

But she shook her head. "I'll just wait in the car."

Damn.

"Okay, then I'm ready when you are." He grinned at me. "You had quite the crowd here with you tonight. It's nice that your parents came here to support you."

"Yeah, it was. I was more excited that Connor came, though."

Grace stood from the chair, and I jumped up to help her.

"I'm not handicapped." But she wobbled on her leg. "Well, not really."

Her dad pressed his lips together. "I'll go move the car."

He walked out the door, and she lifted her face to mine for a kiss. How could something so soft have complete control of me?

I whispered against her lips, "I love you."

She took a deep breath, her eyes sparkling like diamonds. "I love you, too. I always have, ever since we were kids."

"That's good. You're the only one who can put up with me."

She laughed, and I hugged her. Her dad honked the horn.

"Come on. I don't want your dad to come and get us."

I helped Grace into the car, and Pastor King stepped to the door to lock the church.

She reached up through the open door and tickled my lips with a soft touch of her fingers. "Good night. I'll see you tomorrow."

"Go to sleep so you can feel better." I glanced over my shoulder at her dad, then winked at her. "I want you to keep up your energy."

She laughed, and I closed the door.

Her dad jogged over from the building and stopped in front of me. He extended his hand. "Thanks, Asher."

I shook his hand and raised my eyebrows. "For what?"

"For proving me wrong. You did have it in you."

The pieces of my broken self slowly fused together. As hard as changing would continue to be, knowing Pastor King had forgiven me for being an ass lightened the weight pressing on my chest.

As they drove away, Grace waved through the window. I waved, too, and got into my car, already counting the minutes until I could see her again.

****

I went straight home, stomach rumbling. Mom and Terry had left. Her going somewhere with Dad had probably set alarms off in Terry's head. I'm sure he wanted to wine and dine her to remind her he was the right choice.

On my own for dinner, I headed for the kitchen, scrounging up the only thing I could find worth eating in the fridge. Heating cold pizza in the microwave, I leaned against the counter and thought about Grace.

The jumbled pieces of my life fell into place. My parents supported me, Connor had come to the meeting with Chloe, and Grace—the best piece of all—had given me a second chance. The hard part was yet to come with her treatment. But I knew I would save her because Kali had told me I would. She'd promised.

I still wasn't sure how I could save her from cancer, and all I could do was wait for the moment or opportunity to show itself. But I would be ready when it did. I wouldn't let her slip away again. Or rather, I wouldn't throw her away like before.

The microwave beeped, and I took my plate to the table, then grabbed a pop from the refrigerator. I chewed my first bite, and my phone buzzed on the table. Connor's face and middle finger greeted me. I rolled my eyes. *God, I have to give him a new contact picture.*

"What's up?" I took another bite.

"Asher." He sniffled into the phone, and my stomach fell to my feet.

"What is it?" I dropped my pizza on the plate. "What's wrong?"

At the same instant, Kali exploded into my kitchen with an eye-watering wave of mint. Her eyes, black orbs again, glittered with tears. Like the night of the vision, they sent chills racing down my spine, and I almost dropped the phone.

"Asher, hurry!" she shouted and just as quickly disappeared.

I stood like a statue in my kitchen, my heart about to jump from my chest.

Connor said the words I expected. "It's Grace, Asher. She's at the hospital. There's been an accident." He sobbed into the phone. "It's my fault. I'm sorry. I'm so sorry."

Wait, an accident? No, she had cancer. I have to save her from cancer!

Were the Fates trying to intervene? Were they making one last-ditch effort to make it impossible for me to save Grace? Were they still trying to win?

I gritted my teeth, my free hand clenching into a fist as my speeding heart pumped blood through my veins.

No. Not this time.

I abandoned my food and ran to my car. "Calm down. Tell me what happened."

Connor breathed into the phone, repeating, "Shit," over and over like a stupid GIF.

"Asher?" Chloe's shaky voice greeted me. "Are you on your way?"

"Yes, what's going on? What happened to Grace?"

A tornado of silence came through the line.

"Just get here. Fast."

My throat snapped shut. I struggled to swallow and croaked, "Chloe?"

"Just hurry." She ended the call.

I drove to the hospital like Dale Earnhardt on crack. I squealed into the parking lot by the emergency room and ran inside but jerked to a stop at the scene that greeted me.

Chloe held Connor, who still sobbed. I'd never seen him so upset. Not when his dad had broken his arm last year in a fight, not when his dog had died, not even when his mom had left him. He caught sight of me, and his face turned white.

I rushed to them. "What the hell is going on?" My voice was too loud, and my hands shook.

A couple with their toddler sitting nearby eyed me and moved to different seats across the waiting room.

"Where is Grace?"

Connor sank into a chair, never meeting my eyes. He kept saying, "She's dead. She's dead. It's my fault."

My heart stopped. Dead? What was that? The word meant nothing. It didn't exist. But he kept saying it, so maybe it was real.

I grabbed his shoulders and shook him hard. "Stop saying that! She can't be dead. You're lying. Where is she? Where is Grace?" I slammed him into the hard-plastic chair, his head bouncing back and forth.

Chloe grabbed my hands. "Asher, stop. Stop. Grace isn't dead."

I let go of him and clutched her hands, my heart beating again, flooding my throat. "What? Then who's dead? *Where is Grace?*"

I was on the edge of the cliff again, and one more question would knock me over for good.

She squeezed my hands. "They're prepping her for surgery."

I sank into a chair. She sat next to me, still holding my hands. I took a deep breath, trying to calm down. Connor still cried, but at least he had stopped saying *she's dead*, and I didn't feel like punching him anymore.

"Dammit, Chloe. Tell me what happened."

"After the meeting, we went to meet Vikki at the restaurant. We could tell she'd been drinking or something."

Connor groaned, and Chloe let go of my hands to hold his.

"I don't know what she was on, but she could barely walk straight. I don't know how she made it there."

I remembered the night in the shed. She'd done coke with Dan that night. Maybe she'd experimented with more. "Knowing Vikki, it was something strong. So then what happened?"

Chloe wiped her eyes. "Connor told Vikki he wouldn't work with her when she was so messed up. He told her she had to go home."

I glared at him. "You let her get in a car? What the hell, Connor?"

He looked at me and wiped his nose. "No, I said we would take her home. But she wouldn't listen. Chloe and I tried to convince her to give us her keys so I could drive her car for her, and she could ride with Chloe. She ran out the door and took off."

He leaned forward and held his head in his hands. His whole body shook, like he was having withdrawals. He covered his face with his hands. "And I just watched her go."

I closed my eyes, my stomach clenching. "Who is dead?" But I already knew.

His hands muffled his reply. "Vikki."

Bile rose in my throat. Vikki was dead. Gone. Wiped out in a blink after her crappy life. After I'd used her. She wasn't important to me like Grace, but still a piece of me left with her. A piece I'd never be able to fix now.

Chloe rubbed Connor's back. "When Vikki left, she was out of control, driving way too fast. She hit them almost head-on. Grace took the biggest impact." She finally broke down and sobbed. Connor pulled her to his chest.

I rubbed my hands through my hair, heaving air out of my burning chest. The moment had come, but it wasn't what I'd expected. Where the hell was Kali? Why wasn't she here telling me what to do? Telling me how to save Grace?

The Fates, God, Kali—I couldn't trust any of them. All I knew was that Grace wasn't dead, and *I* would keep it that way.

Connor and Chloe still clung to each other, crying. He blamed himself for Vikki's decisions, which was crap—a burden he shouldn't have to bear.

"Connor, this isn't your fault."

"Yes, it is. I made Vikki meet me tonight because I was too afraid to go to her house where I might"—he flashed his bloodshot gaze to Chloe—"do something stupid. If I had just been strong enough to go there, she wouldn't have been driving. She wouldn't have crashed, and she wouldn't be... And Grace would be okay. I'm so sorry. It's my fault she's hurt." He hung his head, covering his eyes with his hand.

I didn't know who to blame, but I knew it wasn't him. "No, it's not."

He looked at me with his red-rimmed eyes, forehead wrinkled. "Then who, Asher? I'm the weak one who made the stoned girl come to me so I could avoid getting stoned."

"Avoiding your addictions isn't weakness," Chloe said.

I nodded. "Vikki made her own decisions. You didn't make them for her. She knew she had to meet you someplace. *She* should have stayed sober."

Blaming Vikki for everything made me feel like a complete ass. But blaming Connor would be even worse and wrong.

He placed his hand over Chloe's and drew a shuddering breath. He looked at me. "Asher, if something happens to Grace, if she…"

"Stop." I held up a hand. "She'll be fine."

He nodded like he almost believed me. Or maybe he thought he'd keep my hopes up.

The doors opened with a swish. Mrs. King ran in, eyes wild and wet. She saw me and rushed over. I met her halfway, hugging her.

"Asher, where is she? Paul called, and I got here as fast as I could. I had to take Joel to my mom's house and…" She burst into tears, and I held her again.

"I don't know. I just got here, too. Come on. Let's find out."

I led Mrs. King to a woman sitting behind the information desk. Her bobbed gray hair flipped up at the ends, mimicking the well-practiced smile on her wrinkled face. How many worried moms and half-crazed boyfriends had she seen in her job?

She spoke with a soft and friendly voice. "Can I help you?"

Mrs. King wrung her shaking hands. "Yes, my daughter, Grace King, is here. She was in an accident." Her voice broke on the last word, and she bit her knuckle.

I laid a hand on her trembling shoulder.

The woman's long-nailed fingers flew across the keyboard, and she glanced at the computer screen. "Yes, she's prepped for surgery, awaiting the doctor. I'll have someone take you to the surgical waiting room." She picked up her phone and spoke softly for a moment, then hung up, her expression unchanging. "Mary will be here shortly to take you back. You can have a seat until she gets here."

I clenched my jaw. We weren't waiting for a damn bus. Mary had five seconds, then I would find my way to Grace.

"Thank you," Mrs. King said. She stepped away from the desk.

I stayed, looking down the hall behind Smiley. *Four. Three, Two.*

"Asher, do you know what happened?"

I turned to Mrs. King and nodded. "It was a drunk driver." The rest of the story could wait until later. After I'd saved Grace.

"That's what Paul said." She pulled a tissue from her purse. "Is the driver okay?"

"It was the driver's fault. Why do you care?"

My shock over Vikki's death faded. What the hell had she been thinking? Why had she driven when she was so wasted? I looked down the hall for Mary.

Mrs. King sniffled. "It's another family touched by

tragedy. More pain. Wishing ill will on them doesn't lessen our own."

"The driver died."

She went where I couldn't yell at her and tell her how ignorant it was to get behind the wheel high.

"That's terrible." Mrs. King closed her eyes, new tears falling. She wiped them away with the crumpled tissue. "Do you know who it was?"

Of course she'd ask the one question I didn't want to answer. "Yes. It was a girl from our class, Vikki."

She covered her mouth and shook her head, sobbing again. Crying for Vikki, the one who'd almost killed Grace.

"It was her fault, Mrs. King. She died because she did something stupid."

She gazed at me, tilting her head. "Yes, but maybe she died because she had a problem and didn't know how to fix it. Maybe she had no one to help her."

Vikki'd had problems, that's for sure. I'd never thought about the reasons behind them, though. And I had been one of those problems, but I'd done nothing to help her solve me. Instead, I'd used her and tossed her aside to run for Grace.

Maybe her family was messed up like Connor's. Maybe it was strong like the Kings'. I didn't know. Either way, I guessed they deserved my sympathy, not my anger.

Footsteps squeaked on the tile floor, and I jerked my gaze up to another gray bob. It must have been part of the job requirements for the hospital. Mary's wrinkled face held the same practiced kind smile as Desk Lady.

"Hello. I'll take you to Grace now. Follow me." She turned and headed back toward the hall.

We followed Mary and her squeaky shoes down a long hall. She walked slowly and asked stupid questions like, "How are you doing today?" and, "Is it getting chilly outside?"

I was about to pick her up and run with my hand over her mouth when she stopped at a set of double doors. She swiped a card in front of a monitor, and they swung open with a quiet swish. A flood of noise interrupted the silence of the hall. We entered a room filled with beeps and clangs and buzzing, passing curtained rooms with people in different states of misery.

In the first curtained room, a man lay silent and unmoving with tubes and wires leading to every visible inch of skin.

In the next area, a woman sat up in her bed, holding a bandaged arm. "I said get me a damn blanket! It's fucking cold in here!"

I frowned and looked across from her. Another woman cried, her hand caressing the hair of a boy lying in the bed with a bandaged arm and leg.

"Mommy, I want to go home," he cried.

"Later, honey. When Daddy is gone."

The police officer standing guard outside smirked at the mother's words.

I stopped looking in the rooms after that.

Mary led us to a door at the end of the corridor and held it open. We stepped in without her, and she closed the door behind us. I glanced around at the eight or nine padded chairs lined up around the peach-colored walls. Pastor King stood from his chair, a white gauze patch on his forehead and his left arm in a sling. He met Mrs. King halfway, and they hugged, both crying.

"Oh, Paul. Are you okay?" She kissed him.

I looked away. *For crying out loud, kiss later. I need to know about Grace.*

"I'm okay. But Grace…" He bit back a sob.

My gaze snapped back to his. "What's wrong with her?"

He gestured to the seats.

I sat across from them, bouncing my knee. "Tell me how she is." How would I help her?

He sucked in a breath. "She took the brunt of the impact. The air bags deployed, which saved her from more injuries, but she has a compound fracture of the tibia from the impact of the wheel. Her right wrist is broken, too, and she has a concussion."

Okay, none of that seemed impossible to fix. There had to be more. Or maybe this wasn't the moment. Maybe this was just the Fates throwing a curveball for laughs.

Yeah. Right.

I glared at him, daring him to lie. "What else? What aren't you telling us?"

Mrs. King frowned. "Paul?"

He squeezed his eyes closed for a moment, then nodded. "She has a ruptured spleen. They're removing it."

"Is that bad?" I asked.

He shrugged. "She can live without a spleen."

He held his wife's hands, and I held my head. I prayed for mint. Where was Kali? I needed to know what the hell I was here for so I could do it.

Pastor King patted my back.

I raised my head. "What now?"

"They'll come out to give us updates during the surgery. We can see her after."

"When? How long has she been in there? When will they come out?" I stood and paced the little room.

"No news is good news," Mrs. King said. "Let's hope we don't see the doctor until it's over."

She leaned her head on Pastor King's shoulder and closed her eyes. He held her hand and leaned his head back on the wall.

I paced. How could they just sit there? I wanted to peel off my skin. Maybe he'd had lots of practice as a pastor waiting with others during shitty times.

Seven, that's how many steps it took to cross the room. After two hundred fifty-four, the door opened, and a man came in wearing green scrubs. Short gray hair poked out from underneath the green cap on his head.

Grace's parents stood.

"Mr. and Mrs. King? I'm Dr. Thomas." He glanced at me, too.

Pastor King answered with a question. "How is Grace? Is the surgery over?"

The doctor frowned. "No, we have a slight problem."

The Fates tapped on my shoulder. Their icy breath slithered on my neck. They seemed to say *here it comes, Asher*. Someone had replaced my lungs with deflated balloons. I tried to draw a breath, and they flapped in my chest.

"What's wrong?" Mrs. King asked. She clutched Pastor King's uninjured arm.

The doctor rubbed the back of his neck. "Well, we've had a few traumas today, and we seem to have a shortage of her blood type. Hers is the rarest—O negative. We're giving her albumin right now while we wait for the blood to arrive. I had to halt the surgery to make sure she didn't lose any more." He rubbed his chin. "We weren't aware of the shortage, or we would have held off on the surgery. We're keeping her comfortable now."

The balloons in my chest melted into rubbery puddles. Was he kidding? How did a hospital run out of blood? This had to be a joke by the Fates. Hospitals didn't run out of freaking blood.

Pastor King frowned. "When will it get here? Is it okay to give her the albumin for an extended period?"

"We're having it rushed. She lost quite a bit of blood with the broken leg." The doctor shifted on his feet, crossing his arms. "I don't mean to worry you, but you should know. There's a chance her heart could stop if we don't replace the blood loss soon. We only have a short window of time for the albumin to help. I'd say another twenty to thirty minutes."

Pastor King whispered, "How far away is the blood?"

Dr. Thomas' Adam's apple bobbed in his skinny throat. "Forty minutes, but they're hurrying."

They all stared at each other. Mrs. King buried her face in her husband's chest. Pastor King held her and squeezed his eyes closed. The doctor pinched the bridge of his nose.

I laughed.

They jumped and looked at me like I'd gone crazy. Was this it? Was this the best the Fates could do? Kali didn't need to show me the way to save Grace.

"You don't have to wait," I told the doctor.

Grace and I had shared a lot when we were little. Two peas in a pod. Same ideas, same dreams, and the same damn blood type.

"I'm O negative. I have what she needs, right here."
I laid my hand on my chest, right over my pounding
heart, pumping the blood that would save her.

Chapter Twenty-Five

Grace's eyes fluttered open and wheeled around the room.

Her dad kissed her cheek. "Good morning, sleepyhead."

"Hey, sweetie." Her mom cried, patting Grace's hand. "It's okay, everything's fine. You're fine."

I stood behind her mom. Grace's eyes were as green as the spring grass outside. Fresh and new, with a promise of better days to come. And that's exactly how I felt, now that the worst was over.

She found me with that emerald gaze, and then her eyes filled with tears.

"What's wrong? Are you in pain? Want me to get the nurse?" My heart raced. I pulled the curtain aside and glanced back and forth, looking for someone.

"Asher." Her voice was a rough whisper after the intubation.

I went back to her side. "Don't talk."

I rubbed her forehead, the only place without something attached or covered with a bandage. Her tears leaked into her temples, and I remembered that night at the quarry, when she'd first told me about the cancer. I swallowed to clear the lump in my throat.

Mrs. King patted my arm. "Don't worry, Asher. Most girls cry coming out of anesthesia. A nurse told me that when Grace had her wisdom teeth out last year and she woke up sobbing."

I looked at Grace.

She still cried, but she nodded. "I'm okay," she whispered. She cleared her throat and reached for me.

I held her hand, and her mom stood. She looked across the bed. "Why don't we go and get coffee, Paul?"

Her dad frowned, like he wanted to argue, but then he stood. "We'll be back in a little while." He leaned over and kissed Grace again on the cheek.

"Okay, Dad. Don't worry. I won't go anywhere." She grinned despite the tears still streaming from her eyes.

I shook my head. "It's my job to make the bad jokes."

Her parents laughed quietly and stepped into the open corridor, pulling the curtain closed behind them.

I sat on the stool her mom had occupied and held Grace's hand to my forehead. Then I brought it to my lips and kissed it at least one hundred fifty-two times. The sweet strawberry smell of her skin bled through the biting antiseptic odor of the room.

She blinked slowly, one corner of her mouth lifting. "I know a better place for those kisses."

I placed a careful kiss on her lips.

"I'm sorry this happened to you." I gestured to her right leg, splinted and supported by traction above the bed. Her right arm was splinted from her palm to her elbow. I lightly touched the bruise below her right eye, frowning at several cuts that marred the perfect skin on her cheek.

She frowned. "Tell me what happened. All I remember was getting hit."

"You can hear about it later. Right now, you need to

rest and heal."

"Not knowing is worse." She held my hand, wincing as she looked at the IV. Then she closed her eyes, and more tears leaked out. "Please tell me."

"It was Vikki." My voice was just a whisper. "She'd gone to meet with Connor for their project. But she shouldn't have been driving."

She was silent, staring into my eyes. The rapid beeping of her heart monitor was the loudest sound in the room. She whispered, "And how is she?"

My throat grew too tight to answer. I pressed my lips together and shook my head, tears for Vikki pooling behind my lids.

She scrunched her face and closed her eyes again. I leaned down and laid my head near hers, kissing her cheek and ear. "It's okay. It's not your fault. It's okay." I whispered this new lullaby, trying to soothe her. And myself.

She grasped my neck with her good arm, and I gently squeezed it, too afraid to hold her like she wanted me to. Her sobs must have hurt, and I tried to think of some way to ease her pain. I brushed the hair away from her face, then kissed her salty lips, resting my forehead against hers.

Movement to my left caught my eye, and mint replaced the antiseptic. I turned to Kali, a peaceful and out-of-place smile on her face. She jerked her head toward Grace. Did she want me to tell Grace about her? Well, if anyone would believe me, Grace *would* be the one.

"I need to tell you something. It sounds crazy, though. Promise not to call the psych ward to get me."

She wiped her eyes and glanced around the room. I

could have sworn her gaze settled on Kali for a moment. But that would lead to nothing but trouble. Then Grace definitely looked at Kali.

"Okay, but I have something to tell *you*, and I'll need that same promise."

Chills raced across my neck, and I shook my head. "Kali?"

Grace's eyes widened, and she inhaled a sharp breath. The heart monitor beeped her surprise. "How do you know that name?"

I ignored her question, and we both looked at Kali.

Her Hollywood smile as bright as the sun, she took our hands and laughed. "Go, team."

My breath sped. What the hell? If Grace could see her, it could only mean one thing, right?

I glared at Kali. "Wait, how come Grace can see you? Does this mean she's still going to…" I gulped.

"No, no. You took care of that, Asher. She's fine." She rubbed her fingers on my hair. "You were perfect and right on time."

I nodded, but a rock still filled my stomach. Then I remembered I could see Kali, and I wasn't about to die. Maybe the reason we saw her was because we'd both been on Kali's to-do list.

Grace's gaze bounced between us. "What does she mean? What did you do, Asher?"

Relief so huge that I almost cried washed over me. So of course, I made a joke out of it.

"Did you know hospitals could run out of blood? What the hell is that about? Lucky for you"—I pulled up my sleeve and showed her the bandage in the crook of my arm—"we have the same blood type."

"You gave me blood?" The beeping increased, and

309

a slow, teary smile spread across her face. "That is the most romantic thing you've ever done."

I laughed. "What about cleaning your kitchen after you turned into a human tornado?"

She wiped her eyes. "I'm never going to live that one down, am I?"

"Nope, I'll remind you of it every year on our anniversary and when I don't feel like cleaning our kitchen." I kissed the tip of her nose and tried to sit up, but she pulled me back, claiming my mouth. I didn't fight her.

Kali chuckled. "I thought you two would have more questions, but I can see I'm just getting in the way."

Grace let go, and I smirked at Kali.

"No, you have some explaining to do. The vision. I thought it meant I would save her from her cancer."

"That's a battle you'll both still have to fight. But you'll do it together."

Groaning, I ran a hand through my hair. "This isn't over? I thought you said if I changed, she would live. That was the plan, right?"

She leaned her head to the side, a wrinkle forming between her eyes. "There was never a plan, Asher."

"It was all random? The cancer. The accident. What's next? Will I have to keep saving Grace until the Fates decide I've battled enough? I thought God had plans for everybody and everything happened for a reason." I rolled my eyes on the last part.

Her cheeks flushed. "The Fates aren't real. And God doesn't decide what you do or what happens to you. *Life* happens. You make your own choices to handle what life gives you."

I rubbed my forehead. Most of my choices had been

terrible. But I had tried to change, did change. Helping Grace and Connor, fighting my addictions, those were my best decisions. Vikki's face haunted me, and I pushed it away. I'd have to learn to live with that regret.

I gazed at Grace. This was my biggest regret—wasting my life away from her. What if the cancer won and I'd thrown away the little time I could have had with her? The weight of my past decisions hit me like an avalanche.

I twisted a strand of her silky hair around my finger. "I shouldn't have walked away from you."

"No, because you still loved me, too. That's what hurt the most, knowing we belonged together but not knowing how to bring you back." She sighed. "So I did what I've always done. I prayed."

I caressed her cheek, trying to erase the bruise beneath her eye. "What did you pray for?"

"I've loved you my whole life, and it didn't end when you left me. I've prayed for you to come back." She bunched the thin, white hospital blanket with her shaking hands and looked down at her fingers. In barely a whisper she said, "You know that I—I tried to kill myself after you left. My parents said th-they told you."

Kali laid her hand on Grace's shoulder.

I tried to breathe past the boulder of guilt in my chest. I wasn't worth that kind of sacrifice. And just the thought of Grace dying because of me… *Nope. I'd never deserve her*. I unwound her fingers from the blanket and held her hands in mine.

She squeezed back. "My dad was the one who found me after I'd taken the pills. But Kali came to me in the hospital after the doctors brought me back." She sniffled and finally met my gaze. "She lectured me about the beauty of life and finding hope. That's when I told her about you. About how much you mean to me."

I wanted to laugh because it sounded like Kali gave all her clients the same lecture, but my gut still rolled with the aftereffects of listening to Grace talk about killing herself. Still, I raised an eyebrow at Kali. "The little bird, eh?"

Her laughter rang out, and a chill filled the air. The warmth of Grace's hand in mine held off the ice.

"Once I found out I had cancer, my only prayer was to help you heal before I died. I couldn't stand the thought of leaving you here broken. But watching you with...with Vikki, I didn't have much hope." Grace's eyes sparkled with tears beneath the bright fluorescent lights. "Then that day we met for the project, you told me you were ready to change. I went to the doctor that day to discuss my treatment, and for the first time, I had something to hope for."

She was still too good for me. But I'd spend the rest of her life trying to earn her. I kissed her. "Well, now you're stuck with me."

She said, "Good, I'll keep you."

Kali's track record for answering questions wasn't good. And I had a feeling it wasn't about to improve. But I needed to know if there would still be a way. "Did you come here to help me so I could save Grace?"

"I wasn't sent here to help you. I helped you *because* of her. I told you before my boss is a nice guy, and he likes to give second chances. And thirds and fourths, however many it takes for a person to live a better life, to make beauty out of tragedy. Some people are too blind to recognize the offer. Others just don't take it. Grace took that second chance." She moved closer, leaning with her hands on my shoulders. "And so have you. Now do something good with it."

Yep, a non-answer. Maybe I should be more specific. "Will Grace beat her cancer?"

Kali gazed at me, her dark eyes inscrutable. "That's not for me to tell you. But have hope, Asher. Without it, life gets too depressing."

I looked at the monitors and the wires that would become a familiar sight over the next few months. My heart ached for Grace's pain.

Grace squeezed my hand. "You and me, that's what matters right now. We can get through this. Together."

Kali rubbed Grace's forehead. "She's right. Don't worry, you'll find a way to help her. Who knows, maybe you already have."

I smirked at her cryptic remark. Hugging Kali, I buried my face in her hair and breathed in her minty scent. "Thank you," I whispered. "For everything."

She squeezed me and then stepped back, wiping her eye. "I have places to go, people to see. But thank *you,* Asher, for letting me help you." She left a tingling kiss on my cheek.

I rubbed it, like Dave, and knew I would forever feel that kiss whenever I smelled mint.

Kali kissed Grace on her forehead and whispered in her ear.

Grace gazed at her with wide eyes. "Thanks."

I opened my mouth, then snapped it shut. *Mind your own business. Not everything is about you.*

Kali exhaled and squared her shoulders, backing away from us. "Don't worry about the things in your past you can't change. Look to the future and do good whenever you can. Just take every day one step at a time."

With one last laugh, she winked and lifted her arms above her head. Flames engulfed her, blinding me, burning away my tears. And then she was gone.

We sat in silence for a few moments, then Grace sniffled. "I'll miss her."

I gazed at her wounded face, my heart like a balloon about to pop. Rubbing a finger along her cheek, I enjoyed the cool smoothness of her skin. "I'll miss her, too. But I'd rather be with you."

The pain pump attached to the IV clicked. She held my hand to her face and closed her eyes. "I love you. Thank you for helping me today."

She breathed deep and kept her eyes closed. Her hand dropped to the pillow, and a quiet snore left her throat.

Smiling, I kissed her lips and whispered, "Anytime."

Epilogue

I sat on the bench and lifted my face toward the sunshine. Another beautiful day. The warm breeze carried the scent of fresh-cut grass, early for the season, but the winter was rather mild leading up to this early spring.

The wood slats pressured my back, and I shifted, making myself more comfortable. The birds chirped noisily in the huge oak tree behind me, its branches already covered with tiny green buds. Soon the leaves would shelter this bench from the sun and give me shade when I came to visit the grave situated underneath.

I only came here twice a year, once on my anniversary—and once on hers. They were only a month apart, and sometimes I felt guilty. Maybe I should come more often. But seeing her name on that stone twice a year was hard enough.

She was my rock, my greatest supporter, and the one ultimately responsible for me giving up drugs and alcohol. Without her, I would have died—and not just physically, but spiritually as well.

I came here to remember her. To picture her smile, imagine her laugh, to feel her kiss. She'd left this earth too soon.

My phone buzzed, and I pulled it from my pocket. Connor's face and middle finger greeted me. Even eight years later, the picture still made me laugh.

"What's up?" I answered.

"Hey. How's it going?" His happy voice still took me off guard. We were years away from the trauma of our youth, but sometimes, I still expected him to be the defensive, angry teen I'd befriended.

I glanced at the gray headstone in front of me. "I'm good. Nothing new."

He laughed in my ear. "Like every other day. I swear, Asher, you're turning into an old man. Maybe you should get out more. No…" He groaned. "Stop, Isaiah. Do *not* put your finger up your sister's nose."

I listened to the new chaos in his life, laughing. "Did you teach him that? You know kids learn by watching their parents."

"Very funny. No, he's fascinated with poking things into holes. Yesterday I caught him about to stick a pencil into the cat's ear." He exhaled a loud breath. "He'll be the death of me. Chloe just laughs and says it's my penance for being a difficult child myself."

"Well, Chloe may be right. But you'd think she wouldn't enjoy it so much, seeing how he's her kid, too."

He groaned again, and I laughed.

"Lucky thing little Ryleigh is an angel. She makes up for all the trouble from her twin."

"Well, one out of two isn't bad. Chloe deserves a good kid like her, too. Speaking of Chloe, she asked me to remind you about dinner tonight. You'll be there, right?"

"Of course. Wouldn't miss it."

"Good, because she's making her father's secret deep-dish pizza tonight. I think she has games planned, too." Connor laughed. "She's feeling a little stir crazy being at home with the twins. I think she needs adult conversation."

"Yeah, I can understand that. Especially since she only has you to talk to."

"Shut up." He sighed. "Ugh. Gotta go. Isaiah just threw his cup in the toilet. Wait! No, don't drink that!"

"I'll see you later. Good luck." Laughing, I clicked end and leaned back on the bench. Watching Connor with the twins, anyone could see he loved being a dad. He was a good one, too, making up for his shitty upbringing, breaking the cycle.

I spoke to the grave beneath my feet. "Did you see that one coming? Not that you would have told me if you did." I rubbed a tickle on my cheek and smiled.

"Are you talking to yourself again? You know, the voices in your head aren't supposed to answer." Grace sat beside me and held my hand.

"Sometimes they do, but that's okay." Pulling her close, I kissed her soft lips and rubbed her silky hair. I gestured to the grave where Kali rested. "Besides, you've heard this voice, too."

"Yes, and sometimes I still miss her." She looked down. "But we'll have plenty to distract us soon."

I leaned in and kissed her bulging belly, resting my hands on either side of our child growing within her. "Yes, and if she's anything like Connor's son, we're in trouble."

"God help us if that's true." She rolled her eyes. "Surely we've had enough trouble in our lives and earned a break." She reached behind my neck and pulled my lips to hers.

The kiss was full of heat, and my heart sped. I rubbed her back. "Connor and Chloe want us to come for dinner tonight," I told her between kisses.

"Hmmm. Then I think we should go home and get ready."

"It's still hours away. What do we need to do?"

I knew what I *wanted* to do. My desire for her hadn't lessened over the years.

"Well, making a baby is hard work, and I get tired easily." She played with the collar on my shirt. "And we'll be there late, so when we get home, I'm sure I'll go right to sleep."

I raised my eyebrows, breathing fast. "So?"

She slid her hands up to my shoulders and around my neck, dropping her voice to a whisper. "So." Her lips touched mine. "I think we should go home now and…"

My mouth watered from her teasing. I gulped. "And?"

She laughed and grabbed her stomach. I stared. Not the *and* I expected.

"She's kicking like crazy. Here, feel it, right here." She took my hand and placed it on her stomach. Her eyes crinkled with her smile.

A tiny foot kicked my hand, saying hello from the inside. My stomach quivered, and I was fascinated despite the unanswered desire still stirring in my blood. "She's strong. But I think I have some bad news."

"Bad news?" Grace frowned, her forehead wrinkling.

"Yes." I nodded solemnly. "She has bad manners."

"Oh, really?"

"Yes, she's already interrupting her mom and dad." I shook my head and pulled Grace closer, kissing her neck. "We shouldn't let her do that, you know. We have to teach her to wait her turn."

Her laughter blended with the birdsong and the

breeze. She kissed me again. "You're right. Let's go home and practice. Happy anniversary by the way."

"Yes, it is." I pulled her in and touched my lips to hers. "Can you believe we've made it five years?"

"I knew we would. And there's lots more to come after this."

That called for another kiss.

We walked through the sunny cemetery toward our car. At the edge of the path, I turned to look back at Kali's grave resting next to Dave's.

Kali hadn't shown herself since that day at the hospital when things were still uncertain. When she'd left us wondering if Grace would beat the cancer. I thought of Kali's final remark to me and the whisper to Grace. *You'll find a way to help her. Who knows, maybe you already have.*

I didn't find the way. The way found us. Donating bone marrow, being a match, hadn't crossed my mind. Maybe it would have eventually, but when I gave blood to save her during surgery, the doctors were already thinking ahead.

They'd delivered the news the next day and told me to think about it. After one surprised blink, I'd told them to sign me up. And the rest was history. Our history. I guessed running out of blood that day was part of the plan. Or rather, the non-plan.

And Kali had known it. She'd known I would save Grace. I'd bet that's what she'd whispered that day, to give Grace hope. Maybe she thought I had enough already.

I'd had pain in my life. Pain brought on by my selfish desires, my self-pity, my bad decisions. But I'd escaped death with the help of an angel and got a second chance at life and love. That was all the hope I'd needed.

Grace squeezed my waist, drawing me back from my thoughts. We'd reached the car, but instead of getting in, I held her close, laying my hands on her stomach. "I hope this little one is good like her mama. I don't think I could take a mini me."

"Well, you know what they say about those preachers' kids." Pressing her body to mine, she kissed my jaw.

With her kissing me and every inch of her body against mine, I sure didn't feel like a preacher. "This preacher's daughter won't be able to fool her daddy like you did."

"Why is that?"

I took a long moment to kiss her before I answered. "Because she has a daddy who's walked through the fire and made it out the other side. He knows the signs, so she doesn't stand a chance." I kissed the tip of her nose. "Not to mention she has a mommy who knows all about bad behavior."

"I guess you're right." She giggled and pushed away from me, her gaze traveling down to my toes. "Speaking of, I thought we were going home to practice."

I raised an eyebrow, then clicked the remote to unlock the doors. "Yes, I think that's a great idea. Let's go."

I drove toward home with Grace on my mind and by my side, thinking of how our lives were about to change. A new addition to our story, but this time, the change was good. And I couldn't wait to read the next chapter.

A word about the author...

B.B. Swann is a mother of three young adults, a wife (of another big kid but don't tell him she said that), and a twenty-five-plus year veteran elementary teacher. She has all the age groups covered and draws on their influence when writing her books. Picture book, young adult, new adult, and beyond, they all have one thing in common—life experiences, both the good and the challenging.

Most nights you can find her reading or writing into the wee hours. She believes in the almighty power of caffeine and battling old age with purple hair and lots of sarcasm.

~*~

Find B.B. Swann online at:
https://www.bbswann.com/